THE DEADLY DOWAGER

More Vintage Thrills and Chills from Valancourt

The Feast of Bacchus (1907) by Ernest G. Henham

The Mummy (1912) by Riccardo Stephens

Benighted (1927) by J. B. Priestley

The Slype (1927) by Russell Thorndike

I Am Jonathan Scrivener (1930) by Claude Houghton

Man in a Black Hat (1930) by Temple Thurston

The Curse of the Wise Woman (1933) by Lord Dunsany

He Arrived at Dusk (1933) by R. C. Ashby

Hell! said the Duchess (1933) by Michael Arlen

The Cadaver of Gideon Wyck (1934) by Alexander Laing*

Harriet (1934) by Elizabeth Jenkins

Wax (1935) by Ethel Lina White

Night-Pieces (1935) by Thomas Burke

I Am Your Brother (1935) by Gabriel Marlowe*

The Birds (1936) by Frank Baker

Fingers of Fear (1937) by J. U. Nicolson

Night and the City (1938) by Gerald Kersh*

The Hand of Kornelius Voyt (1939) by Oliver Onions

The Survivor (1940) by Dennis Parry

The White Wolf (1941) by Franklin Gregory

The Killer and the Slain (1942) by Hugh Walpole

The Master of the Macabre (1947) by Russell Thorndike

Brother Death (1948) by John Lodwick

The Feasting Dead (1954) by John Metcalfe

The Witch and the Priest (1956) by Hilda Lewis

* Forthcoming

THE DEADLY DOWAGER

EDWIN GREENWOOD

with a new introduction by
MARK VALENTINE

VALANCOURT BOOKS

Dedication: To M because she laughed

The Deadly Dowager by Edwin Greenwood
First published (as *Skin and Bone*) by Skeffington & Son in 1934
First U.S. edition published by Doubleday, Doran in 1935
First Valancourt Books edition 2016

Introduction copyright © 2016 by Mark Valentine
This edition copyright © 2016 by Valancourt Books

Published by Valancourt Books, Richmond, Virginia
http://www.valancourtbooks.com

ISBN 978-1-943910-38-0 (trade paperback)
Also available as an electronic book.

Cover: A reproduction of the dust jacket of the 1935 first edition.

Set in Dante MT

INTRODUCTION

The Nineteen Thirties novelist Edwin Greenwood (1895-1939) was the author of six lively and farcical crime novels, characterised by his exuberant imagination and witty repartee. His first book, *Skin and Bone* (1934), which had the better title of *The Deadly Dowager* in the U.S.A., had a foreword by his friend Arthur Machen, the Welsh writer of supernatural fiction. In his characteristically trenchant way, Machen distinguished between the portentously solemn "serious" books that earn praise in their time and are soon forgotten and unread, and the survivors, "who have a story to tell and are not ashamed to tell it", and so are still enjoyed many years later. Edwin Greenwood's book, he proclaimed, "is compounded on the true and ancient recipe: it mixes murder and mirth with immense spirit and success".

They became acquainted probably through theatrical circles – Machen and his wife Purefoy had been actors in the Benson Company, and Greenwood was an early filmmaker, director and actor. However, they were also near-neighbours in the little Buckinghamshire town of Old Amersham, where the Machens lived in semi-retirement at Lynwood, a house in the High Street. Greenwood's home was at 'Longleat', 29 Elm Close, in what was then a new estate of individual private houses built in the early Nineteen Twenties, close to the railway station.

Despite being more than thirty years younger, Greenwood delighted in the Machens' company, and in a kindly gesture, he took them on holiday to Paris in 1937, among the last adventures of their twilight years. He became part of the circle of friends and admirers who gathered at the Machens' home for spirited conversation amid copious libations of the host's lethal punch. In the memoir *Peterley Harvest* (1960), the young 'David Peterley' recalled the sort of soirees that went on at the Machens' place, on this occasion during the town's annual carnival: "When I reached the little upper room and saw our host pouring his punch, I had the impression of a necromancer who had conjured up the unnatural scene outside; and thought that at any moment he might put down his jug and leaning out of the window utter the cabalistic word at which the noise and the carnival would become moonlight in an empty street."

Theodore Edwin Greenwood was born in London on 27 August 1895, and the family home was in Fulham. His father, Alfred, was a music teacher who, however, Greenwood said, "did everything from digging gold in New Zealand to singing at Covent Garden". The young Edwin, as he chose to be known, was a chorister at King's College, Cambridge between the ages of 8 and 14, and later claimed it was this that gave him "an early leaning towards the macabre". This is perhaps a sly reference to the influence of the eminent ghost story writer M.R. James, who was Provost at King's. When it came to choosing a career, Greenwood's father suggested he become a chartered accountant. "I asked him what those words meant and he didn't know," recalled Greenwood: "Neither did I. The idea fell flat, so I went to the Sorbonne and studied philosophy and became a Socialist".

At the outbreak of the First World War, when he was 19, he first served in the French Army "and – other things" he recalled, possibly a diffident reference to intelligence or liaison work, since he was fluent in French. He later served as an ambulance driver. After the war he took up acting, but claimed he was too ugly to get many roles. Pictures do not quite bear this out: he had a long, lean, bony face, true, but one full of character and an evident gentle humour. However, he chose mainly to work behind the scenes instead, as stage manager, producer or director. This led him to get involved in the early silent film industry. "A demon asked me to direct some films," he said, "I did and they were successful. Those were the days! I designed my own set, wrote my own scenarios, sometimes even 'ground the handle'. That is what I love to do. I intend to go on making movies and writing books if any one will read them."

He directed *The Fair Maid of Perth* (1923), based on Sir Walter Scott's adventure novel and starring Russell Thorndike in a swashbuckling adventure. This was followed by the melodramas *A Woman in Pawn* (1927) and *Tesha* (1928), and *The Co-Optimists* (1929), a musical based on the stage version, about a troupe of actors touring seaside resorts: something both Greenwood and Machen knew a lot about from personal experience.

He also worked as a screenwriter, where his credits included the desert thrillers *East Meets West* (1936) and *His Lordship* (also 1936). One of his films as writer, *Lord Camber's Ladies* (1932), was produced by Alfred Hitchcock, and the two became good friends. It is a murder thriller involving a peer, and starred Gerald du Maurier, with Nigel Bruce, better known as Dr. Watson to Basil Rathbone's Sherlock Holmes, as Lord Camber. The mingling of aristocracy and murder may well have seemed a good prospect for a plot when Greenwood went on to write *The Deadly Dowager* just a year or two later. His other novels often have a similar mixture.

He later wrote the scenario for Hitchcock's *The Man Who Knew Too Much* (1934), and was one of the screenwriters for the director's *The Girl Was Young* (1937), based on *A Shilling for Candles* by the noted detective fiction writer Josephine Tey. Greenwood's book *Old Goat*, (1937; *Under the Fig Leaf* in the U.S.) is dedicated to "Alfred Hitchcock ('Hitch'), Good Maker of Good Pictures, Good Judge of Good Things, Good Friend".

Edwin Greenwood's taste for the macabre and experience at working on mystery and melodrama films can be seen in his inventive and irreverent fiction, with its black humour, fast-paced plots and sharp dialogue. Most of his books were issued by Skeffington, a prolific publisher of crime novels, although they also listed books about royalty, exploration and adventures, and self-improvement. Indeed, they had published Machen's *War and the Christian Faith* in 1918, though it had not sold well. It would be fair to say, however, that their catalogue was usually unabashedly commercial in outlook.

The work of very few of their authors (many of them pseudonymous) has attracted a later following. Edwin Greenwood's books, though, deserve to be the exception: they are intelligent, witty and full of sheer gusto. The *New Yorker* called *The Deadly Dowager* "a mystery that is both exciting and very funny" and the *New York Times* thought it "quite the jolliest crime story that has come our way in many moons." It is more of a "howdunnit" than a "whodunit". We know perfectly well that the trenchant old Arabella, Lady Engleton, wants to bump off her largely unattractive relations: the redoubtable aristocrat is determined to restore her family's fortunes by the simple expedient of insuring members of her family, and then seeing to it that the policies deliver. It is the various ingenious methods by which she contrives this, and the increasing understandable wariness of her entourage that provide the zesty black humour of the book.

The other characters are not quite as powerful as the book's eponymous assassin, but Greenwood took care to provide an (as it were) full-bodied supporting cast: the aged, querulous parson Alfred; the domineering, calculating Vera; the timorous Sophie; the old Raj bore, Major Hugh Beamish; the oppressed companion, Miss Caraway; the libidinous Lily. Perhaps only in the gentle hero of the piece, the earnest young Henry, 4th Baron Engleton, does he not quite succeed: in fiction it is hard to make virtue interesting when there is plenty of vice available. More successful is the portrait of the urbane Jesuit, Father Reginald, who intervenes at a crucial point in the plot. Though he is not fully deployed in the book, seeming to hover in the background a bit, he may owe something to G. K. Chesterton's clerical sleuth Father Brown, or even to the priest and author Monsignor R. H. Benson, author of far-reaching apocalyptic thrillers such as *Lord of the World* (1907) and *The Dawn of All* (1911). Accounts emphasise Benson's charm and clear perception, qualities Fr. Reginald also possesses.

Though the plot is not quite the same, there are points in common with Roy Horniman's black comedy *Israel Rank* (1907), later filmed very successfully as *Kind Hearts and Coronets* (1949), with Alec Guinness memorably playing most of the characters. Greenwood's book could also have made a great film, as perhaps he hoped.

In his second novel, *Miracle in the Drawing-Room*, sub-titled *A Daring and Cynical Novel of the Modern World's Reaction to an Old-Fashioned Miracle* (1935), Greenwood again depicted a family trying to save itself from ruin. But this time he essayed the more difficult task of showing this achieved by faith, with a saintly intercession unexpectedly resulting from prayer. In its contrasts between the cynicism and calculation of the modern world and the ancient consolations of religion, the book is somewhat in the tradition of the extravaganzas of G.K. Chesterton, but perhaps more attractive to the converted than to the uncommitted.

The author returned to the flamboyant figure of a *femme fatale*, this time intent on removing obstacles to a title as well as wealth, in his next book, *Pins and Needles, A Melodrama* (1935; in the U.S., *The Fair Devil*). The novel is almost a match for *The Deadly Dowager*. One wonders whether Greenwood might have been inspired in part by the female villains in Machen's fiction, such as Helen Vaughan in *The Great God Pan* (1894) or Miss Lally in *The Three Impostors* (1895). Certainly his anti-heroine is evoked with a similar dark allure, and is also involved in a shadowy double life. It shares a certain macabre atmosphere and flippant tone with Michael Arlen's *Hell! said the Duchess* (1934, also available from Valancourt), in which the demure Duchess of Dove proves to have a sinister secret.

Two more novels were to follow in his lifetime: *French Farce, A Tale of Gallic Lunacy, Murder and Mirth* (1937) is a murder mystery involving English and French detectives working together to solve a crime complicated by twins. The author's delighted sympathy with French manners and customs enlivens the ingenious, vigorous plot. But *Old Goat*, published later in 1937, with another lively sub-title, *A Fantasia on a Theme of Blackmail and Sudden Death*, marked a departure. It is a satire on the dictators of the Nineteen Thirties in which a British peer attempts to impose his vision firstly on the local villagers and then on the country. However, he has one redeeming but fatal flaw for a would-be autocrat: an incurable sense of humour. He even finds his own followers funny. The mockery of the militias, back-to-the-soilers and little Englanders of the era is sly and the more effective for being under-stated.

A final novel was published posthumously as *Dark Understudy, A Modern Crime Story* (1940) and again shows the author moving into new ground with the portrait of a shell-shocked serial killer who conceives it is his mission to combat sin in the world by removing individual sinners. The story is told with gravity and pity, as brisk and vivid as his other books but with a serious interest in understanding the protagonist and his visions.

Purefoy Machen called Greenwood "a most singular and lovable character", and he seems to have attracted the slightly bewildered admiration of many others. Mary Butts, also an admirer of Machen, and the author of modernist fantasies such as the Grail novel *Armed With Madness* (1928), had a fierce unrequited love for Greenwood from about 1917 onwards, and he remained her friend and confidante. The formidable actress Mrs. Patrick Campbell, Purefoy recalled, described Greenwood as "the gentleman who looks like a dusty cathedral". Purefoy explained that "he was long and thin, and had certainly something Gothic about him."

In September 1934, Greenwood had married Mollie Collett-Jones: both were keen admirers of Machen's work. But they did not have long together. Edwin Greenwood took the minor part of Dandy, a smuggler, in Hitchcock's *Jamaica Inn* in January 1939 and it is said that the filming, in cold and arduous conditions, took its toll on him, though he tackled it with his usual full-blooded vigour and good humour. However, his death aged 44 on 17 September, 1939, at his home in Amersham, was caused by endocarditis, an infected heart valve. Later, Mollie went on to marry another close friend of Machen, Oliver Stonor (who also wrote as Morchard Bishop) and together they made their home in Devon.

His early death was a great loss to the Machens and his many other literary and theatrical admirers, and those who enjoy the zest and original outlook of his books will also regret that he did not live to write more. In the seventy years and more since his death, his novels have been largely lost to view, but it is high time they delighted a fresh readership. As Machen forthrightly averred of *The Deadly Dowager*, these are real books with a story that *is* a story, and that from him was high praise indeed.

Mark Valentine
February 2016

(Thanks to Godfrey Brangham for his kind help with information about Edwin Greenwood)

THE DEADLY DOWAGER

I

THE FAMILY

In the days prior to the Tudors the de Birketts weren't very important, but in the reign of Henry VIII one Hugh de Birkett was rewarded for some piece of dirty chicanery by Thomas Cromwell with the lands and revenues of no less than three monasteries. This was the start of the Family fortune—or misfortune. We can forget about them for a couple of hundred years or so until we meet Charles de Birkett who, born in the year 1781, managed to be made first Baron Engleton by a grateful Prince Regent. On his death he left two sons to mourn him, Edward, who was born in the year 1820 and Alexander, who saw the light a couple of years later. Alexander didn't matter to anyone and his only effect on this story is that in the year 1853, after being duly married for a year, he had a son, Alfred.

At the opening of this story Alfred was exactly eighty years of age and very stupid. For nearly half a century he had been incumbent of a small living near Salisbury—Preston St. Pans. He had spent a large proportion of that half-century finding out who St. Pans was and writing a life of the good if rather elusive man. Also he had written many excruciatingly dull sermons; but most of the time he had just pottered—pottered from the church to the rectory and pottered about the village, whose inhabitants grew to look upon him rather as they looked upon any other act of God.

The elder son, Edward, on his father's untimely death, had duly inherited the title and the sadly depleted fortunes of the de Birketts, and so far from trying to restore them had made further inroads. The probability is that Edward, second Baron of

Engleton, would have blown the lot had it not been for his wife
Arabella who, apart from being extremely attractive in her youth,
had a shrewd head. She was born on January the first, 1850, and
was therefore literally *fin de siècle*. She was the daughter of one Sir
D'Arcy Brainton, the holder of numerous state sinecure offices,
and from her earliest days had been trained to regard money and
honours as the two necessaries of life. It is doubtful whether she
would have married the plain and rather evil-minded second
Baron had she not thought him considerably richer than he was.

So at the age of eighteen she duly married Edward, who
was thirty years her senior, and in accordance with the Family
tradition promptly had three children at intervals of two years
between each; Claude, the eldest, Arthur, and lastly a rather
colourless daughter Adela—"poor dear Adela," as she was called.
Edward was a real Victorian "chappie," side-whiskers and all. He
took to staying out late and smelling perpetually of brandy. This
was his undoing. Startlingly unpleasant things happened to his
liver; thus, when he took a bad chill one day he had no stamina
left and incontinently died.

Left a widow and Dowager Lady Engleton, Arabella made
unpleasant discoveries about the family finances. To all intents
and purposes, they didn't exist. Engleton Priory, one of the monasteries acquired from Cromwell, was badly mortgaged and just
paid for itself. The house in Mount Street was somewhere to live,
but there was precious little to live on. But she was shrewd, was
Arabella, and gambled fairly successfully on the Stock Exchange.
Though not rich, she made enough to send the two boys to
Eton and Harrow respectively, and thence into the Army. There
had been far too many de Birketts who had frivolled about and
wasted money. "Poor dear Adela" was a bit of a problem and
kept her mother awake at nights, but like so many problems, this
one suddenly and quite unexpectedly solved itself. She married
as well as could be expected of one so colourless, a certain John
Trefusis who fell in love with her at an "At Home," bore her away
to Cornwall where he had estates and tin mines (since defunct)
and married her. "Poor dear Adela" died in giving birth to a son
in 1894. Arabella, while secretly pleased at her daughter's being
got out of the way, professed displeasure at the marriage, a dis-

pleasure which saved her having to buy her daughter a wedding present. Adela had committed the unforgivable sin of marrying a Papist and had even become one herself. The son, Reginald, went a step further and became a Jesuit. This was a disgrace that the Family found hard to stomach.

Her sons, Claude and Arthur, did moderately well at Sandhurst and in due course passed into the Army, attaining fair rank by virtue of the de Birkett blood. Arthur was killed by a Boer sniper at Magersfontein, but having married a moderately wealthy woman there was no difficulty in letting Bertram de Birkett go in his father's footsteps, and Hamish, the other son, put a plate up in Harley Street after the usual preliminaries.

Claude, the third Baron, stayed with his mother in Mount Street, completely under her thumb. In fact, he did everything he was told to do, even marrying a girl called Helen Beamish, who, every one thought, was rich and who proved to have nothing. This made Helen an object of acute dislike to Arabella, who felt cheated. This dislike persisted even after the birth of a grandson, Henry, destined to be the fourth Baron.

When the Great War broke out, Claude rejoined the Army and a stray airman dropped a stray bomb which blew him all to pieces. His wife pined away and died early in 1916, leaving Henry, then aged three, on Arabella's hands.

Arabella did her duty by her grandson and lavished all the affections she had ever had on the boy, who was generally liked by the other survivors of the de Birketts. When this story opens, Henry was twenty, good-looking and (for a direct de Birkett) quite intelligent and, though he had been ruled with the same rod of iron that had driven his grandfather to drink and his father into a vacant imbecility, the rod was now antique and rusty and not too severely wielded. For all Arabella's sixty-five years of active scheming to restore the fallen fortunes of the de Birketts, the result had been little or nothing. As fast as the old lady had built them up, so did some unexpected blow of Fate send them hurtling down again.

So it came about that Arabella, one day in the autumn of 1933, summoned the Family to solemn conclave. It was hinted that she had some Plan, some Scheme that would somehow set the

Family on its feet again, enable Henry to wear his coronet in the House of Lords and look his peers in the eye without the stigma of poverty hanging round his head like some disreputable halo. Others might work, be clergymen or scientists or soldiers, but Henry was to be a legislator.

The entire Family was summoned and the entire Family came, some to humour grandmother, some out of curiosity, and some because, coming from a distance, they enjoyed Lady Engleton's meagre hospitality gratis at Mount Street, and it gave them an excuse for a jaunt up to London. Even Old Uncle Alfred had been prevailed upon to grace the conference with his white, hirsute presence. He disliked coming; indeed, a twelve-mile journey into Salisbury was much to his distaste, but there he was. So were the three nephews, Hamish and Bertram de Birkett and Father Reginald Trefusis, S.J. In addition, Sophia and Vera Beamish were there. These two spinsters were Helen de Birkett's sisters and not, of course, de Birketts in any real sense. They lived in a Norfolk village, Mellingham Parva, in a small house. Their brother Hugh was also present, ponderous and fifty, self-constituted squire of the village where he lived in the Big House. He was a military man of means, who had seen service in India and now ruled the roost at Mellingham Parva. The Beamishes had been mildly surprised at having been invited to a Family conclave. Lady Engleton had paid no attention to them since Helen's rather ill-timed and stupid death.

The Beamishes did everything but beam. Helen had been the youngest and nicest, and certainly the best looking, and Sophia and Vera had never really got over being passed over in favour of their younger sister. Edward de Birkett had met Major Hugh Beamish in happy pre-War days at some military club and neither of them having much to speak of in the way of brains, they had chummed up. Edward had gone to stay with his friend and had there met Helen. Old Man Beamish was alive in those days, reputed to be enormously rich. He had a mania for inventing health foods of all sorts, which were put on the market with reckless abandon. "Beamish's Brain Bread," "Beamish's Bran," "Beamish's Blood Builder," were only a few of them. The old man developed a monomania and took to eating nothing but his own products, and died during the War at an expensive private asylum. It was then found that he had been living on capital for years and that his health foods were a complete failure. Enough was left, however, to allow Hugh to live in fair comfort at Mellingham Parva. His sisters lived in the same village but not in the same house. The Major had seen to that. Sophia was thin and small and Vera large and fat, and reversing the usual order of things, it was Vera who was the dominant factor. Vera was definitely an unpleasant woman; she made her sister do the work, plagued the life out of the Vicar, and thought of various and varied methods of irritating the inhabitants of Mellingham Parva, who called her the "interfering elephant," and, of course, other things as well.

It was Vera then who opened the coroneted envelope which arrived from Her Ladyship, though it was addressed to Sophia. The letter was brief and to the point. Her Ladyship had important family matters to discuss and would be glad if the Misses Beamish would give her the pleasure of stopping at Mount Street for a day or two. Would they arrive in time for lunch on such and such a date? Vera sniffed.

"A somewhat late touch of conscience," she said. "The minute Her Ladyship wants help and advice she turns to me for it. I must think it over. . . ."

"But of course we'll go," Sophia said mildly. "We haven't been to London for years. It'll be something to talk about." She was frank in her snobbery.

"After the way she treated dear Helen I'm not at all sure we *should* accept, Sophie; not at all sure! I repeat, we must think it over. There are our duties in the village to consider."

She had no intention of refusing, really, and Sophie, knowing it full well, refrained from arguing.

"I wonder what she wants," she contented herself with asking. Vera wagged her huge head and looked mysterious.

"Perhaps it's about her Will," she said slowly.

"But Lady Engleton won't leave *us* anything. She'll give it all to Henry."

"There may be one or two trinkets, a few things of dear Helen's which she might want to give us before she passes over." Vera was one of those women who always talk about "passing over" instead of dying. She had a hazy vision of being given a tiara: in fact, the trinkets were assuming large proportions. "Depend upon it, that's what it is—a few trinkets."

Further talk was interrupted by the Major, who had come over post haste.

"Good morning, girls," he boomed. "I've just toddled over. I've had the most extraordinary letter."

"Not from Her Ladyship?" Vera asked.

"That's right. How did you know?"

"We've had one too. Not so much a letter as a royal command."

The Major gasped. This was without precedent.

"But why on earth does she want *you* to go?" he asked.

"She evidently wants to ask our advice about Henry," Vera said snappishly. In her opinion her brother's question and astonishment bordered upon being rude.

"Vera thinks she may want to give us a few trinkets before she is taken to avoid death duties," Sophie put in timidly.

"Taken to avoid death duties?" the Major asked blankly. "What on earth do you mean?" Vera explained. "Oh, I see. No, I don't think that's likely. Far more likely she wants something out of *us*. And she can't want to give *me* trinkets."

Vera agreed cordially that it wasn't likely.

"I'm not at all sure we shall go," she said.

The Major produced his letter. It was almost identical except that he had not been asked to stop at Mount Street, for which he was secretly very thankful. He made a grievance of it, however; he was made that way.

"I'm not sure that you're not right, Vera. After all, why should we be ordered about? Depend upon it, the old woman is after something. I don't like it. And she might have put me up. Not that I want to stop in her house after the way she treated poor Helen."

They all three wagged their heads over poor Helen, reposing quietly in the de Birkett vault at Engleton, and then fell to arguing again. Vera even went up to the Vicarage to ask the vicar's wife about it; ostensibly, that is; really to boast about being invited by Lady Engleton to her town "place." The vicar's wife was almost too eager for the Beamishes to accept. It was their duty to an aged woman, a Christian charity and all the rest of it. This nearly tilted the balance in favour of refusing.

They went, however, all three of them, much to the delight of the vicar and his wife. As the car went away to the station, five miles away, Mellingham Parva heaved an enormous sigh of relief.

2

THE CONFERENCE

The Misses Beamish arrived at Mount Street precisely at the right minute for lunch and after having gone up to their respective bedrooms, descended in stately style to meet Arabella. Vera had a set smile of forgiveness firmly moulded on her face, a sort of smile that said: "You may have treated me shabbily, but I'm a good, kind person and bear no malice." She had to take it off again, however, as Arabella did not put in an appearance. There was a message to state that Her Ladyship much regretted her inability to greet the Misses Beamish, but on account of her great age, felt sure they would understand. She sent Miss Caraway, her companion of many years, as deputy. The real truth was that Arabella was having a little woodcock all to herself in her private room. The other lunch was of the cold meat variety, and not much of it at that. Arabella saw no reason to feast the Beamish women on poultry and told Caraway so in no uncertain terms. "Old Uncle Alfred" was present, having arrived the previous day over three hours late. He had had trouble at Waterloo Station, flatly refusing to get into a taxi-cab, or indeed any form of motor vehicle. He had loudly described them as "the Devil's chariots" and quoting Holy Writ in support of his allegations, had aroused the sympathetic interest of an atheistic porter, who had finally managed to rake up a growler, nearly as old as Uncle Alfred himself. Into it he had been bundled, swathed in numerous mufflers, rugs and overcoats, his huge white beard tucked in, adding further warmth to his aged blood.

"The old bird's a gent, anyhow," the atheistic porter had said, as he regarded the half-crown that gleamed on his palm.

On arrival at Mount Street the "old bird" had been unswathed rather as they unswathe mummies, and put to bed promptly by the footman, who administered hot milk and a book of Robertson's sermons. Thus it was that Uncle Alfred put in an appearance at lunch with the Misses Beamish and Miss Caraway. Incidentally he appeared to have completely recovered from his wild adventures of the previous day, but displayed unmistakable signs of senility. True, he chatted away brightly about the complete decadence of England, the Book of Revelation and similar light topics of conversation, but while consuming the very inferior soup he several times mistook his huge white beard for his dinner napkin and used it accordingly. However, he couldn't talk all the time. Conversation languished till Caraway discovered that the Miss Beamishes were truly Norfolk and remembered that once, as a girl, she had spent a week at Cromer. Thus was a common bond established. Even so, the small talk only just held out till the rice and stewed fruit had been consumed. No one ate much except Uncle Alfred, who was heard to remark that cold mutton was "one of the nicest of viands." He was determined to enjoy his visit to the great wicked Babylon, and proceeded to do so, even to the extent of the filthy lunch that disgraced an uncomplaining board.

The conclave had been fixed for four o'clock, and every de Birkett was mutually surprised at meeting so many other de Birketts or near de Birketts. In the sombre and rather mouldy-smelling library they were gathered like hens at dusk. The Beamishes sat in a row on the oak settle, puffing up their feathers, Hamish and Bertram exchanged a few polite words as brothers, as in duty they were bound to do, and then relapsed into silence. Hamish was there under protest. He was a bony, busy man with a string of patients who paid three guineas each for the privilege of talking to him, and he very much disliked throwing away good money. Uncle Alfred was embedded in the leather chair with two mufflers on, each in faded colours reminding the world in general that countless years before he had been both to a public school and a university. He felt the cold, poor old soul!

The door opened and the butler announced a newcomer:

"The Reverend Father Trefusis."

The Misses Beamish glanced at each other in alarm, rather expecting to see something enter with horns and a tail. Vera even sniffed, as if endeavouring to detect a smell of sulphur. The result was disappointing from that point of view, for Reginald Trefusis was good-looking, and shook hands pleasantly with every one, especially with Hamish de Birkett, who welcomed him as an old friend. Reginald then went to greet Uncle Alfred. Strictly speaking, he should have greeted him first, as the patriarch of the party, but like a sensible person left the good wine till last. Uncle Alfred regarded his great-nephew suspiciously and ignored the outstretched hand.

"You the Papist fellow?"

Father Trefusis nodded brightly, as one found out in a base act.

"You ought to be ashamed of yourself, my boy. Look here, I'm an older man than you are. I don't want to be hard on you, but have you ever read the Book of Revelation? I don't suppose you're allowed to do that. What about the Scarlet Woman seated on seven hills, eh? If that's not Rome, what is it?"

He cupped a gnarled old hand and put it to his ear, waiting for a reply. Reginald Trefusis ignored the question by asking another.

"What does Aunt Arabella want? Do you know?"

"No, I don't. But if I'd known you'd been asked, Reginald, I should have stayed at home. You're after my living, that's what you are, but let me tell you this—no one gets Preston St. Pans till I'm dead. If you fellers ever get in the saddle again, then God help England."

Try as he would, Father Trefusis could not suppress a fleeting grin.

"That's right; laugh at me!" the old man piped. "If you'd read the Book of Revelation, you would know about the ten horns? That's a poser, eh?"

Trefusis bowed gravely and crossed over to Hamish, who was getting more and more impatient.

"Glad to see *you* here, Reggie," he growled. "Any idea what it's all about?"

"Not the remotest."

"That old ass, Alfred, is in his dotage; ought to be lethalled, like a worn-out dog."

"He's not too bad, Hamish," said Trefusis. "Of course he's a bit dotty, but our dear great aunt isn't, and I'm curious to know what she's up to. Probably something to do with the Family. I can understand her asking *you*, Hamish, in that case, but why *me?* Or those dried-up Beamishes? You're a de Birkett and we aren't, strictly speaking."

"I dislike all the de Birketts except myself," Hamish said. "Even Henry. The lad's a prig. Where *is* he, by the way?"

"What about the Douai version?" Uncle Alfred called out suddenly. "What about Bloody Mary?"

Hamish wriggled as if he had crumbs in his vest.

"Silly old parrot," he muttered. "Shut up, you old fool!" He raised his voice for all to hear. Even Uncle Alfred heard it, in spite of his deafness. Ripples of rage coursed up and down his bald pate, which grew pink and then began to shine. Bertram, who had preserved a stolid silence, thought it fit to intervene. He always considered himself a broad-minded man. He read Aldous Huxley and thought there was "something in the feller."

"Hamish!" he said severely, and as befitted the elder. "You shouldn't lose your temper. Live and let live, Uncle; live and let live." He added this to the old man, who seemed to think it was a reasonable contention. His domed head gradually paled.

"I don't expect anything but rudeness from atheists," he mumbled.

"That may apply to Hamish, Uncle, but whatever Reginald may be, he's not an atheist," Bertram went on. He felt like human oil on troubled waters. "Come now!"

"Ah! There are worse things than atheism," the old man retorted. "What about the Massacre of St. Bartholomew?"

"How right the reverend gentleman is, in spite of his age," Vera murmured. "How very right."

"Bosh!" said Hugh simply. "You talk through your toque, Vera." He laughed at his own joke, and Uncle Alfred, thinking he had been "got at," began to grow pink again.

Reginald was vastly amused, but Hamish, thinking of lost fees, was chafing.

"What a crew!" he muttered. "What a bunch!"

Further argument was stilled by the sudden entrance of the

Lady Arabella. It was more like the state entrance of a judge. Supported on the left by Caraway and on the right by her walking-stick, she came upon them. Not that she was feeble, but she wasn't taking any risks at her age. Henry and Mr. Merry brought up the rear. Mr. Merry was seventy odd and had been the de Birkett legal adviser for years. He was senior partner of Merry, Meldrum and Isaacs. Mr. Merry piloted Arabella to the large chair that stood at the head of the long table. She appeared in a very good humour, bowed and smiled to every one collectively, not forgetting the Beamishes. She was elegantly dressed as becomes an old lady, in violet silk with a shawl and cameo. On her head was perched a huge lace cap, adorned with festoons of ribbon. An impressive sight. She took her chair and lowered herself into it. It was noticeable that Henry kept out of the way and answered the greetings of the others with standoffish nods.

"I'm sorry to have kept you all waiting," Arabella said, "but must plead old age. It is so good of you all to have come to gratify an old woman's whim."

There was a buzz of appropriate murmurs.

"I should not have asked you here and put you to all this trouble had the matter not been very important—very important indeed. Perhaps we'd better all draw up to the table; we shall feel more *en famille*."

The next few minutes were occupied by chair finding and individual greetings. The atmosphere began to be almost jovial. The only fly in the ointment was Uncle Alfred who, still smarting under Hamish's insults and the presence of Father Trefusis, affected to have a fit of deafness. He had found this trick very convenient during the last twenty-five years, when he wanted to make a thorough nuisance of himself. It was infallible.

"Eh?" he shouted suddenly, not moving from his chair. "What's all the commotion? What's Belle talking about? Why weren't you down to lunch, Belle?"

Major Beamish boomed in his ear that Her Ladyship wanted them to gather round the table.

"Why?"

"More convenient."

"Is it?"

"Yes!"

"Oh!"

It took a good five minutes to get the old gentleman to sit at Arabella's right hand. He developed the idea that as the oldest living male de Birkett he should sit at the head of the table.

"But you haven't called this meeting, Uncle," Hamish said irritably, as the minutes went by.

"Haven't I?"

"No!"

"Oh!"

It was all very difficult, but at last they were all sorted out, Uncle Alfred being put at Arabella's immediate right hand. They then grouped themselves in an informal order of precedence right down the table, the Beamishes being at the end. Henry took the bottom of the table, facing his grandmother; he was noticeably uneasy. Mr. Merry occupied a hard chair in the no man's land at Arabella's elbow, and began to undo a dispatch case in which he scratched about, looking for a memorandum. At the last moment, Uncle Alfred created a further diversion by making the discovery that his deaf ear was next to Arabella, and had to be changed over with Bertram. Under cover of the resulting confusion, Father Trefusis gave Hamish a nudge.

"It's just like one of those scenes that never happen," he said with a grin.

"How d'you mean?"

"Like something from a modern novel by Walpole or some such. Matriarch, Uncle-arch, Family Solicitor and poor relations. It's irresistibly funny."

"Glad you think so. I'd like to bomb the whole lot, wouldn't you?"

"Remember my cloth . . ."

At last the scene was set and Uncle Alfred cupped an expectant ear.

"What are we waiting for?" he asked.

Caraway was still hovering round, hoping against hope to be asked to join in. She had a certain right, she thought, having occupied her present job for over thirty years. Arabella motioned her to go, thus nipping the hope in the bud.

"Go away, Caraway!"

Caraway went, and the door bumped softly behind her. She exercised her moral right, however, by listening at the keyhole.

There was an expectant hush.

"You'd better say your piece, Merry," Arabella said, "and save my breath till later."

Mr. Merry rose, put a pair of old-fashioned folders astride his nose, and looked at his memorandum.

"Her Ladyship has asked you all here on a matter which she considers, and rightly in my opinion, one of extreme urgency."

Here Henry suddenly rose in his chair, very red and self-conscious.

"Before Mr. Merry goes any further," he said rapidly, "I want you all to understand that this business has got nothing to do with me."

"Don't be a prig, Henry," his grandmother said sharply. "Sit down and try not to be a fool!"

Henry sat down. One does, when the Arabellas of this world insist.

"The boy's just romantic," she went on. "Pay no attention to him. Go on, Merry."

Merry went on obediently.

"The one interest that we all have close to our hearts," he said, "is the welfare and prosperity of the de Birkett Family. Yes," he added, for the benefit of those who were not de Birketts, "even those of you who are only connected with the Family by marriage. You are, as it were, de Birketts by adoption. In these days, when Jack's as good as his master, when the idea of Family and its traditions . . ."

"You can cut that chatter and come to the point," Arabella said, rather snappily.

"In any case," Reginald said silkily, "not being a de Birkett, I have a certain dislike for the de Birkett tradition."

The old lady threw a venomous glance at him.

"Your mother had the honour to be a de Birkett," she said icily. "Do you forget that, Reginald?" Reginald smiled.

"She was a de Birkett," was all he said, waving the question of honour.

"I hesitated as to whether to include you at this meeting," the old lady said, her beady black eyes sparkling with memories of long dead squabbles with Adela. "I never have liked you. You were a most unpleasant baby, and the passing of years has seemingly brought no improvement."

"I wouldn't offend you for anything, my dear Great Aunt," he said, "but it's unfair to rope us all in as de Birketts. We aren't."

His glance included the Beamishes. It was Vera's looked for opportunity to chip in.

"I and my sister," she said heavily, "—I will not include my brother who can speak for himself—but I and my sister are only too honoured to be included, even remotely, with such a wonderful and distinguished Family."

Major Hugh opened his eyes rather widely at this. It hardly tallied with all that had gone before. He was not an agreeable man, but to do him justice, was not such a snob as all that. He grunted in a non-committal way. Arabella beamed on Vera and Sophie through huge horn-rimmed glasses, specially put on for the purpose.

"Thank you, Miss Beamish," she said, with her pleasant though rather forced, old-world smile. "I shall do myself the pleasure of visiting you in the country some day."

The Misses Beamish both squirmed together.

"What's it all about?" Uncle Alfred quavered suddenly. He had been indulging in extraordinary gyrations to bring his serviceable ear in range of each speaker. "I shall want my tea in a minute. What do you want to do, Belle? Read us your Will?"

"It's not usual," Arabella answered, "to read a Will without a corpse. I am not yet a corpse! Far from it. I have no intention of being a corpse for many a long year."

"Spoken like a true de Birkett," said Reginald. Arabella ignored him.

"No," said Arabella, "the point I wish to make clear is this. The fortunes of our house are at a low ebb. I have done my best to restore them, but the Great War and Greedy Governments, and, it must be admitted, the foolish profligacy of one or two of our ancestors, have made my efforts of little avail. The House of de Birkett is at this moment represented by that boy there." She pointed a ringed and clawlike hand at the self-conscious Henry, who was unable to deny it. "There is little or nothing with which he can sustain the past glories of our House, or take his rightful place amongst his peers."

"He might work," Hamish suggested. He had long given up hope of getting back to Harley Street to collect fees. "It's not a bad notion. I have to work. Even Bertram has to go on parade."

"That's just what *I* say," Henry began eagerly. "I don't want to be a legislator. I should enjoy a job." Reginald and Hamish glanced at the lad with new interest. The old lady rapped the table with her rings and her eyes blazed.

"I will not have it!" she said. "You owe me everything, Henry, including obedience. You owe your country something too. You are a Peer of the Realm. I expect the others to support me."

Henry subsided. Like his father, he usually took the line of least resistance.

"But, Aunt," Bertram asked, "how can we help?"

"Money!"

The word came pat. No beating about the bush with Arabella. Her directness was almost indecent, and produced a sudden hush.

It was, strange to relate, Major Beamish who spoke next. He heaved himself forward.

"But," he protested, "I don't suppose any of us have got a couple of coppers to jingle. I'm sure I haven't, with all this taxation. And dash it, I'm a Beamish!"

"I'm in debt as it is," Bertram murmured. "Can't seem to help it somehow—what?"

Uncle Alfred's hearing had improved vastly.

"My stipend is very small," he croaked, "very small indeed. Barely four hundred a year—I can't do anything! Anyway, I'm too old."

"Four hundred and forty pounds per annum with a Vicarage and coals," Arabella said, correcting him.

"Coals? Coals? What's coals?" Uncle Alfred muttered irritably. "Coals don't signify."

"I don't mind helping Henry a bit with University fees," Hamish said slowly. "But it won't be much. I'm making a decent income when I'm allowed to, but I want it for myself—for good dinners, good cigars and old brandy. I earn it. Then I'm selfish; I admit it gratefully."

Reginald Trefusis had been studying the ceiling, finger-tips together.

"Go on, Great Aunt," he said suddenly, "I feel you've not done yet. You've something up your sleeve."

"For once, Reginald, you're right," she said. "But everyone's making such a noise; I'm given no opportunity."

Mr. Merry intervened.

"One moment," he said, "one moment! Her Ladyship has a plan whereby you may help her without incurring any personal expenditure."

They all looked relieved at this important addition to the per-emptory word "Money." Arabella leaned back in her chair, folded her claws and regarded them like some very ancient owl.

"This clatter is quite unnecessary," she said. "Of course I know you are all poor as mice, poor as I am myself. I don't want your money, I want your lives."

"Holocausts and offerings of rams," Reginald murmured. The Misses Beamish looked frightened, as well they might.

"I want you to let me insure your lives for the ultimate benefit of His Lordship, my grandson."

"So that's the cat that lurks in the bag," Hamish said reflec-tively. "Good Lord, what an idea!"

Arabella held up her hand for quiet. Once launched, she was not to be stopped.

"Engleton Priory is mortgaged," she said. "It just supports itself and the agent, and supplies us here with fruit, vegetables and eggs."

"No chickens, eh?" Uncle Alfred asked maliciously.

"An occasional fowl as well."

"I'll guarantee it didn't produce that mutton we had for lunch. Oh, dear, no!" He cackled with laughter.

Arabella turned on him with strangely youthful ferocity.

"Silence, Alfred! This house is the property of the Family, but what with monstrous taxes and excessive rates, I am barely able to sustain it. Henry, to take his proper place in the world, must have capital. I propose with your consent to insure your lives up to twenty thousand pounds."

The silence that greeted this was one of sheer astonishment.

"But, Aunt," Bertram said at last, "may I ask a question? I'm no business man, but if things are as bad as you say, and I can quite believe it, where are you going to find the dough to pay the premiums? See what I mean—what?"

Arabella sighed impatiently.

"Tell them, Merry."

Merry put on his folders again.

"I must hark back a bit," he said. "When Her Ladyship married His Lordship, her father, the late Sir D'Arcy Brainton, made a settlement which luckily—at least, that is——"

"Go on. Say it, Merry," Hamish said impatiently. "Which luckily our late Great-Uncle Edward couldn't get his teeth into. Tied up, eh?"

"That is correct, Mr. Hamish. Tied up! It was ten thousand pounds, which was carefully invested and reinvested in the Funds. That money has more than doubled itself during the last sixty years—more than doubled itself. Her Ladyship had to part with a little of it on one occasion, but in the main it was untouched. Her Ladyship proposes to utilize about five thousand pounds of this money on paying premiums."

"It'll cost every penny of that," Hamish said, inspecting the company with a professional eye. "Every solid penny—and a bit more."

"When the policies mature," Merry went on ghoulishly, "when the policies mature, with the addition of this dowry, Lord Engleton should have about forty thousand pounds with which to sustain his position in the world and his dignity in the House of Lords."

"I wish you wouldn't talk like that, Merry," Bertram said peevishly. "You make me feel as if I were dead already. You roll that word 'mature' round your mouth like—like a liqueur!"

Uncle Alfred had been listening with a blank expression.

"This is all beyond me. Why do you want to insure me?" he said suddenly and began to cough. "Wait a minute—wait a minute. I must go outside and spit a bit."

This was a habit he had contracted at Preston St. Pans, where the garden was conveniently situated for the purpose. Miss

Caraway had to beat a hasty retreat; in fact, she hid in the alcove under the stairs. Uncle Alfred got out into Mount Street and "spat a bit," to the amusement of a taxi-driver.

In the library Hamish suddenly laughed boisterously.

"You don't propose to insure that old bag of rubbish, do you?" he asked. "The premium would be a cold million! I wouldn't give him ten minutes myself, all muffled up and spitting. The idea is a joke."

"We have other views with regard to the Reverend Alfred," Merry interposed.

"I've no illusions about Alfred. The old idiot has been paying a hundred a year in premium on a life policy for the last forty years," Arabella said frankly. "I propose to get him to transfer the benefit to Henry. At present he has made it over to the Charity Organization people."

"But I don't want his money," Henry said piteously. No one paid any attention. Hamish was amused by the whole thing and not unsympathetic, in view of the fact that it would cost him nothing. The Beamish girls were rather shocked. Bertram didn't like it, because he didn't like thinking of dying. He said as much.

Uncle Alfred floated back. He had put on an overcoat to go out into Mount Street, and had forgotten to take it off.

"You'll find me a tough nut to crack, Belle," he gasped as he sat down again. "I can pick a chicken bone with any one. By the way, isn't it tea time? I've asked for dripping toast. I don't think I want to be insured any more," he added inconsequently.

"I'll talk to you after dinner, Alfred. Go on, Merry."

"The appointments have all been made with the various companies concerned and the sums fixed—that is, of course, subject to your consent, and I cannot see how such consent can be reasonably withheld, when we think of the worthy object of these policies. Have you any valid objection to raise, Major Beamish, against having your life insured?"

Directly appealed to, Major Beamish stroked his chin and got rather red. He was flattered, though, that he had been asked first, before the real de Birketts. Merry had carefully selected him to be a bell-wether.

"I can't say that I have," he said slowly.

"Excellent! And doubtless your sisters share your very sane and charitable views?"

But Vera didn't, not by a long chalk! She felt she had been dragged up to town, given an uncomfortable bedroom and fed on frozen mutton under completely false pretences. Her heavy cheeks waggled a negative.

"I think Life Insurance is wicked," she said sombrely.

"But, my dear lady, why?"

"It's tempting Providence. Who are we to say when our end is to be?"

"Death is inevitable."

"Yes, but God is not mocked!"

All of which is undeniable.

There was a solemn pause. This was an unexpected jolt to otherwise smoothly running plans. Even Arabella was at a loss. She swallowed her irritation at what she considered (and rightly) the maunderings of a fat and hypocritical woman. There was more in it than met the ear.

"'Heaven helps those that help themselves' used to be a dictum in my young days," was all she trusted herself to say. Vera seemed in an ecstasy which puzzled the other Beamishes.

"We had hoped you had invited us here, Lady Engleton, for very different reasons."

"What reasons?" Arabella asked sharply.

"Our poor dead sister was, after all, our dear nephew's mother." She spoke as if the matter had been seriously questioned. "We *had* hoped that you were going to give us some little trinket in memory of her."

The old lady's throat worked. So that was the game! It was blackmail! Sophie gave her sister an admiring glance which Arabella put on the slate to her debit account, and then forced her celebrated smile.

"But my dear Miss Beamish, why didn't you say so before. Of course, if there is any little thing of Helen's that you care for, I should be only too pleased to let you have it. Anything that may have belonged to your mother," she added.

This was a fortunate afterthought, a saving clause. The only thing that Arabella could recall that fulfilled that condition was a hideous gold wire brooch with a huge crystal in it, under which reposed a lot of faded and mouldy hair in plaits. Vera could have that and welcome; if she had to go to a ring or so, it would be worth it.

"That's very gracious of you, Lady Engleton." Vera warmed up again and descended to earth.

"And about this insurance policy?" Merry asked rather tactlessly.

"If my brother thinks that it is quite a suitable thing to do, I shall be swayed by his advice. So will my sister." Sophie wasn't asked even.

"And you, Mr. Hamish? What is your view of this matter?"

"Yes, and what about my tea?" Uncle Alfred asked shrilly. "It's long past my usual hour for a collation." He always referred to tea as a "collation."

"Ring the bell, please, Merry," Arabella said.

After a decent interval Caraway appeared, having first tiptoed away from the keyhole.

"You rang, my lady?"

"Yes. Take the Reverend Alfred into the little drawing-room and see that his tea is given him at once."

"Yes, my lady."

Uncle Alfred heaved himself to his feet by a mighty effort of will power and pottered out. Directly he had gone, Hamish spoke.

"I think the whole affair is completely grotesque and unnatural," he said, "but for the life of me, I don't see how I can object. I must warn you that I'm a first-class life and you'll make nothing out of my dead body for many years."

Mr. Merry bowed from the waist.

"I'm sure I hope not, Mr. Hamish. Long may you be spared to carry on your excellent work. I take it you have no objection, Mr. Bertram?"

Bertram wriggled uneasily.

"I don't know why I don't like the idea," he said. "I just don't and that's all there is *to* it—what?"

"Being insured won't help you to die, Bertram," Arabella said quickly. "You're old enough to realize that, surely. Don't be a fool!"

Bertram blushed. He hated being called a fool, and Arabella knew it.

"I suppose if it's good enough for Hamish, it's good enough for me," he acquiesced humbly.

There was no one left but Reginald Trefusis, who was still examining the ceiling. Mr. Merry became almost playful in his anxiety to placate.

"And last, but not least, what about you, Mr. Reginald?" He held his breath. He had always maintained to Lady Engleton that it was altogether unwise, inviting Reginald to this gathering. There was something rather uncanny about him. He was the only one of the de Birkett blood capable of meeting Arabella on her own ground.

"Father Trefusis to you, Mr. Merry," Reginald said primly. He knew that this would draw Arabella, who snorted accordingly.

"Father, indeed! Rubbish!"

Reginald smiled.

"A title, my dear Great Aunt," he said, "a title I try to deserve. As to the insurance business, I think you had better count me out. To start with, I don't think any company would take my risk."

Mr. Merry showed elaborate concern.

"I'm sorry to hear that, Father Trefusis. Nothing wrong, I hope?"

"Oh, no. On the contrary, I'm very well. *Mens sana in corpore sano* is one of the precepts of my Order, and I hope I have both, but I'm a bad risk. You see, I live under perpetual orders like any other soldier." He bowed gracefully to Bertram, who felt pleased. "I might be ordered to China on a mission—or even to Wales. My life is not worth a moment's purchase. I'm a worse risk than dear old Alfred even."

Arabella knew she was thwarted at this point in her great effort to rehabilitate the de Birketts. Argument was useless. She hated intensely this suave, genial person who seemed to have a secret in which she did not share. She tried to stare down his bland smile and failed.

"I said just now that I always disliked you, Reginald. I now repeat it!"

"I shall not pretend I am deeply grieved," Reginald continued, enjoying the sound of his rather mellifluous voice, and then added with cold vigour: "I think the whole idea is outrageous and abominable."

"Come! Come!" This from Major Beamish.

"I do! You want to turn this lad—forgive me if I seem patronizing, Henry—into a do-nothing. I refuse point-blank. The boy wants to work and be a man. Let him, in God's name! Let him be owner and agent at Engleton Priory. I should like to see him Prior, but that's only by the way and a private prejudice."

Arabella began to get to her feet.

"Send for Caraway," she said. "I've nothing more to say. We have been near neighbours for some time, Reginald, and yet this is the first time you have taken the trouble to visit me."

"I was waiting for the summons, my dear Great Aunt. I have frequently seen your bath chair in the neighbourhood, but hardly dared approach."

"You can take it from me, Reginald," said Arabella, trembling with temper, "that if Caraway ever does push my chair down Farm Street again, it will be as much as her job is worth. You have no sense of family pride, or sense of duty. I never wish to see you again!" She turned to the others. "Thank you," she continued. "You will none of you regret your kindness in acceding to my wishes."

Caraway entering at that moment, the tirade came to an end, and Arabella, Dowager Lady Engleton, retired on her companion's arm and in glory. The minute the door shut, Henry turned to Father Trefusis.

"Thank you, Cousin Reginald," he said simply.

"That's all right, Henry."

Father Trefusis had only a short way to walk and left the gathering with a genial good-bye in company with Hamish, for whom he had a certain regard. Hamish was not a man to inspire affection, but Reginald felt that there was something commendable in his frank selfishness, quite apart from the fact that he had a first-rate brain.

"That aunt of ours is a bad old woman," Hamish announced, after they had gone a few yards.

"I'm afraid you're right," Reginald said reluctantly, "but it's the lad that worries me. What's going to become of him? What I said wasn't just mere oratory, you know."

The other gave a grunt.

Back in the library, Major Hugh was grumbling that he had not been asked to dinner. Not that he wanted to be asked. He had ideas of a little tag round Shaftesbury Avenue on his own. After all, he wasn't often in London. He accepted Bertram's invitation to have a drink at the club, with dignified alacrity. Mr. Merry refused to accompany them. He *had* been asked to dine as he had certain business papers to go over with Her Ladyship. He thanked them all the same.

Vera and Sophie went up to change for dinner, and put on different cameos.

"She *did* want something," Vera said, snapping her jaws together. "I was right. I'm always right when judging others."

"I hope we've done correctly in consenting to be insured," Sophie said. "I wonder if it *is* tempting Providence? I hope not, I'm sure."

"There's still the matter of the trinkets to be considered," Vera said. And there the matter stood.

3

UNCLE ALFRED

Dinner at Mount Street was over and had passed without incident, except that Uncle Alfred had twice inadvertently blown his nose on his dinner napkin.

"Poor old gentleman—very absent-minded," Sophie had murmured to Mr. Merry.

"Nonsense," Alfred had shouted back, his deafness seemingly miraculously cured. "When you get to my age you just grab what's handy."

The dinner itself was of the same category as lunch. Much of the food was the same, except that it was called by fancy names on a handwritten menu card. The mutton, for instance, appeared curried, but was called *Mouton rechauffé à l'Indienne*. It was an insult to the great Empire of the Moguls. Uncle Alfred had a bit of trouble with the boiled fowl (*poule bonne femme*), one of the "occasional fowls" from Engleton Priory. His false teeth suddenly ran amok and played havoc with his ancient uvula. He explained at length and with vivid details that they had as a central pivot one gigantic and hollow dental relic of bygone years. It was not until the ladies had withdrawn and left him and Mr. Merry over some cheap port that he regained his equanimity and could discuss any other topic. He removed the offending denture and proceeded to wash out the hollow relic. This ritual was accompanied by strange whistling sounds.

Mr. Merry coughed, preparatory to coming down to brass tacks.

"That's easier," said Uncle Alfred at last. "If I don't wash him, he gives me gyp!"

"Don't you think Her Ladyship's plan altogether admirable?" Merry asked tentatively.

"No," was the uncompromising reply. "Very silly idea."

This put Mr. Merry in a quandary. Somehow or other he had to induce this old man to sign a new will, already drawn up and reposing in his bag.

"Belle should have thought of it years ago—like I did."

"Of course, as your legal adviser, I know the terms of your policy and of your will, Mr. Alfred."

"Not bad, eh? What shall I cut up for?"

"Your policy is worth, with increments, about £6,500, which together with your other investments should mean about £8,000 all told."

"You know it all pat, don't you?" the old man said suspiciously.

"It is my duty," the other answered solemnly. He almost bared his bosom to die in defence of duty.

"Shocking port this is. . . ." Uncle Alfred was a realist at heart.

"Her Ladyship feels that you could not have been aware of the impoverished state of the Family when you dictated the terms of your last will and testament."

"So *that's* why I was asked up to town and asked to travel in motor cabs? To make me change it? Belle was always a deep 'un. Thought she could gammon the old man, eh?"

Uncle Alfred turned a crafty eye on the solicitor, who reflectively sipped his drink.

"I should hardly have expressed myself like that, Mr. Alfred," he said.

"No, I can well believe that. You were never truthful, Merry, never! No—I'm leaving my little bit to charities. You can tell Belle to put that in her pipe!"

"Surely you feel, sir, that charity should begin at home?"

"Just remembered that, have you? No, Merry, I'm eighty and three-quarters, and I'm too old to go altering things."

"But, Mr. Alfred——"

"That's final! I'm feeling shivery and I'm going to bed. You think I'm an old fool, Merry. I ain't!"

He tottered to his feet and began to shuffle to the door. Merry felt that he had handled the matter badly, which was true.

Back in the drawing-room, Sophie was singing "Juanita" in a faded, but not objectionable voice. The piano was rather out of tune, as Arabella didn't favour music as a rule. On this occasion, however, conversation had languished. They had discussed the weather, Cromer, the wickedness of Governments, and Arabella had once more expressed the hope of visiting the Misses Beamish at Mellingham Parva. Caraway was also present, sitting apart and doing some mending—darning stockings, to be precise, though she camouflaged this side of her labours to such an extent that she might have been doing embroidery. Vera had suggested "a little music," and Sophie had begun her one parlour trick. Arabella had disliked it, but agreed, since it gave her time to think and obviated the necessity of talking to two spinsters she disliked. Uncle Alfred blew in, flushed with temporary victory, and applauded heartily during a pause, thinking the song was over.

"Bravo," he said. "*Bravissimo!*" And going over to the piano, pressed his ear firmly against the case and added: "Put the pedal down and play loud—a schottische or a gallop or something!"

Merry in the meantime had caught Arabella's eye and shaken his head ever so slightly. Arabella's tight lips grew tighter.

"Stop that noise the woman's making," she told Merry in a sharp undertone. Merry was spared this ordeal by the termination of "the piece."

"Do it again," said Uncle Alfred. "Do it again! It makes my gums tingle." But Arabella was having none of that.

"You must be very tired after your long and exhausting journey, Miss Beamish," she said in a high-pitched voice.

There was no mistaking this remark. It was a definite command which even Vera could hardly ignore. She did not give in without a struggle, however.

"I thought, Lady Engleton, that you were going to show us poor Helen's little trinkets, but perhaps we are all too tired. The morning will do, and you mustn't get over-tired at your great age." That was a nasty one, Vera thought, and Arabella took it as it was intended. She had no objection to using her great age for her own advantage, but disliked others using it for theirs.

"Never felt better in my life. You shall see the trinkets in the morning. I'll have them brought from the bank." They weren't at the bank, but it made the stuff sound more opulent. "Good night, Miss Beamish. Good night, Miss Sophie."

The sisters, after the usual formalities, drifted out, accompanied by Caraway, who was heard in the hall asking them if they would "take anything."

"As many of Helen's jewels as she can lay hands on!" Arabella said with heavy sarcasm. "Let 'em wait!"

Uncle Alfred tried to go out with them. He knew his Arabella.

"I'll be going along as well. I'm shivering. You've told 'em to put in a hot-water bottle, I hope, Belle?" He began to get up from his seat by the piano.

"Sit down, Alfred. I want to have a word with you."

"What about?"

"Money!"

These two ancient de Birketts eyed each other, and Merry had the sensation of feeling as if he were about to be an eye-witness of an awe-inspiring ordeal by combat. Caraway came back into the room and stood hesitating.

"Don't go, Caraway; I shall want you."

"Very good, m'lady." Caraway sat down well away from the battlefield. For all that, poor old Alfred felt closed in on every side. He was game, however, and faced his sister-in-law.

"Fat bulls of Bashan," he said, indifferent to sexual questions.

"Merry's told me what you want," he added, "and you ain't getting it. He knows where it's going."

"I think your will is both selfish and stupid," Arabella said. "You are one of the few real de Birketts left; in fact, the oldest and most direct in descent, and you leave your money to clerical charities! Have you no pride of race and breeding?"

The old man snuffled and displayed his breeding by wiping his nose on the back of his hand, but he actually did feel a little mean and into his old brain there gradually percolated the knowledge that this iron old lady really and truly did believe in the de Birketts. It was an overpowering passion with her; had been so all through her life. He was slightly awed by it and not a little scared.

"Edward never did much for me, nor my father before me," he muttered.

"And so you propose to visit their sins on your grandnephew?"

"Nonsense! But I won't have *you* having a penny of it, Belle!" he said fiercely. "Not a sou! I don't mind leaving the boy a hundred."

Arabella's lip curled.

"To pay off the mortgage on the Priory?" she asked.

"No—just to amuse himself."

"I forbid any such thing! I intend that you shall leave your money where it rightfully belongs and not leave it to be squandered aimlessly in so-called charity."

The old man flared up.

"You take too much on yourself, Belle. I won't be dictated to by you. Oh, dear, oh, dear, I'm too tired to argue. I'm shivery!"

Arabella ignored his attempt to beat a retreat. If he were tired, so much the better.

"To clerical charities!" she cried shrilly. "When your own flesh and blood must starve! What has the Church ever done for you?"

It never occurred to him to answer that it had kept him in comparative comfort for purely nominal duties for nearly sixty years. Arabella went on, seeing that his non-advancement was a grievance with him. The old man ruminatively worked his false teeth about with his tongue.

"Have you ever been made a Bishop—or even a Canon?"

"No, I can't say that I have ... I can't remember it, anyway!" It had long been Uncle Alfred's secret ambition to be styled "the

Hon. and Rev. Canon Alfred de Birkett." The old lady pressed her advantage.

"If you had been made a Bishop, it would only have been of the Cannibal Islands!"

"I should have refused such preferment," Uncle Alfred said haughtily, somewhat scared. "Anyhow, it's too late to be a Bishop now," he added with a certain relief. Uncle Alfred had no wish to win the martyr's crown. "But I think my services might have been recognized. I've sent every Bishop a copy of my *Life of St. Pans*."

"You should have had a stall in the cathedral ages ago. Your *Life of St. Pans* is just silly, Alfred. It was tactless of you to push it down the Bishop's throat. No, you should have been made a Canon just because you are a de Birkett. Heaven knows there's no other excuse."

"You've got a very nasty way of putting things, Belle. I want to go to bed with some hot milk, please."

"How would you like to have a stall for the last year or so of your life?"

"Last year? What d'you mean? I shall live to be ninety!"

"I'll speak to the Prime Minister about it—on one condition." She did not add that she barely had met the Prime Minister, nor did she know whether he had anything to do with Cathedral Chapters. She knew that he appointed Bishops in some way or other. That was good enough for Uncle Alfred, anyway.

"The condition being that I alter my will, I suppose? I don't want to be bothered."

There was a cold pause. Arabella spoke like the whistle of an east wind.

"I never thought that you would be so selfish as to refuse, so I instructed Merry here to draw one up for you. Get it out, Merry, and let him sign it. Caraway here can witness it, and so will I."

If Merry felt a few qualms about "undue influence," he kept them to himself. Uncle Alfred's beard worked convulsively as he chewed his annoyance.

"I don't like you, Belle," he said. "Never have, though you were decent looking as a girl. But you'll never let me go to bed till I've signed the thing. Give it here, Merry. I want to go to sleep."

The new will was placed before him. It was short and to the

point, simply revoking all previous wills and leaving everything to his dear grand-nephew, Henry. He signed it and watched it witnessed by Arabella and Jane Caraway. The old man snarled at them.

"I feel like a rabbit being torn to ribbons by dogs. Now I'm going to bed."

He began to move to the door at tortoise speed. Once there, he turned and wagged a lean finger at his sister-in-law and delivered his Parthian shot.

"I can always invalidate that," he wheezed, "by making another. Understand *that!*"

He laughed nastily and they could hear him shuffling upstairs and coughing at intervals. Arabella paid no attention.

"Is that document legal, Merry?" she asked.

"Absolutely, m'lady."

"Good. Is his lordship in yet, Caraway?"

"I haven't heard him, m'lady."

"H'm. I'll talk to him in the morning. I don't like him being out late like this, wasting his energies. It's nearly ten o'clock!" Then for the first time she began to droop a bit. "I'm tired too. Give me your arm, Caraway. And by the way, get a fresh hot-water bottle for the Reverend Alfred. Bring it to me first—to test the temperature."

4

DORA

The minute the conference had finished that afternoon, Henry had dashed from the house, pawned his watch and rung up Dora Winslow.

"Is that you, Dora? I've had a ghastly, unthinkable afternoon. Have a spot of dinner with me!"

"But can you afford it, Henry? Let's meet afterwards . . ."

"No, now! And we'll have some grub in peace. Please, dear!"

"Why, of course. Same old place, where they cook mussels so nicely?"

"The same. Good-bye, sweet!"

It had been a lucky day for Henry when he met Dora. She was the daughter of a Permanent Official in the Foreign Office—one of those men who did the work while others talked about it. She was the only possible antidote for Henry, to counteract his grandmother, and he sought her with unfailing regularity.

Dora was a modern girl all right, but not obtrusively so. Nature had given her a bountiful supply of good looks, but she helped Nature just sufficiently to be extremely attractive as well. Dora had definite views and was older at nineteen than Henry at twenty, older, possibly, than Henry would ever be. She was in love with Henry, but sensibly in love; she knew his weaknesses, realized that he was easily led, and determined to do the leading. He was her man, and she was out for him tooth and nail. Yes, Henry was decidedly lucky when he met Dora. It was rarely enough that Henry had any money: Arabella saw that his allowance was microscopic and refused to let him earn. The result was that going out together was a genuine and very real treat to these young people. They met at a small restaurant just off Wardour Street when they held high holiday, a pleasant spot, just expensive enough to be really good. Dora was not mean, but liked value for money; her ideas on home-making being very definite. At that very period she was taking a cookery course, so as to be able to tell any cook on earth "where she got off," if necessary.

They were eating the mussels for which the restaurant is justly famed, and Henry was pouring out the whole, horrid business. Dora listened carefully without interruption.

"Let me get this right," she said, when he had done. "Lady Engleton wants all these relatives and oddments to let her insure their lives for your benefit. Is that right?"

"Yes, that's the idea. In order that I needn't work or do anything useful."

"Running Engleton Priory on modern lines as a farm might do no harm."

"That's what Reginald Trefusis said, more or less. I could at least be my own agent. But that's not the idea. I've got to be a real lord and behave like one, whatever that is."

"I don't like the notion of rebuilding the House of de Birkett on a foundation of dead bodies."

"It's hateful! It's ghoulish! My dear, what am I to do about it?"

Dora looked up and met his appeal with honest grey eyes.

"I don't know, Harry. I shall have to think it out."

"There must be some solution!"

"Sure. But at the minute, you can only play a waiting game."

For a moment or two neither of them spoke. They were full of the problem of Harry's future.

"I must ask Edouard how they do these mussels," Dora said at last. "Nary a bit of grit in any of them."

"I don't care tuppence," Henry said suddenly, "what happens as long—well, as long as you don't think me a cad, Dora—don't think that I want to loaf around and do nothing but behave like a lord."

Dora laughed lightly and her soft eyes met his.

"You're rather a darling, Harry. I know you well enough, my dear, to know you aren't a cad."

Henry leaned over the table and touched her hand.

"Dearest, you know I love you, don't you?"

"All girls know when a man's in love with them."

"I haven't any right to ask you, dear, but I want to marry you some day. Don't say 'No' in a hurry. Think it over and let me know."

"But, Harry dear, I've been thinking it over for a long time. I love you, that's flat, but loving someone and marrying them are different things. I'm glad you've asked me formally, Harry, and I'll marry you ever so gladly."

"My darling . . ."

"Wait a sec.! But I want it open and above board. Got me? I want you to take me to your grandmother. I don't like secrecy."

Harry's face hardened at the thought of Lady Engleton, who probably had views about the disposal of his affections. He was weak; he hesitated, but Dora was not hurt. She was prepared for it, and appreciated his sudden resolve.

"Neither do I!" he said, and thumped the table. "We'll go to her to-morrow morning and just announce it as a fact."

"You'll leave it to me, dear," Dora said quietly. "I'm rather looking forward to tackling the old girl. I'm jolly hungry. Can you run to a mixed grill, Harry? If not, I've got some money. Anyhow, we'll go halves."

"Nonsense!" Harry cried with unusual vigour. "We'll damn' well celebrate. Waiter!"

"Sir?"

"A bottle of champagne!"

"No, Harry, nothing of the sort. We'll have a bottle of Lieb-fraumilch of 1923. That's quite expensive enough."

"Ver' good, Madame."

"You mustn't run riot like that," Dora said gravely. "The de Birkett blood is not famous for abstemiousness."

The Liebfraumilch was well on the road down which all good wine eventually goes when they suddenly looked up on hearing a voice.

"Well, well. If it isn't my young cousin."

Reginald Trefusis was standing at Henry's elbow, very bland and aristocratic.

"I didn't know that you patronized this excellent spot," he went on. Henry jumped up.

"Let me introduce you," he said. "This is my cousin Reginald Trefusis, whom I was telling you about, and this is Dora Winslow."

Father Trefusis found himself subjected to a rapid but very searching analysis by Dora. Apparently he passed muster, since she held out a firm, cool hand. Father Trefusis, used to summing up his fellow-creatures, liked Dora on sight.

"Won't you join us?" she asked.

Trefusis hesitated.

"To be quite candid," he said, "I'm due here to meet my publisher, poor man. Oh, yes, even *I've* got a publisher. He's producing a heavy volume called *The Significance of Matter*. He thinks it too flippant in tone. But he doesn't appear to be here; probably backing out. I should be delighted."

He sat down and ordered fish and chips. Despite his protests, Dora insisted on his having some of the precious wine.

"We're celebrating," Henry explained.

"In any case you've earned it," Dora added, "by being decent to Harry at that filthy business this afternoon."

Father Trefusis raised his eyebrows.

"But I declined firmly to participate," he said.

"You tried to help Harry to be a man," Dora said gravely. "I've not much use for clergymen as a rule, but I liked you for that."

Father Trefusis liked Dora more and more.

"Well, you see," he explained apologetically, "I'm not a proper clergyman." His urbane smile suddenly vanished. "But I agree with you, Miss Winslow, when you describe the whole affair as a filthy business." His smile came back. "But why are you celebrating? Is it because . . . ? Don't think I'm being nosey."

"Why shouldn't you know?" Henry said. "I'm proud of it. Dora says that some day she'll marry me."

"I think that's the best news that the de Birkett Family has had for four centuries," Trefusis said with his smile. "But—forgive me introducing a disagreeable topic, but does your grandmother know you're out, as they say?"

"She'll know to-morrow morning," Henry replied grimly.

"And I mistrusted your moral courage! My dear boy, I apologize."

"Oh, Henry's got guts all right," Dora said. "The trouble is his grandmother. What's he to do about all this, Mr. Trefusis? Forgive my not calling you Father, but it sticks in my throat."

Trefusis brushed this aside.

"You can call me cousin if you like, or even Reginald." He ordered coffee for three and three liqueur brandies of '58. Dora looked alarmed, but he intercepted the look. "That's all right," he said. "I'm in the chair. After all, it is an occasion. You've asked me what I think Henry ought to do? It's a poser! I honestly don't see that he can do anything. If those gentry this afternoon don't mind the scheme, I don't see how Henry can validly object."

Dora seemed disappointed.

"I object to having my future built up on dead bodies!" she said. "I've already told Henry that."

"Unfortunately, all life is built like that. But I agree; I don't like it. Lady Engleton gives me the creeps. The whole thing was a Dance of Death with Uncle Alfred as Nijinski! The best thing to do is to carry on for the moment. Wait."

"I suppose you're right," Dora said slowly. "We shall need a lot of courage, though."

"Being in love gives one courage," Henry said, and she smiled gratefully. "You wouldn't understand that, Cousin Reginald."

Reginald grinned at the slight note of patronage.

"I wonder," he said. "I'm a human being, you know. But I wonder if you're right. Surely, falling in love doesn't require courage, but founding a home does. Marriage does. Ask any woman."

"You're right Reginald," Dora said quickly. "Men in love don't realize that. I could have half a dozen lovers in as many months. Oh, yes, I could!" she added, as Henry started to protest. "Easily! But a husband is different. I want children."

"Good!" said Reginald. "Jolly little people who'll turn cartwheels and hand-springs in the name of the Lord. I understand perfectly. Well, cheerioh!"

They drank their good brandy and were at peace with each other and the world in general. Reginald called for the bill.

"All on one, please," he said to the waiter. The others protested, but he wouldn't hear of it. "No," he said. "My turn. My contribution. When you're married, you can ask me down to stay at Engleton."

He rose to go and took Dora's outstretched hand.

"This afternoon," he said, "I was afraid for my young cousin, body and soul. I'm not so scared now. If I can be of any service at any time you know where I hang out. I'm outside this tangle, which is perhaps just as well. Good night, both of you, and God bless you."

He turned to go and then stopped.

"By the way," he added, "if you're walking home, there is a dark patch just at the corner of Bruton Street, about half-way down. You may find it booked already, but I don't think so—not if you hurry."

He walked out unobtrusively.

"I like that priest person," Dora said dogmatically, "though he is just a shade too urbane—just a shade. But I liked that about turning cartwheels."

They took his advice about Bruton Street, however, and it was nearly midnight before Henry was admitted into Mount Street by a Caraway that yawned like a chasm.

"Her ladyship has gone to bed," she said primly.

"What do I care?" Henry said recklessly. "I don't care if

she's gone to hell. I'm sorry to have kept you up, though, Miss Caraway."

Caraway, shocked and delighted by Henry's outburst, nearly forgot herself sufficiently to say "No such luck," or her equivalent for that phrase, but refrained. After all, she was used to Arabella, and where would she get another job if this one failed?

Henry sat on the edge of his bed, and threw his clothes at the armchair.

"All the courage we've got," he kept on muttering. "All the courage we've got! We'll need it!"

He was more right than he knew.

5

POOR OLD UNCLE!

When he awoke, Harry's love-found courage had ebbed somewhat. He dreaded facing his grandmother, and, to do him justice, dreaded even more the possible insults that Arabella might hurl at Dora. He had intended to tackle his grandmother and then send for Dora and confront them; as it was, he might just as well not have bothered. His telephone message to Dora was quite different. Uncle Alfred had been taken ill and the doctor sent for. Any meeting, or broaching of the subject of Dora, would, therefore, have been ill-timed.

When Henry went down to breakfast he found that the Misses Beamish had already finished. He had not expected to see his grandmother, but from all accounts Uncle Alfred never rose later than eight o'clock, and was nowhere to be seen. Sensing that something was wrong, he made his way upstairs to the old man's room and knocked at the door, but received no reply. Then, remembering that he was deaf, went in without further ceremony. There was small doubt that something was wrong. The old man was sitting up in bed with an ancient dressing-gown draped round his shoulders. His wrinkled old face was red and blotchy and his enormous beard stuck out in all directions.

"At last, at last!" he wailed, "someone has come! I'm very ill.

Send for a doctor. I'm very shivery. Fetch a doctor. Fetch a . . ."
Uncle Alfred started to cough. Henry supported the withered
old frame till the fit passed, and then laid him back on the bed,
arranging the bedclothes as best he could. Henry had not realized how immensely aged he was; he remembered Hamish's
phrase about "the old bag of rubbish."

"Feeling more comfortable, Uncle?" he asked with artificial
cheerfulness.

"No! Give me my teeth." Uncle Alfred gestured towards the
washstand, and Henry fished the denture out of a tooth-mug. He
watched the old man fit the teeth in. It was a great effort for him,
and he fell back on his pillow exhausted.

"Fetch a doctor," he said feebly. "Better now I've got my teeth.
You can't have your temperature took with no teeth. The thing
slips out."

"How do you feel, Uncle? What's wrong?"

The old man squirmed with impotent annoyance. "I've told
you, haven't I? Hot and cold and ill. It's that hot-water bottle.
It's been leaking all night. Fetch a doctor—but not Hamish! He
called me names. Thought this old fool couldn't hear. But I'm
not so deaf that I can't hear an insult. Make me Bishop of the
Cannibal Islands, will they? Let 'em try. They won't put *me* in a
pot—though I feel roasted and toasted . . ."

He began to meander inconsequently and Henry, feeling
rather frightened, left a footman in charge and went in search
of his grandmother, who was having breakfast in bed as usual.
It was one of Caraway's countless tasks to piece her together
for this ritual. Henry found the old lady propped up in front of
her breakfast tray. She looked witchlike and rather sinister in an
immense mob-cap.

"You were late last night, Henry," she said at once without
preliminary. "You know I dislike late hours."

"I'm sorry, Grannie. I'll explain later. I came to tell you that
Uncle Alfred is ill. He seems very bad and wants a doctor."

"He was always greedy," Arabella said tersely, "always over-
eats himself. He gobbled disgustingly at dinner."

"I don't think it's that. It seems to me like a bad chill. He said
his hot-water bottle was leaking. Shall I send for Dr. Grantley?"

"No. If he must have a doctor, send for Hamish. He won't charge anything."

"But he's a specialist!"

"Surely even a specialist knows how to treat a chill!"

"But he refuses to see Hamish. Worked himself up into a passion about it."

"Very well," Arabella said grudgingly, "send for Grantley, but let him be sure and keep the account separate. Run along, do. Have those detestable women been fed?"

"Yes, Grannie."

"Off you go!"

So Dr. Grantley was sent for and arrived within the hour. He found the Rev. Alfred very querulous and slightly delirious. He was sitting up in bed again, keeping the well-meaning footman at bay with well-directed abuse. He eyed the doctor fiercely.

"Make a canon of me, will they?" he piped. "Boom! Boom! No, not that sort of cannon. I forgot. Oh, dear, oh, dear, I'm very chilly. But no leaky hot-water bottles; mind *that!* I wish I was back at Preston St. Pans," he added pathetically. "Then I could go into the garden and spit a bit!"

The doctor joined Henry later in the library, the scene of yesterday's family council. His face was grave.

"I've given the old boy a sedative," he said, "and shall send round some medicine. His temperature's high and he's got a bad chill. He must be kept warm and quiet. Just let him lie. We ought to have a nurse, by the way."

"Is he in danger?"

"When you're over eighty you're always in danger. Let me know at once if his breathing gets queer. At the minute, there's nothing more to be done."

He took his leave and hurried off.

"Don't forget about that nurse," he said over his shoulder as he boarded his car. "Skilled attention is very essential."

Henry reassured him and went to report to Lady Engleton. This time he was not permitted to enter, and he had to wait forty precious minutes to be granted an audience. When this at last took place, Arabella proved adamant. No nurse! A chill was of no significance.

"Is the whole house turned upside down when *I* have a chill?" she asked. Neither the ever-present Caraway nor Henry could ever remember such an event, so they naturally remained dumb. "Just doctors' talk! Caraway, you will look after the Rev. Alfred. Take it in turns with Alice. But you needn't neglect me. See you don't!"

"But, Grannie, the doctor . . ."

"Does Dr. Grantley run this house or do I? Do you understand, Caraway?"

"Yes, m'lady."

"Before you go to the invalid give me that leather-covered jewel case, and then tell those two Gorgons to come in here."

Henry felt his grandmother's attitude rather nauseating, so went to the library and rang up Dora to tell her the news.

Meanwhile, Arabella was interviewing Sophie and Vera. They interchanged insincere greetings before Arabella indicated the leather box before her. She inserted the key. None of the best de Birkett jewels reposed in it—just throw-outs. The real jewels, such as they were, Arabella kept in a separate box for her own use and for the future Lady Engleton; she was giving nothing away to these harpies without a *quid pro quo*. She opened the box slowly in happy anticipation of its valueless contents.

"Do you recall anything that belonged to the late Mrs. Beamish —anything in particular? Poor Helen had very few jewels, except what my son, or myself, gave her."

"Just some little trinket for old times' sake," Vera said hardly. She could see it was going to be a struggle. "I've a sentimental nature, I'm afraid."

"What do you mean by trinket, Miss Beamish?" ("Sentimental nature, indeed, you fat vulture!"—this to her own soul.) It was an awkward, leading question which Vera found difficult to answer. The situation was saved, unconsciously, by Sophie.

"Just a gewgaw—a fal-lal," she gushed. Poor Sophie really did want a memento of her dead sister. Arabella stared at her glassily for a full second, the ribbons on her cap trembling in the breeze of her displeasure. She pushed the box over to them and displayed the contents with a smile of victory. Vera sniffed. It was exactly like "the shilling tray" at an antique dealer's. "Beat that if you can!" Arabella's face seemed to say. Vera breathed hard, like an organ bellows in a village church.

"Was it really necessary to keep these at the bank?"

"Yes," Arabella lied hardily. "These sentimental trinkets are treasures as much as objects of real value, I always think. Don't you?"

Vera swallowed a camel after straining at a gnat; she disliked the stress on the words "trinket" and "sentimental."

"Yes," she said. There was nothing else to say.

Sophie was eagerly and happily turning over the rubbish.

"Look!" she cried. "There's the jet necklace that belonged to dear Aunt Cuthbert Carewe! Our mother was a Carewe, you know."

"Indeed?" said Arabella. "How nice! You may have it, dear Miss Sophie." First blood to Arabella! Vera scowled. It was a hideous piece of early Victorian Whitby jet, of no value to any one but the dustman. She dreaded that it might be the sum total of Arabella's idea of what constituted Helen's trinkets. But Arabella was cleverer than that. These two women had got to be inveigled into the offices of an insurance company the next morning. Arabella wondered whether they realized that they would have to be examined by a doctor, and for the first time felt a wave of sympathy for the medical profession.

"Here," she said triumphantly, "here it is! The brooch that belonged to your mother!" There it was, sure enough, an affair of twisted gold wire and plaited hair. "Whose hair is that? Aunt Cuthbert Carewe's?" There was veiled laughter behind it, and Vera boiled—but not over.

"Oh, how I've longed for that brooch!" Sophie cried sincerely, almost childishly.

"Take it, dear Miss Sophie. Take it!"

Sophie took it with a cascade of thanks and added it to the jet necklace. Vera fumed, and with a fat finger scraped around the leather case which she had by now appropriated. There seemed absolutely nothing of any value. There were even a few stones labelled with strange and cryptic remarks such as "Given me by dear Mr. Dovell at Babbacombe, 1864. Such a happy afternoon!" "Taken from Stoke Poges churchyard. The curfew tolls, etc."

Vera could have slung the stones at Arabella's creased, triumphant face. But *was* it triumph? Or did she see a shadow cross it, a shadow of anxiety? It struck Vera that her ladyship had just thought of something—something in that box. Ah, that was it! The bottom of the box was false, was in reality a tray. There were the two little slips of tape. Vera groped for them, and her thick fingers and thumbs closed over them in triumph. Before anything could be said she lifted the tray and displayed the underneath. There were a set of garnets and a small diamond ring. The garnets consisted of a dog collar, ear-rings, necklace and a tightly fitting bangle. Sophie gave a squeak, and Arabella could have bitten her tongue out with mortification. True the set wasn't of great value, but was a cut above the other rubbish. She had by some freak of memory forgotten them. Vera determined to possess them and flaunt them in Mellingham Parva. Her eyes flashed with battle.

"So poor Helen *did* have those garnets after all! That just shows. Sophie and I suspected a housemaid of taking them. What was her name now? Edith! Didn't we, Sophie?"

Sophie had never set eyes on them before and floundered.

"Yes, we suspected—no—yes— That is, your memory is better than mine, Vera."

"I've very little doubt on that point," Arabella said shrilly. "You're making a mistake, Miss Beamish. That set of garnets has been my personal possession for the last forty years. My daughter-in-law never even wore them. I mean them for Henry's future wife."

Poor Dora!

"Surely you're in error, dear Lady Engleton."

"I'm never in error."

Vera played her ace. She leaned back in her chair as if forgetting garnets and folded podgy hands on her great chest.

"Sophie and I have been wondering whether we *ought* to insure our lives—whether it's quite *right!*" She had determined to go into ecstasy again—if necessary.

This was too much! Arabella came out into the open at once. The interview for the Misses Beamish had been fixed for to-morrow with the insurance people, so there was no time left for finesse, for meeting blackmail with counter-blackmail, and certainly no time for ecstasies.

"Am I to understand, Miss Beamish," her ladyship said, "that these garnets will influence your decision?"

Vera laughed as if Arabella had made a really good joke.

"Oh, Lady Engleton, how funny you are! The sharp tongue of the Old Regime! But those garnets were Helen's. She wished me to have them. They were given her by . . . dear me, I forget now!"

"By Aunt Cuthbert Carewe, I should imagine," the old lady said nastily.

"That's quite right, now I come to think of it. By Aunt Cuthbert!"

Arabella, like all good generals, realized defeat. She almost respected Vera for her sheer mendacity.

"Very well, Miss Beamish," she grunted, "take them. You can have the ring as well."

"Oh, thank you *so* much, dear Lady Engleton."

"Don't thank *me*. I'd forgotten they were there." Her generosity about the ring was not difficult to explain; it was paste. The others gathered up the spoils.

"You'd better have the whole lot," Arabella said irritably as they fidgeted about. "Case, stones and all. There's nothing mean about me, I'm glad to say."

She wasn't therefore in a particularly good temper when she sent for Henry to report on Uncle Alfred's condition, nor did she seem particularly delighted to hear that he was no worse. In fact, she was very peevish when informed that he had bitten the clinical thermometer in half, forgetful of the fact that he had put in his teeth.

"Did he swallow any of it, Henry?"

"No, Grannie. Miss Caraway retrieved both sections."

"How tactless of her! Tch-tch! Four and sixpence thrown away."

"Poor old Uncle."

"Poor old fiddlesticks! It's no good being sentimental, Henry. Your Uncle has outlived his utility, if he ever had any. He has altered his will in your favour, by the way."

"I don't want his money."

"Perhaps not, but the House of de Birkett needs it, and it belongs by right to them. You needn't worry; he made the alteration of his own free will and generously."

Henry wondered, but did not argue the point. He needed all his courage to tell his grandmother about Dora. The very thought of her clear grey eyes sent a flood of moral bravery rushing through his veins. As a matter of fact, Arabella took it more calmly than he had thought she would.

"You were very late last night, Henry. Whom were you with? An actress?"

She had memories of her late husband, who was frank about his infidelities, and remembering them, thought the stage scandalous.

"Good gracious, no, Grannie. I was with—with Dora Winslow."

"A woman! I knew it! Who is she? I'm not going to buy her off."

"There's no need, Grannie. I want to marry her."

"Good Heavens, you'll do nothing of the sort. You're much too young."

"I don't mean now. Some day."

"Who is she—this girl?"

"She is the daughter—only child—of Sir Creighton Winslow." The old woman sat up and took notice.

"The Foreign Office fellow?"

"That's right."

"Hm. No breeding; no real family; but not counter-jumpers. That's something. Have they money?"

"I should imagine so."

"That sounds interesting. I'll make inquiries. But you'd no business to get yourself tangled up like this at your age."

"I'm not tangled up. Dora wants to see you first; have your full permission. You see, Grannie, she hates secrecy."

This was tactful of Henry, if not altogether accurate. Arabella was not too sure of her grandson's truthfulness, as she judged her fellows by herself, but honour at least was satisfied. She reflected that it might be worse. It might have been an American out for a title with a bank balance to barter. Or a cinema star—that would have been horrible. Much as she worshipped Mammon, she worshipped Breeding more. The Winslows were not poor exactly, though she had heard that Sir Creighton was tight-fisted, not a bad trait in any one's nature. But even Foreign Office Officials must die, and then the Winslow money must be added to the gradually growing de Birkett fortune. She must make sure that this Dora girl was a proper mother for the future line; none of your cocktail girls who drank, and talked nastiness and then proved barren.

"Well, Grannie?" Henry asked with flattering anxiety.

"I don't approve of your knocking about with girls. This one at least seems respectable, which is more than could be said of your ancestors' choices for first flutters. I'll see her and pick her over."

Henry disliked the last phrase, but on the whole she was more accommodating than he dared expect.

"Thank you, Grannie."

"Don't thank me. I've not settled yet. In any case, you'll have to wait till I'm dead, and that may be years."

Henry felt that any further expression of happiness or gratitude would be out of place.

"I'll ask her to drop in this afternoon. . . ."

He dashed away and told Dora the news, and it was with justifiable pride that Henry took her, very tactfully dressed, into Arabella's little private sitting-room at four o'clock that afternoon. The old lady took careful stock of the girl, but her thoughts were not apparent. Arabella never betrayed her own confidences.

"This is Dora Winslow, Grannie."

Arabella didn't hold out her hand, but merely indicated a vacant chair. The gesture was not rude, merely regal.

"Sit down, Miss Winslow."

Dora was not in the least awed or intimidated by this, but being a tactful young person, arranged herself as indicated with due diffidence.

"Thank you, Lady Engleton."

"Henry, you may go away."

Henry looked a bit blank; he rather dreaded leaving his love to the tender mercies of Arabella. He needn't have worried; Dora was more than a match for the old lady. She gave him a tiny glance which counselled obedience, so he went without further question. Directly Henry was safely out of the room, Arabella adjusted her huge glasses and peered at Dora with magnified eyes.

"I understand from my grandson that he wishes to marry you . . . or is, at any rate, in love with you. You must understand that I don't take the matter too seriously. The de Birketts are well known to be precocious. It's probably calf love."

"I'm quite content to wait, Lady Engleton."

"That is as well. But calf love has been known to persist in an aggravating manner. My late husband fell in love with an actress at the age of seventeen and the attachment continued for nearly half a century. It was at times embarrassing, but Victorian gentlemen were more faithful than the modern generation."

Arabella kept up a steady and gentle flow of conversation, rather as if she enjoyed the sound of her own voice. Why she should enjoy it was by way of a puzzle to Dora, who didn't find it a pleasant voice. Dora interposed finally.

"Henry's calf love for me may be of the same quality, Lady Engleton."

"It's just possible, but the de Birketts have predilections for low life. But before I even will consider sanctioning any engagement between my grandson and yourself, I intend to be satisfied on certain points."

"I'm here to answer questions."

"Henry is Lord Engleton. You will be Lady Engleton and the future mother of a whole line of de Birketts. The Family is unfortunately impoverished. What are your prospects of heritage?"

"My father is a comparatively rich man, I believe, and he has always given me to understand that he would leave me his estate."

The trend of the talk was rather nauseating, but Dora managed to endure it.

"My own father, Sir D'Arcy Brainton," Arabella went on, "occupied a permanent Government position, but was not called upon to perform any duties. The wretched Gladstone put an end to such sinecure posts which constituted the sole source of revenue for stupid but well-born people. I will discuss your financial position with your father. Does he make you an allowance?"

"A very small one."

"I suppose that Henry has been wasting his pittance on buying you dinners and cocktails and so forth?"

Dora felt a wave of indignation, but swallowed it down—partially, at any rate.

"We always go halves, Lady Engleton. I pay my share, and I don't care much for cocktails."

Dora spoke with a certain inevitable tartness which definitely pleased Lady Engleton.

"Good!" she said. "You hold your own, my dear girl. I was waiting to see if you'd get snappy or irritable. Come here!"

Dora was puzzled and at a loss. What did the old wretch want?

"Come here!"

Dora rose obediently and approached the old lady.

"Closer!" Arabella poked her intimately with a bony finger. "Not much of a figure," she said. "Turn round!" She repeated the process. "Same shape all the way up, like a Wellington boot. Though you're not so bad as some. There appears to be a mania nowadays for having no flesh on your bones."

Dora turned rather resentful and flushed.

"I don't think I like being handled like a prize sow, Lady Engleton."

"Nonsense. It's just ridiculous to be squeamish. Can't think what's come over this generation! And they pretend we're fogies. You know the facts of life, I presume? Well, then, don't be silly. Had any lovers?"

"No." Rather shortly.

"That's sensible of you. Neither had I when I was married. Men can say what they like about forgiving and forgetting, but they have a habit of remembering when it comes to the point, and it's no good trying to suppress facts—someone always tells them, and then they've got you under their thumbs for ever. Do you think I'd have ruled the de Birketts if I'd had lovers? Never!"

"I happen to be fastidious, Lady Engleton."

"Rubbish! Take the credit for being sensible, but don't prate about morals or fastidiousness. That's just vicar's talk."

"I don't agree, Lady Engleton. I want to belong to my husband and to no one else. I'm made that way."

"Hoity-toity! I'll take your word for it, but good heavens, child, what do you do in the evenings?"

"I go to the Polytechnic twice a week for cookery classes, and domestic science. Once a week I go out with my father, and the rest of the time's my own to go gay in on thirty shillings a week. That's my allowance, but I could earn three times that if I set out to do it, and I could get men to pay for my meals and sleep with them if I wanted. It just so happens that I don't want. Is there anything else you'd like to know, Lady Engleton?"

Dora had spoken quietly but with quiescent vigour. For a moment Lady Engleton was taken back. People didn't usually talk to her like that.

"Impudent little minx," she said, but without rancour. "I suppose you're what's called a modern girl? Just the sort to be terrified of having babies . . ."

"I'm not terrified of anything, Lady Engleton. Not even of you!"

The old lady grinned like some human gargoyle.

"Hoity-toity," she said again. "Bless my soul! You don't show much respect for age, but that's the way nowadays. All the same, I like your spirit: If those harpies hadn't blackmailed me out of the garnets, I'd have given them to you. You'll keep Henry in order, that's one comfort. I'm not sure I don't like you."

"I'm quite sure I don't like you, Lady Engleton." Dora was in a temper by now, and yet half-amused. The old lady laughed.

"I don't care a snap of the fingers about that," she said. "I want Henry's wife to remember she's a de Birkett, and of the ruling class." She was serious enough when she spoke the last sentence. "Now ring the bell for tea and Henry. Wait a minute first. Open the door suddenly."

Dora did as she was asked.

"What's the matter, Lady Engleton?"

"I suspect that companion of mine of eavesdropping. She was listening yesterday when I was talking to the Family. I heard her breathing through the keyhole. You can take it from me, young woman, that precious little escapes me! So don't get trying any tricks. I don't want you to love me, but don't think I'm a fool, that's all."

Tea and Henry arrived simultaneously. He looked questioningly from one to another of these two women so oddly contrasted. He noticed that Dora was flushed and rather on her dignity, and for a moment feared the worst. Arabella seemed all smiles, but she was frequently happy when she had been blackguarding someone.

"Well, Henry," she said, "I suppose you want to know whether I'll consent to this mooncalf love affair. Provided that Sir Creighton has no objection to making a proper settlement and providing you aren't married until I'm dead, I've no objection to you imagining yourselves to be engaged."

"Thank you, Grannie."

"The girl's got sense and won't be bullied. I'm sorry for you, Henry, but that's your lookout. But there," she went on, "you're both prigs, so you may quarrel less than most."

She spent the rest of the time in regaling the young people with scandalous stories of previous de Birketts, notably her late husband, giving a wealth of detailed candour in a manner peculiar to mid-Victorians. Then Mr. Merry was announced, and she turned them out with scant ceremony, and without introducing Dora. Merry bowed with what he would himself have described as old-world courtesy.

"Who is that young lady?" he asked when they had gone.

"Dora Winslow. Know her?"

Merry raised his eyebrows. "Sir Creighton's daughter?"

"Yes. Has he any money? Henry wants to marry her."

"He is a man who is very well thought of . . . well thought of indeed. On the board of many charitable institutions—Homes for Children, and so forth."

Arabella's face darkened.

"That sounds bad," she said. "He might go leaving them money, like that old fool Alfred tried to do. He's ill, by the way. Now let's go into these insurance details."

In the library, Dora had lost nerve. She clung to her lover with an abandon that Henry had never before perceived. It was the abandon of sheer fright.

"I'm scared," she whispered, "scared stiff. Oh, my darling, what are we going to do?"

Henry smoothed her sleek hair, watching the patch of light that glowed on the gloss of it.

"My sweet," he said, "the old girl's old and eccentric and has a sharp tongue, but there's no real harm in her."

"There is, Harry, there is! She's wicked! I'm sorry to hurt you. I don't mind her being rude and coarse. She only does that for effect, but she gives me the creeps. It's like spending a night in a haunted room. But she shan't get at *you*, Harry. I'll fight her!"

She clung to him with all the possessiveness of healthy love.

"You're mine! You're mine, and I'm afraid for you."

"Well, darling, I'll slope off and find a job—if I can. The estate is all entailed; it'll be mine when I'm of age. Then we'll go and work on it."

"No, Harry. There's no running away. Yesterday I'd have said Yes, but not now. We've got to fight."

Harry took her in his arms and kissed her gently—as he did most things. Dora flung restraint to the winds and taking his head in her hands, kissed him frantically again and again, as if he were a soldier off to the war. They broke apart suddenly as the door opened. It was Caraway, who stammered an apology.

"I beg your pardon, I'm sure," she said. "I didn't know any one was in here. I wouldn't have dreamed of coming in without knocking."

"That's all right, Miss Caraway. Please don't apologize. This is Miss Winslow. We're engaged."

Miss Caraway smiled suddenly and fleetingly. It dawned on Henry that years before the woman might have been pretty, might have had a lover of her own instead of being offered up on Arabella's altar.

"I do hope you'll be very happy!" Then the smile vanished. "Does her ladyship . . . ?"

Henry nodded. Why was the whole world frightened of an old lady?

"Excuse me," Caraway said suddenly, "but I'm looking for a sheet of paper and a pencil. The reverend gentleman wants them. He is most insistent. He seems better—more himself. I'm afraid of a relapse if I don't do what he asks."

In her private sitting-room Arabella and Merry were carefully going over a list. It was a list of de Birketts and Beamishes with a sum of money marked against each.

"I wonder if that girl would consent to be insured?" Arabella mused, more to herself than to Merry.

"I shouldn't ask her—yet, at any rate. Sir Creighton might object. Believe me, Lady Engleton, it wouldn't do ... wouldn't do at all."

"She wouldn't cost much," Arabella went on. "She's a healthy young creature. I prodded her to see, and you never know in these days of motor cars. But perhaps you're right. I'll sound Sir Creighton first. Perhaps he'll make Henry residuary legatee." She scanned the list before her once more. "Why have you made that Vera Beamish person only worth two thousand?" she asked. "I said three!"

"Well, m'lady, I'm afraid you may find the premium rather more than we thought. So I wrote her down, as it were."

"Why should she cost more than her rat-like sister?"

Merry gave his usual deprecatory cough.

"Miss Vera," he explained, "is, from the Company's point of view, not such a good risk, I fear. She is—well, may I say—unduly corpulent."

"Talk English, Merry. You mean unhealthily fat, and that therefore she runs a good chance of dying. A good risk from *our* point of view. Put her back again at three. What's worth doing is worth doing well."

"Miss Vera may live many years ..."

"I think not, Merry. I should imagine she'd be murdered by an outraged villager very soon indeed. That Anglo-Indian brother is, of course, pickled and germ-proof and lives in the open air. From our point of view, not such a good risk. Make him two thousand. Have you written to them, by the way, and made the appointments?"

"Yes, m'lady. Mr. Hamish was difficult, but I've arranged for the insurance doctor to call at Wimpole Street. I think you'll find that Mr. Hamish is an A.1 life, as they say. But on the whole the matter is satisfactory. His lordship will benefit to the tune of forty thousand pounds, including, of course, your own bequest and the Reverend Alfred's new Will."

"He's ill, by the way."

"Indeed? I'm sorry to hear that."

"Don't be a fool, Merry."

6

EXIT UNCLE

It was about half-past seven that night. The dressing-gong had gone and the house in Mount Street seemed silent and expectant. Arabella had dressed early for dinner and gone in to see her brother-in-law. She had sent away Alice who was on guard at the time, and the two old people faced each other alone. Arabella sat near Alfred's head so as to avoid shouting at him. What she had to say was best said softly. Alfred lay back, propped up for comfort. The doctor had called and had been more cheerful. The old man's temperature had dropped nearly to normal; he had in addition absorbed some nourishment, in the shape of a little broth resultant from the fowl that had appeared at dinner the night before. Traces of it were spattered about on the sheet, as he had insisted on feeding himself. In fact, the old boy seemed to have rallied.

Arabella leaned forward and spoke almost in his ear.

"They tell me that your time has come at last, Alfred," she said. "Well, we've all got to go."

The old man shot a venomous glance at her.

"You're a very wicked woman, Belle," he croaked. "You're only saying that to make me feel low. You want me to die, but I ain't going to. I'm cheating the hangman. Who said it, anyhow?"

"Dr. Grantley and Henry and Caraway, and looking at you myself, I don't think you're long for this world. You'll have your reward soon."

The old man quailed in spite of his courage. There was an appalling certainty in Arabella's statement.

"Reward my foot!" he snapped. "Grantley said I was better. Don't believe a word. I've found you out, Belle. You're a wicked woman. It was you who unscrewed my hot-water bottle and soaked the bed." His voice grew shriller. "You're a murderess, and I hope you'll get *your* reward. You make me wish I believed in Hell. You're a murderess."

"It would take more than a leaking water bottle to kill me," Arabella answered coolly.

"Yes, but you don't suffer from toobs. I do! Suffered from toobs for the last thirty years. Now go away. Doctor says I'm not to be worried or I'll get the shivers again. Go away, do! I don't feel safe with you about. Oh dear! I'm tired. Go away—go away!"

He waved a feeble old hand at her as if he were brushing away a fly. But Arabella didn't budge; she just leaned back and grinned at him.

"Don't laugh like that. You look as if your head was coming off!"

"You were always a selfish man, Alfred," Arabella said evenly, as he fell back exhausted with his effort. "You've just lived in the country, never married, preaching a religion in which you don't believe to a village that doesn't care."

"Balderdash! If you want to know, I had eight communicants last Easter. Put that in your pipe!"

Arabella laughed softly.

"And all members of the Blanket Club," she sneered. "You make me retch, Alfred. You preach silly sermons about the Book of Revelation and write a *Life of St. Pans.* You're a selfish man, Alfred."

Uncle Alfred snarled at her like a sick dog.

"You're trying to work me into a fever," he piped. "That's what you're doing. Murderess! But there's life in the old dog and you won't kill him. Devil a bit! Go away, Grimalkin! That's what you are—Grimalkin!" Heaven knows from what obscure corner of his mind he had pulled out this term of abuse, but he evidently liked it because he kept on muttering it. Arabella was unperturbed. "Grimalkin! Grimalkin! . . . You're a bad woman, Belle! Even that Papist feller, that son of the Scarlet Woman, could see that, which proves it, don't it?"

He started to cough and his "toobs" made queer, creaking sounds. His bald head was getting pink again.

"There," he gasped, "what did I tell you? I'm getting feverish. Dear, oh dear!"

"I suppose you want to bite up another thermometer at four-and-sixpence?"

"You wish it had choked me . . . but you're not so clever as you thought you were, Belle; not so clever as the poor old fool! I've done you after all."

Arabella's expression changed suddenly. The half-piteous, half-contemptuous twist on her lips vanished to give place to hatred. Her thin claw shot out and gripped his wrist with quite surprising strength.

"What do you mean?" she asked. "What do you mean?"

"Over the Will. I've done you, that's all. I said I'd make another, and I have!"

He chuckled delightedly.

"Try and murder me with a hot bottle, would you? You wait. Now perhaps you'll leave me in peace."

Arabella stood over him; her hands became talon-like and she shook with rage.

"Give it me," she said. "Give it me!"

He cocked an eye at her like some outrageous old vulture.

"Not likely," he said. "D'you take me for a fool? You won't frighten me with your temper."

"It won't be legal. It isn't witnessed."

"Ain't it? Haven't I had a couple of gals in here?"

"Caraway, eh? I'll turn her into the street for this. But I'll have that Will. Give it to me!"

Arabella actually started to grope under his pillow, but Uncle Alfred only laughed feebly. His eyes were feverishly bright and his laughter was unpleasant to hear.

"It's no good, Belle. I've done you. I'm sitting on it like a hen on an egg. Now get it!"

Arabella said nothing. She went laboriously over to the window and began to fumble with the latch.

"What are you doing, Belle?" There was a squeak of sheer fear in his voice. "Good God, you'll kill me!"

The window was slowly going up and fog was drifting into the room, cold and chilly like some ghost. The old man coughed and wrapped his old Wadham muffler round his mouth. His voice became muffled and incoherent. Slowly but inexorably Arabella went to the washstand and filled a sponge with water. Then she crossed over to the bed. Uncle Alfred became livid with fear.

"Don't do it. Belle, there's a good girl. Don't do it!"

His cry for help was muffled by the sponge which Arabella put in his mouth. She squeezed it, and the ice-cold water went in a stream on to his flannel nightshirt and on to his chest. The poor old wretch shuddered and began to blubber senile tears. He was too exhausted to shout. Arabella said nothing at all. She had wielded power over her fellows for years, but this was her first attempt at trifling with Death. With hands that trembled with rage, she replaced the sponge and closed the window. Then she went straight to Caraway's room. It was an effort, but well worth it. Caraway met her on the stairs and fluttered forward to help her.

"You needn't go to the Reverend Alfred. He's gone to sleep. Tell Alice to leave him alone for an hour or two."

"I'll see to that, m'lady."

Arabella eyed her for a full ten seconds before her next remark.

"You signed a paper this afternoon, Caraway. Yes, you did."

"But, m'lady . . ."

"You'll get that paper back and hand it to me in the drawing-room at half-past nine, do you hear?"

Caraway shrank back from the menace of Arabella's eyes.

"Are you deaf, woman?"

"No . . . no . . ."

"See to it. If you want to know where it is, he's sitting on it like a 'hen on an egg.' You'll get it, or you'll get out!"

For the last fifteen years Caraway had lived in hourly dread of hearing those words. She could only stammer her acquiescence.

Dinner was a sombre affair that evening. Henry was silent and oppressed. Dora's anxiety had eaten into his mind. It was unlike her to be panicky. Vera and Sophie chattered fairly brightly. They had spent the afternoon "looking at the shops" and were full of the improprieties of modern fashions. Vera lashed herself into quite a fury about a nightgown she had seen "in the shop window for all the world to gape at." But they had enjoyed themselves for all that. Caraway was comparatively silent. Even her subservient monosyllables were hushed. It was not until the sweet was on the table that Vera asked after the Rev. de Birkett.

"How is the dear old gentleman, Lady Engleton?"

"When I last saw him he was nearly asleep."

"Such a *quaint* character; such a saintly old face!" Sophie said. Arabella selected a salted almond with nicety.

"We had a most interesting chat," she said. "*Most* interesting. On religious subjects."

"I always like discussing religion," Vera said with ponderous solemnity. "As long as it is with Church people. Argument is a very different thing."

"The Reverend Alfred de Birkett," Sophie said, "struck me as a deeply religious man."

"Deeply religious," Arabella echoed. "His knowledge of sacred matters increases every hour."

Henry nearly choked. He had heard his grandmother call Uncle Alfred some strange things, but "deeply religious" was a novelty in the repertoire. She was laughing at those Beamish women; that was it. How he longed to escape from it all, to get out into the clean air of his love for Dora! Right out of this cruel, jeering atmosphere. He was seeing things from Dora's point of view, waking from his spiritual coma. Dora was right, as usual. There *was* something widdershins about Arabella, sitting there huddled and wrinkled like a walnut.

Immediately dinner was over, Arabella addressed herself to Caraway to the effect that it might be advisable just to peep in on the Reverend Alfred, to see how he was getting on, whether he was still sleeping; and at twenty minutes past nine precisely Caraway came back to the drawing-room where they were all seated, politely discussing nothing.

"And how *is* the reverend gentleman?" Sophie asked.

Caraway looked confused, and Henry noticed that she seemed anxious and white about her thin chops.

"He—he—seemed a little restless," she said. "Not quite so well."

"Dear, dear!" from Sophie, who seemed genuinely concerned.

"A chill has its ups and downs," Vera remarked fatly.

Caraway crossed over to Arabella and handed her a half-sheet of note-paper.

"This is the—the letter you asked me to find, m'lady," she said steadily. The finding had been a loathsome ordeal, poor woman!

"Thank you, Miss Caraway, thank you *so* much!"

Arabella glanced at it and gave a sigh of relief. It wouldn't have mattered anyhow, evidently written when the old man was not quite himself. It was a short document, leaving all of whatsoever he died possessed "to my dear old friend, St. Pans," and was duly witnessed by Caraway and Alice. Arabella regretted that she had lost her temper over a document of that sort, and had been driven to extremes. It couldn't be helped, however, and the silly old fool had brought it on himself. Why on earth couldn't he have been reasonable and remembered that he was a de Birkett, bred and born?

"I think, m'lady, that I had better go back to him."

"Who is with him?"

"Alice."

"Indeed?" Arabella said sharply. "You had better go back at once. If he is not quite himself he may say things that aren't quite fit for a young girl to hear."

Vera actually pricked up her elephant's ears, that usually lay flat to her head. They seemed to move outwards as if in a breeze.

"Shall I sit with the old gentleman for an hour or so?" she asked. She limited the time deliberately. No sitting up all night with peevish invalids for Vera.

"Certainly not, Miss Beamish. You are a guest, I couldn't think of such a thing."

It would never do for Vera to absorb the old man's babble. It didn't matter what he said to Caraway, who was a poor fish anyhow. Caraway turned to the door, casting a piteous and appealing eye in Henry's direction. He answered by a slight nod, and a minute or so later made for the door in a nonchalant manner.

"Perhaps it *would* be better, Henry dear, if you went as well," he heard his grandmother's voice. There was precious little that escaped Arabella!

Henry found Caraway at the foot of the stairs. Even in the dim light shed by the tiny and super-economical electric light he could see that she was trembling. She was badly frightened, so much so that her usual subservience had gone.

"I'm so glad you've come," she said. "I'm terrified. I didn't know what to do. Poor old man! He's very ill; much worse. I didn't like to tell her ladyship. He's saying—saying the most dreadful things. He's breathing as if someone were crumpling tissue paper."

Henry could see the woman was suffering badly; her thin throat was working convulsively, beads of sweat were clustering round her nose and on her forehead.

"Ring up Dr. Grantley," Henry said quickly. "Tell him to come round at once."

He didn't wait for her reply, but dashed up the stairs two at a time. He found Alice, the housemaid, outside the door, waiting anxiously.

"Oh, sir," she began, but Henry pushed by her.

The room was illuminated by a red table lamp, and Uncle Alfred was sitting, pillows piled up behind him. He looked like some ancient Demon King in a pantomime: the red light streamed up his face, casting fantastic shadows on the wall behind. Alice followed Henry in, but kept back near the door.

"Enter Third Murderer," the old man croaked. His breathing crackled just as Caraway had said. "Come to finish me off, eh?"

"It's Henry, sir . . ."

"Oh! Come here, my boy. I don't believe *you're* in it. You're not a bad lad."

Henry crossed to the bed and leant over the grotesque figure.

"Put your ear closer. Your grandmother's a murderess, d'ye hear? A murderess!"

"Ssh, Uncle!"

"Don't try and shush me! It's true, I tell you. She opened the window and let the fog in; then she tried to choke me with a sponge. She's a murderess. I don't remember no more—till—I felt a hand big as a leg o' mutton groping about the bed to get my Will . . ."

"You mustn't say such things, Uncle. You dreamed it."

"Oh, dear, I'm hot as hell . . . hot as hell . . . Prop me up, my boy . . ."

Henry heaved him up higher on his pillows and the old man gasped frantically and began to waggle his head from side to side.

"Take it away," he muttered. "Take it away, you devil. You murderess! Grimalkin!" There was a pause and Uncle Alfred became more still. His breathing seemed feebler but not crackly.

"Oxford Movement," he said suddenly. "Bah! Rubbish! Manning's a knave, Pusey a fool and Newman an old woman. *Scarlet* Woman! Go on! Pick up your feet, girls!" He began to whistle some music-hall tune of the seventies and beat time with his hand. He imagined he was back in Leicester Square in the old days.

"That girl on the left, second from the end? See her? Fine pair of hips. Pick up your feet, girls. Kick 'em up!" he began to applaud.

Henry gently held his hands and tried to quieten him.

"That's all very fine," Uncle Alfred muttered. "Why shouldn't a curate have a bit o' fun. Innocent fun, that is. No harm in it." He began to sing.

"Daisy! Daisy! Give me your answer, do."

But the effort was too much for him. Then he appeared to notice Henry again.

"Belle's bad. Rotten as an elm tree! Tractarians? Bah! What are they, anyway? I know! They *eat* tracts. Fruitarians eat fruit, don't they? Vegetarians eat—eat veget—— Don't fit, do it? Kick 'em up, girls! I like a fine pair of hips, like a fine pair of . . . *You* don't remember Lottie Collins!"

Henry gave him a little sympathetic squeeze, not knowing what to do and wishing to Heaven the doctor would come. The poor old thing's body was burning hot.

"Squeezed a sponge in my mouth, she did. Hymn No. 540," he announced. "Fight the good fight with all thy might. No breath to sing."

He fell back and fought a fight for breath.

"A vicarage and coals. Coals? What's the good of coals?"

"Gently, Uncle, gently. Try and keep quiet."

The old man seemed to take his advice, for he lay quite still.

Then a fit of shivering seized him and he began to shake from head to foot. Henry felt the tears well into his eyes. It was all so pitiable. Caraway slipped silently into the room and gestured the terrified and useless Alice to go.

"Dr. Grantley's here," she said tonelessly. "Her ladyship is very annoyed that we didn't tell her."

"Why doesn't Dr. Grantley come up?"

"He was using the telephone . . ."

"Pick up yer feet, gals! Kick 'em up! That's better."

It was by now only a feeble croak. Henry met Caraway's glance over the bed.

"Miss Caraway," he said quietly, "what was that piece of paper you gave Lady Engleton?"

It seemed to Henry that the woman blenched, but it was difficult to say under the red glow of the lamp.

"Oh . . . nothing. Just a . . . just a letter she wanted."

"Why did Uncle want paper and pencil this afternoon?"

"He—he tried to write, but—couldn't——"

"He's been saying some terrible things . . ."

"I heard them too. He's delirious . . ."

"Thank you, Miss Caraway."

At that moment, Dr. Grantley came in, very businesslike, and after a glance at the invalid, busied himself at the washstand with a hypodermic syringe. There was no need to listen to the old man's breathing, which rustled and crackled stertorously.

"I was afraid this might happen," the doctor said, "though he was a good deal better this afternoon. I can't understand it."

"What's the matter?"

"Pneumonia, of course."

He reached for the emaciated arm. Uncle Alfred turned his beady old eyes on the doctor.

"Puseyites," he muttered with unutterable scorn. "Bah! There's no harm in a curate—fun—innocent fun. Kick 'em up, girls. She tried to murder me. Squeezed water into my mouth. Keep her away! Keep her away!" he yelled suddenly and pointed a finger at the door. There was Arabella leaning on a stick, silhouetted by the light of the passage.

"Keep her away! She's a murderess—a crocodile!"

Henry noticed that the old man's eyes were unseeing; he was lapsing into a merciful coma. His breathing crackled more than ever.

Arabella regarded him for a few seconds in silence.

"Poor dear Alfred," she said. "Death rattle——"

Dr. Grantley looked up and studied her. Slowly the old lady drew out a small cambric handkerchief and wiped her eyes.

"Crocodile," Uncle Alfred murmured. "Murderess! Mrs. Peacey! Mrs. Maybrick!"

"I think, Lady Engleton," the doctor said, "it would be best if you and Lord Engleton were to go. He has some delusion and you disturb him."

"If he's dying," Arabella said coldly, "I should like to be present at the end. It's my duty."

"He's desperately ill," the doctor said stiffly, "but not dying—yet."

"I think we'd better go, Grannie." Henry gave her his arm.

A few minutes later another doctor arrived—a specialist—and a trained nurse, and for hours they fought for Uncle Alfred's life. They pumped oxygen into him, did all that medical knowledge could suggest to keep burning the feeble flame that flickered and fell. The Beamish women were bundled off to bed and after a decent interval, Arabella followed. Caraway undressed her and went through all the usual ritual. At last the old woman was ready for the night, a rice pudding at her side in case she woke and felt hungry, her box of lozenges in case her throat tickled and a glass of weak lemonade.

"There's no need for me to make myself ill," she said, "because Alfred has a touch of the 'toobs.'"

"No, m'lady."

"You've done very wrong, Caraway, in signing that paper—not that it mattered, but it was disloyal."

"I'm sorry, m'lady, but I didn't know."

"Ignorance is no excuse. Did my brother-in-law babble a lot of nonsense to you?"

"He talked very wildly . . ."

"Exactly. Don't repeat it to any one. If you do, you can go and you'll find it difficult to go anywhere else except the workhouse, because I shan't give you a reference. I shall tell people you pilfered. You understand?"

"Yes, my lady."

"That at least is satisfactory. Now go to bed."

For a wild moment Caraway had the impulse to push the old lady's head into the pillow and sit on it, but it fled.

"Good night, m'lady."

Henry sat in the library waiting for news. The house was very still except for the occasional opening and shutting of the door, and once there was an interruption when the oxygen arrived. He was troubled in his heart. What change had come over his grandmother? She had always been sharp-tongued, but hitherto there had been something admirable about her ancestor worship, her obsession for the welfare of the family. Obsession? Vaguely he wondered if the old matriarch was not actually a little mad. All that stuff that Uncle Alfred had talked about the sponge—was there anything in it? Of course not. He dismissed the thought angrily as being foul and indecent. But just supposing—obsession—money! He fell into a troubled sleep in the chair, the chair where a few hours previously poor old Uncle had taken root.

He awoke with a start to see someone standing over him. It was Caraway. She was in a dressing-gown and he noticed with queer wonderment that her flannel nightgown had ornamentation on it, feather stitching round the wrists and at the throat. Fancy that! Why on earth should Caraway want to ornament her nightdress? Her head was covered with a good dozen miniature gridirons, contraptions meant to curl or wave the hair. Henry hardly recognized her. She was crying as well.

"It's all over," she sobbed. "He's gone! He's dead!"

7

THE REMAINS

Henry jumped to his feet and grabbing the sobbing woman by the arm, lowered her into a chair.

"When did it happen?" he asked.

"Just now, about five minutes ago. I couldn't sleep; I was listening at the door."

Henry glanced at the ormolu clock on the mantelpiece. It was nearly four o'clock. What did one do on such occasions? Ought he to go up? He had had no intimate connection with death before. He went uncertainly to the door and stood for a moment, listening. Then he heard the door upstairs open and close, and the muffled voices of the doctors as they came down. Grantley was speaking.

"Of course he was very old, Sir Stephen, couldn't put up a fight, but it was very sudden and rapid. Can't understand it . . ."

"You did everything possible, Grantley. You can't tell in these cases. A younger man might have shown earlier symptoms . . ."

Henry slipped back into the library where a few minutes later they joined him. They both looked tired and haggard, as well they might. Sir Stephen Worth, the consultant, didn't mince matters.

"Ah, Lord Engleton," Sir Stephen said, "I'm sorry to tell you that your great-uncle is dead. We did all we could, but his age was against him—sudden congestion of the lungs."

Henry swallowed noisily. He wasn't exactly sorry, but there would be a gap. Not that he had seen Uncle Alfred often, but he would miss his childish prattle about St. Pans and all the rest of it.

"Miss Caraway has already told me," he said.

"Eighty, wasn't he?" Grantley asked.

"Yes, eighty and a half," Henry replied, remembering the old boy's precision. "Eighty and a half. Poor old chap."

"Well," Sir Stephen said, "we'd better go. I've had a tough day. We've done everything necessary, and of course Dr. Grantley will give the certificate and attend to the formalities. Nurse Fawcett will stop here to-night. I'm so sorry, Lord Engleton," he added gently. Henry pulled himself together.

"Thanks," he said. "Have a drink? I dare say you could do with it." Without waiting for their answer he brought out the tantalus which by good luck was open, and a siphon and glasses. He poured out four generous doses, one of which he handed to Caraway.

"I don't think I'd better," she said. "I haven't touched anything for years."

"Do you good."

The doctors were duly grateful for Henry's consideration.

"Had I better tell my grandmother?" Henry asked. "Now, I mean?"

"You know best," Sir Stephen answered. "But I don't see that it will do any good to wake her up and give her a shock. I should break it to her in the morning. Gently and tactfully, of course."

Henry was relieved. He dreaded telling her; he was afraid she might be—glad.

"Very well, I'll do that," he said.

"Good night, Lord Engleton. I'm sorry we could do so little. Can I drop you at your place, Grantley."

"Thanks."

More hand-shakings, not excluding Caraway, and they were gone. Henry listened to Sir Stephen Worth's car hum away out of hearing.

"Well, Miss Caraway," he said at last, "I think we had better go and get some rest."

Caraway rose a little unsteadily, unaccustomed to whisky.

"Oh dear," she said, "I'm dizzy. I don't think I'll ever rest again." She stood swaying slightly, her hair curlers catching the light like small silver toast racks.

"Nonsense," Henry said kindly. "You're just tired out, and small wonder."

She faced him with a courage born of alcohol and fatigue.

"Mr. Henry," she said, dropping titles for the moment, "I've been with Her Ladyship for nearly thirty years. It was I who told her when you were born down at the Priory. Mr. Henry, I'm afraid! If anything happens to me, I've left you all my possessions. You'll find my Will in my workbox."

Henry was genuinely touched, realizing for the first time that he was an object of love to this faded woman.

"That's very dear of you," he said, "but don't let's talk of Wills. I'm sick of the word." But Caraway was not to be checked thus easily.

"Mr. Henry, Her Ladyship has threatened to turn me out. She thinks I'd starve, but I shouldn't. I've saved half my fifteen shillings a week for years. But I won't go. I want to look after you and that sweet girl, I saw—was it a hundred years ago? I was a sweet girl once and a man loved me . . ."

Henry put his arm round her shoulders and led her to the door.

"Believe me, I appreciate all you've done for the Family. Her Ladyship doesn't mean half she says. Bark and bite, you know."

"I didn't know that whisky made one feel so calm," she said, as Henry piloted her upstairs.

"Poor old gentleman," she said, as they passed Uncle Alfred's door. "She murdered him."

Henry, thinking of the whisky, offered no comment, just left her at her bedroom door.

"Good night," he said and with a sudden impulse, leaned forward and kissed her thin cheek.

"Thank you," she said. "I'll look after you . . ."

He flung himself down on his bed and slept till morning.

When he awoke, he was momentarily surprised to find himself in a dinner jacket, but it was late—past nine o'clock, and after a quick change and a shave and bath he went down to breakfast. He went down to find the Misses Beamish wrapped in gloom and hastily assumed touches of mourning. Vera, for example, was wearing a black jet necklace, and Sophie had a piece of black ribbon tied round her wrist. They were both appropriately downcast.

"Very sad, very sad indeed, and so sudden," Vera said, as she helped herself to some more scrambled egg.

"Such a dear old gentleman," Sophie murmured. "Has it been broken to Her Ladyship? I'm afraid we shall be in the way."

"Please ask her if she would like us to leave by the next train," Vera said sombrely. "We don't wish to intrude into a House of Death."

Henry swallowed a cup of coffee and went up to Arabella's room. Caraway, quite normal again, opened the door and let him in. Even Arabella had done something to display formal grief. The ribbons in her cap were black!

Henry hardly knew how to begin.

"You've heard, of course, Grannie," he said at last.

"Caraway told me. It was not unexpected. He's probably

happier where he is. He called me some hard names last night. Crocodile, I believe, was one of them. But of course I shall never forget that he was ill and very aged."

Arabella seemed to have forgotten that she was three years her brother-in-law's senior. She touched her eyes with her cambric handkerchief, and Henry felt somehow that the gesture was genuine.

"You did quite rightly in not waking me; I could have done nothing. . . . You must make the necessary arrangements, Henry. The remains must be sent to Preston St. Pans."

"I'll see to it. Dr. Grantley is due any minute. He's an awfully good chap. The Beamishes want to know whether you'd like them to go at once."

Arabella straightened herself.

"Certainly not," she said. "Life must go on quite normally. Alfred would have wished it. Tell them to pull all the blinds down."

Truly an amazing old woman! Henry went down to communicate this fact to the Beamishes, who interpreted it rightly to mean that they were to call on the Insurance Company as arranged.

Henry rang up the various members of the Family and broke the news; even Major Beamish was included in this. He was at an hotel and it took a few minutes to locate him.

"Well, well," Henry heard his sleepy voice say. "Well, well, I suppose it's all for the best." The Major, having had a night out, wasn't feeling any too good. Luckily he wasn't due for his appointment with the Insurance people till the afternoon.

"Pore old basket, pore old basket," was all Bertram had to say. The comment was not disrespectful in intention, but he was due to attend a State function and was changing into full uniform. "Another link with the past broken," he added as a palliative. "If there's anything I can do, of course . . . ?"

"Is Grantley giving a certificate?" Hamish asked from Wimpole Street, "or are they going to have a P.M.?"

Henry wondered vaguely what a P.M. was. He had heard political nobs refer to the Prime Minister in this way.

"Post-mortem, my boy," Hamish said impatiently in answer to his query.

"Oh! I hope not. They say it's pneumonia . . ."

"Grantley knows what he's at. All the same, I should like to have had a squint at those 'toobs' of his. I always suspected a form of T.B. Where are they going to plant him. St. Pans? Good. That lets me out of going. So long!"

Hamish hung up and Henry felt resentful. Why should Hamish be so astoundingly selfish? Doctors had no business to be like that; they worked for the good of humanity, or at least one was given to understand as much. Hamish just didn't fit into the picture. Father Trefusis was out, but a rather confused maid, after asking whether another priest would do, undertook to deliver a message. Henry deliberately left Dora till last. She said little enough, except to call him "her poor darling" and say she was coming round at once, whereupon he went to report to his grandmother, who was being got ready for her morning ride out in her bath chair.

"There's no use, my dear boy, and no good purpose is served by departing from routine. It's fine and sunny, and air does me good."

Caraway placed an immense bonnet on Arabella's head—a positive cornucopia. In deference to the Great Reaper, black ribbons had been hastily substituted for the brighter of the many fruits that covered it.

"The jet ornaments those wretched women stole would have come in handy after all," Arabella said. "Have they gone, by the way?"

"The Beamishes?"

"Who else?"

"Yes. I heard them set out while I was on the phone."

"That is satisfactory. They have gone to the Insurance Company. Off we go, Caraway."

She was helped into the bath chair, which it was one of Caraway's endless duties to push about the more secluded Mayfair streets. True, Arabella didn't weigh much, but Caraway found it one of the more humiliating of the day's jobs.

"How did the Family take the sad news?" Arabella asked as she climbed into her chariot. Henry allowed himself one of his few minutes of bitterness.

"They seemed to think it was all for the best," he said. "Except Hamish, who was sorry that they weren't going to have a post-mortem."

"Very sensible of them. I think so too. So will you, when you hear his Will. No, Henry, please! Don't start to argue. Dying is inevitable when you're eighty, and you are benefitting by a perfectly natural process. Push on, Caraway."

Caraway gave a forward heave and the bath chair moved off majestically. Henry was appalled at the news about the Will. He had heard the old man's maunderings, but had set no store by them. It seemed ghastly. The poor old wretch had doubtless been hectored into it. He would refuse to touch the money, refuse before any one could bully him, refuse while Arabella was out of the way. If he had been informed anywhere else but in the street he would have told Arabella then and there, but one can't do those things in Mount Street. As it was, he went to the phone again and rang up Merry. In any case, someone ought to tell the family solicitor.

"And understand this, Mr. Merry," Henry said directly he had broken the news. "I won't benefit by his Will. I refuse! He talked when he was dying."

"One must allow for mental wandering, my lord."

"I don't believe he *was* wandering; at least, not when he blathered about being forced into making a Will . . ." He added this proviso, remembering that Uncle Alfred had talked of being murdered. For a moment Mr. Merry did not answer. Henry could hear him breathing heavily and indignantly.

"I must make every allowance for your youth and inexperience," he said at last, "but at the same time must inform you that you are speaking very rashly. I was at Mount Street the night before last, when your late great-uncle made his Will in my presence. Do you think that I, or any other reputable solicitor, would tolerate any undue influence being brought to bear? Such a thing would be a criminal offence. You are not yourself, Lord Engleton —not yourself!" Mr. Merry's voice shook with scandalized indignation. Henry saw that it was going to be no easy matter to refuse Uncle Alfred's money. He heard the front door bell ring. That would be Dora! He made a half-hearted apology to Merry and rang off. It wasn't Dora, however, it was Dr. Grantley. Henry buttonholed him at once and took him into the library.

"I'm very worried about my great-uncle's death, doctor," he said at once, before he should have time to think better of it. "What I say is confidential?"

"Of course. But why are you so worried?"

"All that talk about—about being murdered—and about his Will. It's very disturbing. I don't like it."

Grantley smiled tolerantly.

"My dear Lord Engleton, you needn't give such things two thoughts. It's part of my job to attend dying people and I assure you that the things your great-uncle said were as water to wine to some of the things I've heard. That's all right, my dear boy, your nerves are shaken up. I'll send you round a bottle of physic, and take it easy for a bit."

Henry didn't for a minute believe that Uncle Alfred had been helped in his passage to the next life, but he *did* have a suspicion that Arabella might have bullied the old man over his money. There didn't seem, however, to be any method of differentiating the two points. If Uncle Alfred had been lucid about the Will, then he might have been equally so when he jabbered about being murdered—which was ridiculous on the face of it. The doctor took him by the arm which he squeezed in a manner meant to be reassuring, but which Henry only found exasperating.

"I've made arrangements with the undertakers," he said, "and here is the certificate."

Henry glanced at it and gathered, after discounting the professional verbiage, that the old man had died of bronchial pneumonia. That was that! There was a lot of talk about toxæmia and so on. It seemed very learned and satisfactory. Henry rubbed his forehead as if to try and ease his own thoughts.

"Take it easy, my boy," the doctor said kindly. "There's nothing to worry about. The undertakers will see to everything. They'll arrive unobtrusively after dark. How did Lady Engleton take it?"

"Her Ladyship has gone for a walk."

"Very sensible too. I advise you to do the same."

A few minutes later Dora arrived; in fact she met the departing

Grantley on the doorstep. At last! Henry clung to her eagerly and with a certain desperation. At last there was someone to whom he could talk, could pour out his unworthy thoughts, who would not treat him like a petulant little boy. He sat at her feet and exulted at the cool, firm hand that stroked his forehead. He told her everything, all he could remember of the dead man's delirious chatter, Oxford Movement, Lottie Collins, equally with the more serious matter; nor did he forget to mention Caraway's cryptic utterances.

Dora listened, hardly making a comment of any kind, but the very touch of her hand told him that she at least understood his difficulty. When he had at last finished, he looked up into her steady eyes.

"My darling, what do you think about it all?" It was a cry of sheer necessity, clamouring for an answer. She stooped over him and kissed his lips.

"I think," she said, "that you are an unutterable darling. I think I'm the only girl who has ever loved a man before."

She held him to her breast and almost rocked him, maternal yet possessive and loverlike.

"For all that," Henry said, "and bless you for it, my sweet, you haven't answered my question."

Dora instantly became practical.

"I'm not at all sure about that," she said. "You're so scrupulous, Henry. I love you for it, my dear; there's not enough of it in these days; but perhaps you imagine things. I only say perhaps."

"I'm worried about the money," Henry said.

Dora suddenly put him gently but firmly from her. "I've got an idea. We'll go and see that Trefusis chap."

Henry didn't seem too keen.

"He was out when I rang up."

"Anyway, the walk'll do you good. It's no good mooning and being bitten by a conscience all the time."

As it happened, Reginald was at home. They were shown into rather a bleak little room with uncomfortable wooden chairs and a dingy table. Over the fireplace hung a large Crucifix; a white figure on black wood. The cheerlessness of the place rather damped the enthusiasm of Henry and Dora, who only conversed in whispers. After about ten minutes, Reginald blew in. He shook hands cheerily.

"Thank you for ringing me about Uncle Alfred, Henry," he said. "The maid got it muddled. She thought that you wanted a priest—not just me. It was very sudden."

Henry explained that the chill had developed and that sudden pneumonia had just blown the old candle out. Reginald nodded his understanding.

"Smoke?" he asked, handing them his case in turn. He flashed his sudden smile on them. "Now then," he went on, "out with it! Something's bothering you two, and I've not forgotten that I offered to be of assistance. Won't your respected grandmother consent to the engagement? Is that it?"

Henry shook his head.

"She behaved fairly decently about that," he said slowly. "It's not that."

"Henry's conscience is worrying him. I thought that might be in your line, Mr. Trefusis. I persuaded him to come round."

Underlying her flippant note, Reginald detected anxiety, saw the strained look in her eyes. His mind became alert, though his smile remained unchanged.

"To see an expert or a cousin?" he asked.

"It was the combination that made me think of you," was the ready answer. "I expect Henry is fagged out with the whole business, so I'll tell you just what he told me. Stop me if I'm wrong, Harry."

Once more the circumstances of Uncle Alfred's death were gone over in detail. Dora missed nothing. Just as she was finishing, a gong sounded somewhere in the depths of the building. Henry jumped up in alarm.

"I must get back," he said. "I'm awfully sorry, Reginald, but I simply daren't be late. Tell Dora what you think about it all and she'll tell me. You do understand, don't you? It seems odd, coming to you like this and then dashing away. Don't bother; I can let myself out."

"Naturally I understand. Don't worry."

He saw Henry to the door and came back to find Dora hesitating whether she should follow.

"Don't go, Miss Winslow. Don't go."

Something in his manner reassured Dora that Reginald's lunch was not at that moment a prime consideration.

"I'm glad Henry has gone," she said. "We're friends, aren't we?"

Reginald nodded.

"Thank you," Dora said simply. "I'm going to anticipate a bit and call you Reginald." She sat down again. "It's a rum business, isn't it?" she went on. "You see, I have to comfort Henry; we're lovers; but I can talk straight to you. What's to be done?"

Reginald stroked his well-shaven chin and sighed.

"Dora," he said suddenly, "there is one reality in this world that people won't face, and that is Sin. Henry doesn't like to think that his grandmother bamboozled Alfred de Birkett into making a fresh Will; he doesn't like to face it."

"I think you're wrong there. But do *you* think it?"

"Yes. Lady Engleton is a very unscrupulous old woman. She is obsessed by the de Birkett Family; it's what doctors call paranoia, a monomania. As you know, I had reason to disagree with her on the point. I think the old man gave in for peace and promptly made a new Will, which was subsequently destroyed. It is Miss Caraway's behaviour that makes me think that."

"And do you think that—that there might have been something more than just delirium in—in the other accusation?"

"It's a point that I hardly dare ask myself, Dora."

"It's a question I've *got* to ask myself."

"Lady Engleton is possessed of a devil; mad, if you like. On your young shoulders rests a fearful responsibility. You must fight that devil for Henry's sake, for the sake of the love it has pleased Almighty God to pour into your heart." His smile had gone and he spoke with a fierce, almost theatrical intensity. "I don't say," he continued, "that Lady Engleton is responsible for anything criminal, but she is capable of it."

"I think so too." She rose and smoothed out her skirt. "I'll take on the job," she said. "That job of fighting the devil."

She laughed suddenly.

"Perhaps we're both being fantastic, thinking evil."

"I trust not, and hope we are wrong. But watch, watch carefully. May I say watch and pray?" He held out his hand. "God's blessing go with you," he said. "I wish I could do more, but Lady Engleton loathes me, I'm afraid. Count on me if you're in any sort of bother."

"Thanks," she said. "Go and have your lunch. Even clergy must eat."

But Reginald made a poor lunch. He was anxious. . . .

Reginald wasn't the only one who made a poor lunch. On his arrival at Mount Street, Henry found the whole house in a state of suppressed temper and indignation. In fact, every one seemed to be having sandwiches or "just a little something" in their respective rooms, much to the annoyance of the staff who had to cart it about.

It appeared that Vera and Sophie had come back from the Insurance Company in a taxicab, Vera purple and Sophie pale and trembling. They had actually rung the bell and ordered "stimulants"—just like that. "Stimulants," on the butler's reading of the word, had resolved itself into meaning cooking sherry, which they duly drank in the darkened drawing-room. Here Arabella had caught them in the act. Vera rose majestically.

"Lady Engleton," she said, "would I had known what this Insurance meant! Never, never I repeat, would I have consented to suffer such indignity. The questions I was asked! An outrage. By a man, too. I told him we were maiden ladies!"

"There was a nurse present," Sophie said timidly, "but it was dreadful. I shudder even now! This doctor asked me if I'd ever had——"

"Please, Sophie, please!"

Vera held up a huge hand like a prophet in a stained-glass window.

"Don't," she said, "let us dwell on it or even think of it!"

"I shall dream of that examination for the rest of my life," poor Sophie murmured. The sisters shuddered in concern and Vera poured out more cooking sherry. Arabella leaned on her stick and watched them, like some old gnome. It was difficult to know whether her face was amused or sympathetic.

"What was it the doctor asked you if you'd had?" she asked, eyeing them suspiciously. "And had you had it?"

"Certainly not!" Vera stormed. "Dear me, I'm so upset. I was forgetting that there is Death in the house."

"But what *was* it?" Arabella reiterated.

"A—a—baby!" Sophie wailed with sudden abandon.

"Oh, is *that* all?" Arabella said, relieved.

"But it wasn't all, Lady Engleton. Not by any manner of means."

"That's enough, Sophie. Quite enough."

"I didn't know it was going to be as bad as that," Arabella said softly and untruthfully. "I deeply regret your humiliation. But it was in a noble cause—the cause of your dear sister's child. Let that be our consolation."

Vera disliked the use of the word "our" and nearly said so, but refrained. After all, a "Lady" is a "Lady," and she still hoped she would come down to stay at Mellingham Parva. What a feather in the Beamish cap! What a smack in the eye for the rather exclusive and snobbish County that was apt to cold-shoulder the Beamishes.

"Yes," she said, almost visibly swallowing her vexation. "After all, it is worse for the poor old gentleman upstairs." She pointed a huge finger to the ceiling.

"I'm sure I hope not," Arabella said, "but you never can tell with a de Birkett."

It was always a puzzle to people who knew her to reconcile Arabella's contempt for individual de Birketts and her almost passionate regard for the Family, but there it was!

"Perhaps," she went on, "you'd like some more sherry. I'll give you a bottle, and bring some down with me when I look you up in your lovely country home." Arabella had recognized the cooking sherry and made a mental note to thank the butler.

"And you must taste some of my home-made wine," Sophie chimed in. This was her hobby. She made wines of the most unpromising materials, carrots, parsnips, potatoes and even mangel-wurzels. She gave these bottles of stuff away as presents, and the liquid usually found a last resting-place down a drain. But of course they drank it themselves and complained of subsequent attacks of giddiness.

"I shall be delighted to do so," Arabella said politely, but with an inward shiver. "De-lighted!"

Vera thought they had been too easily side-tracked, that their great act of sacrifice for "dear Helen's child" was not being recognized sufficiently. She rose from her chair, thus creating a miniature draught by the sheer misplacement of air.

"Come, sister," she said, "let us go to our rooms. Pray forgive us, Lady Engleton, if we are absent from luncheon. I simply could not face food so soon after my ordeal." She had got her cue from the gong.

Arabella had no objection to any sort of household economy.

"Shall I have something sent up to you?" she asked.

"Just a little something," Vera said. "Just a little something."

And it was a little something too! The sisters lunched off a small cup of very weak Bovril and a water cracker each. This did not include memories of the morning, which was after all only food for thought, and hasty food at that.

Arabella found Henry depressed and morose, and said so.

"A bottle of physic came from the doctor for you," she said. "Be sure and take it."

"I'm tired," he said.

"You'd be tireder still if you'd had those squeamish Beamish women to deal with. They made as much fuss about seeing a doctor as if they had been violated. I nearly tore the lace collar from the fat one's neck. I'm afraid, Henry, you don't appreciate all I'm doing for you."

"I do—really I do! Sometimes I wish you wouldn't."

"Don't be absurd, boy, I only hope you'll never know all I've done and *am* doing."

Henry glanced up sharply. Did he detect a note of malice? Why should she hope such a thing? But Arabella met his glance with a clear eye and tackled her food with her usual picksome greediness. Henry put down his knife and fork. It was obnoxious to eat in a half-darkened room; odious. He felt sick.

It was not until tea time that the atmosphere became something approaching normal. The Beamishes having had what amounted to no lunch at all, and having spent a couple of hours lying down, rose refreshed and ready for tea, which they tackled like starving, but well-trained, dogs. Their feeling of outrage on the sanctities of sex, the sensation of violation, had abated and

they appeared to themselves and each other rather in the light
of young brides, knowledgeable women of the world, almost of
the half world. In fact, the more the thin bread and butter went
down the more their spirits rose. Arabella even rang for a further
supply of food. Henry thought them both revolting. Arabella's
handling of them was impressive, though she privately described
the tea-party as a disgusting spectacle.

A sudden hush, however, fell on them when a maid, entering,
informed Henry that there was "a gentleman to see him," and
a black frock coat was discerned standing literally a "mute" in
the hall. He had come to take the measurements. Later it was
suggested that the two visitors might care to see "the remains."
Nothing could have pleased them more. At Mellingham Parva
they viewed all the remains of every one—a final coroner's court,
as it were—and gave suitable advice to the bereaved, inquiring
when the deceased had last had a meal which, when taken in
conjunction with the cause of death and the weather report,
settled the date of the funeral. Such delights were of course out
of the question when it came to Uncle Alfred. He was of noble
blood and had died fortified by Harley Street and oxygen. They
stood over the corpse and gazed down at it, hovering like vul-
tures. Henry wasn't given to hating people, but a wave of intense
dislike of the Beamishes, Vera in particular, swept over him. Why
did they need to pull long faces? Why couldn't they admit that the
dead man meant less than nothing to them, that he had been a
bore and bother?

"He has battled with life's storm and is now at rest in harbour,"
Vera murmured with unction. As if she knew whether he had
ever battled with anything!

"So beautiful! Such a delicate pink flush!" There never was and
never had been any beauty about Uncle!

"In the midst of life we are in death," rumbled up from Vera's
depths. Would they never stop?

"A long life well spent." Rats! Henry nearly screamed it aloud.

At last it was over. The two sisters went in solemn procession
to the door and left Henry alone. It was his first experience of
death. He looked down on the dead face. It was singularly unim-
pressive, this business of being dead. Uncle Alfred had been none

of the things that the Beamishes had said, had lacked all the attributed qualities. He had never been a fighter, never a champion of
Christendom; neither good nor evil—nothing! His life had been
neither particularly well nor ill spent. And yet there lurked in the
dead face a dignity. The pettiness had gone.

Henry's mind reverted to the Other Figure he had seen that
morning, a white figure on a black cross. Dead—yet living. Alive,
like his love for Dora. Vaguely he understood the love that will
suffer, the love that will hang on a cross, its shadow spreadeagled
over the world, mysterious and terrifying! Poor old Uncle Alfred!
He touched the cold forehead. Was Uncle Alfred somehow swept
away in that torrent of love, the torrent of which his own love for
Dora was but a symbol, a minute fraction?

"Oh God," Henry muttered, half-ashamed of his own voice,
"make me worthy to live, worthy to love, worthy to die!"

He tiptoed from the room.

The next day the Misses Beamish and their brother went back
to plague Mellingham Parva, and the remains set out by the
last train to Preston St. Pans. The coffin was pushed aboard the
train and the few who saw it had vague feelings about it being
misfortunate to travel with a corpse. The grave was dug in the
churchyard at Preston St. Pans, and that was the end of Uncle
Alfred. A young curate sent over as a stop-gap read the service
and wondered whether he could get the living. It was a good vicarage and coals. ("Coals? What's coals? Coals don't signify!")

Arabella was there with of course Caraway and Henry. The
others had all wriggled out of it somehow. Mr. Merry was there
too, in the highest hat that Henry had ever seen, but solely for
the purpose of reading the Will. A representative of one of the
Charities that had hoped to benefit came down to "pay a last
tribute," but was sent empty away, save for three sandwiches and
a glass of sherry. Henry listened to Merry's monotonous voice. In
a year's time, when he came of age, he would become possessed
of nearly nine thousand pounds and the contents of the vicarage,
which heritage was in the meantime to be held in trust for him
by the firm of Merry, Meldrum and Isaacs. Henry felt that his
responsibility was at least delayed. Perhaps had Dora been there

he would have repudiated the legacy, but as it was, he did not even know whether he could legally do so. It became his by default, as it were.

It was Arabella who scoured the vicarage for loot. She enthroned herself in each room in turn, settling what should or should not be sold. She even inspected her brother-in-law's personal wardrobe. With quite unexpected vigour, Henry put his foot down and insisted that these should be distributed among the villagers, and for many years afterwards aged inhabitants of Preston St. Pans had a semi-clerical look, a dog-collar here and a black waistcoat there. In an attic were found hundreds of copies (almost the entire edition) of Uncle Alfred's *Life and Legend of Good St. Pans* and *Sermons on the Apocalyptic Prophecy, or Roman Pretensions Dismissed*. These were quite simply pulped, and in the strange theosophy of paper strove to become something else, something more useful.

Henry grew to like the old man posthumously, liked him for his rubbishy bric-à-brac, for his use of quill pens—there were hundreds of these!—for his forty-years-old croquet set. He saved these and sent them to the Priory.

The sale realized one hundred and seventy-three pounds fourteen shillings and threepence—the threepence being the price put on Uncle Alfred's published works by an ungrateful paper merchant. He had wanted to charge for taking them away, but this was vetoed by Arabella, who demanded at least some form of payment.

Poor old Uncle Alfred!

8

THE MOUTH OF BABES

The gratification felt by Arabella at the complete success of her Insurance plan and the quick demise of Alfred de Birkett with its consequent testamentary benefits, seemed to infuse her with new vitality. She became almost genial and raised Henry's weekly allowance of a pound by yet another pound immediately they returned from Preston St. Pans. This was to be paid "out of the estate." The conferring of this extra benefit assumed the importance of a function. Arabella's one misgiving was that Henry might be tempted to "keep an actress" on it. She alluded to the subject just as others might refer to keeping a dog: it was part of the de Birkett tradition. It says something for Henry's mental development and Dora's training that he laughed, and pointed out that a pound wouldn't go very far in that direction. There was even talk of sending Henry up to Cambridge. A year ago he would have jumped at the idea, but now it just didn't mean anything, and he discouraged the notion, rather to Arabella's secret joy. She hadn't meant it seriously as she was fond of Henry and didn't want to lose him. In any case, even pretended scholarships formed no part of the de Birkett tradition. Eton, yes, but that was breeding, not learning. The extra pound, however, gave the boy a certain freedom, which he exercised by going down to Engleton Priory for the day to "have a look round" with Dora. After all, if she were to be mistress of the place, she might as well have a look at it. They met on Waterloo platform early in the morning, happy as children off to a picnic, which is exactly what they were. Engleton Priory was in Wiltshire, in that lovely stretch of country that flows like a green river from Salisbury in waves towards Shaftesbury. Henry had spent a large part of his youth there and knew it intimately, loving every stone of it, knowing every tree, very nearly. He became enthusiastic about it in the train, his rather delicate face flushing with happy anticipation. The girl smiled in sympathy and they held hands surreptitiously under a newspaper.

"In some ways my grandmother is right," he said. "If the de Birketts mean anything, they mean Engleton Priory. They acquired it by robbery and have done their best to ruin it, ever since. But when the Priory goes the de Birketts finish. They have no other claim to survival."

"And if the de Birketts finish, the Priory will vanish," Dora said thoughtfully. "It gives an added zest to having children; 'jolly fellows, turning cartwheels in the name of the Lord.'"

He squeezed her hand very tightly.

"I used to envy chaps at school sometimes, boys who were

going into businesses or the professions. Sometimes I've even envied that dummy Bertram. They seemed to have impersonal work to do. But the land is different. I'm not going to talk about trees and sheep as if they had any relationship or intelligence; don't think that."

"The cow is not my sister," Dora interpolated.

"Exactly. But to do justice to the land, one must *love* somebody. I felt that fact at Uncle Alfred's funeral. All those present seemed to have someone to love . . ."

"Surely that's true everywhere in the world, in cities and back streets as well as fields."

Henry shook his head obstinately.

"No," he said, "that's not what I mean. Isn't there an order of monks or something who work and plough for the love of God?"

"I haven't the vaguest idea."

"I do know," Henry said, "that my love for you is somehow tied up with my love for the Priory. You're very beautiful, Dora," he added irrelevantly.

"Thank you, Harry," Dora said simply. "You make me *feel* beautiful."

They left it at that and ate penny sticks of chocolate.

At Salisbury they were met by the agent, a Mr. Bean. He had with him a Morris-Cowley of immense age—a relic. Not only was it bull-nosed, but it had a radiator that resembled a portcullis. It seemed to typify the Priory; it was aged, dirty and ragged—but it went.

Mr. Bean apologized for the state of the car and smiled his approval of Dora, who was good to look at. He was a grizzled, tanned person who had a hopeless job. There seemed to be no chance of making the Priory into a paying proposition. He had even convinced Arabella of this fact—no easy task. Mr. Bean had taken a degree at an agricultural college and had a perpetual grievance in that unlettered farmers knew more about it than he did, and that the only person who really knew how to tackle sick cattle was the village idiot, who had been removed to a Home for Mental Defectives. He had told all this to Henry long before they had reached Wilton. He pulled the car into the side of the road

and pointed to that astounding piece of militant Christendom—
the vast spire of Salisbury Cathedral.

"Defective indeed!" he snorted. "Look at that! Probably the
man who built that would have been locked up in one of their
blasted homes."

He was an excitable man, was Mr. Bean, with unorthodox
ideas about peasant ownership. He was popular, though regarded
as more than a little mad, but not even Arabella's eagle eye could
detect errors in his accounts. Dora liked him at once. There was
something pleasant about his dirty clothes and lack of reticence,
something that gave one confidence and lent colour to Harry's
innate love of the land. This man loved the soil. Almost at once
they were discussing potato wart and kindred subjects with an
almost passionate intensity.

At Wilton he stopped again, this time outside a neat hotel, and
wiped his mouth with the back of his hand.

"I shan't be a minute," he said. "We supply this place with eggs
and I want to know how many they propose to take next week."

He jumped out without opening the door.

"Just a minute, Mr. Bean," Dora said. "We like beer, too!"

He gave a sudden grin.

"Can't do without beer," he muttered apologetically, "though
I wasn't lying about the eggs."

Soon they were raising tankards with mutual expressions of
goodwill.

"Forgive me being rude," said Bean, "but are you going to be
the next Lady Engleton, miss?"

"Yes," Dora said promptly. "I am."

"I'm glad. We can do with your sort." They shook hands all
round and ordered more beer.

Thus was a friendship signed and sealed.

The Priory itself was an architectural jumble. The ancient
ruins lay apart, dumb monuments of the pillage; a grand arch still
remained, pointing a reproachful finger heavenward. The house
was in the main Tudor, but a bad Georgian architect had added an
Italian portico. The stucco had begun to flake within a few years
of its erection, and a Victorian architect had then done his worst.
Edward de Birkett had not been inclined to pay out money for the

mere preservation of his ancestral halls. It was a patchwork affair which required even further patching, and required it urgently; but in spite of its dishevelled appearance, perhaps because of it, it was lovable. Henry watched Dora's face anxiously to see what impression it had made on her.

"It's not," he said humbly, "the best time of year to see it . . ."

"I think," Dora said at last, "that we'll start by having that portico pulled down."

Henry breathed again. She had taken possession already.

"It won't want much pulling," Bean said, scratching his crimson neck. "Go and give it a shove now. The three of us could do it. I'm afraid it's the same story everywhere. The fences are rotten, there's no game to preserve, the sheds and outhouses are falling to bits. Those old monks are having their revenge all right."

He gestured towards the Abbey ruins. Silence fell on them. It was late autumn, leaves lay in profusion, rotten plants smelt acidly, and the air was tinged with the pleasant smoke of bonfires.

"What a job, eh?" he went on, "if there was only a spot of cash to do it with." The mention of the word cash made him think of Arabella. "How is Lady Engleton? I should have asked before, but I didn't think of it," he added truthfully. "Last time she was here, she said it stank of decay and poverty, and she never wanted to see it again. That was three years ago, and we've gone farther downhill since then."

"My grandmother is much as ever. She doesn't get any older."

"It would hardly be possible, would it?"

Bean glanced at the two eager young faces and heaved a sigh.

"You won't mind if I trot off, will you?" he asked. "There's always something wants doing. In any case, I dare say you'd rather be left on your own. Mrs. Barber is getting you some lunch."

He bowed to Dora and took his leave. When he was out of sight, Dora suddenly put her arms round Henry and kissed him.

"He's right," she said. "It's going to be a job. But we'll do it, Harry! It's worth it. If we only keep ourselves and our kids by working all the time, we'll do it. It'll be our very own. . . ."

She slipped her arm through his, and thus did they take possession, as it were. They walked to the front door, where they could see the stout Mrs. Barber waiting to give them a welcome, a tiny figure in the distance.

"You know, darling," Henry said, "Uncle Alfred's death has taught me things; things that I can't put into words. Artists and musicians put the things into colour and sound. I want to interpret them by loving you and . . . all this. Just simple things."

Dora laughed happily.

"I know," she said. "You want to sing songs, not jazz tunes. I'm going to enjoy marrying you, Harry."

They passed through the old ruined Gothic arch, picking their way over the rubble through which rank grass pushed its faded autumnal green.

"Perhaps," Henry said, "that's what those monks were doing when they built this arch, singing a song, possibly the same song I'm trying to sing. They may have been bad landlords, but they lived here at least; they were part of it. In any case, they could not possibly have been worse than the de Birketts. They had ruin brought on them; they didn't bring it on themselves."

"I think they would have liked you, Harry."

"They would have loved you, adored you, like I do!"

"I'm sure I hope not."

Suddenly Harry took her in his arms and held her tightly, roughly. He kissed her till she fought for breath. Never before had he done such a thing.

"I'm sorry," he said humbly. "Did I hurt you, dear?"

"Yes. But you needn't be sorry."

"I've never been so happy in my life."

"I'm sure I haven't. Harry, nothing could ever part us, could it?"

"One of us might die . . ."

Dora made a sudden impatient gesture.

"That's not being parted. The most important thing about living is dying; you can't help it. I don't mean that. I mean . . . people . . . things."

"What things?"

"Well—your grandmother, for example."

"I *will* be truthful. A fortnight ago she might have managed it. She is so dictatorial and successful. But not now, not after to-day, not since Uncle died, not since I learnt things. . . ."

Mrs. Barber was affability itself. Any visit from one of the Family was an event, but the young lady—so pretty too—made it a high festival. There was a glass of sherry and a biscuit waiting for them—real sherry, one of the few remaining bottles in the devastated cellar. Then Mrs. Barber insisted on taking Dora all over the house. His Lordship of course knew it, every nook and cranny. It seemed to Dora that they walked miles, in and out of countless bedrooms, through low archways ("Mind your head, miss"), and down passages ("There's a step, my dear"). Some of the rooms, it must be confessed, were very damp and dusty, "but it's hard to keep a place clean with only me and two lazy hussies from the village." Dora was shown the actual bed on which Henry had first seen the light, and not much light at that. Looking out of the corner of her eyes, she noticed with amusement that he blushed, as if slightly scandalized at the indelicacy of having been born.

After lunch, they wandered over the estate, the poor neglected Priory. Wherever they went they could see Mr. Bean. He was not spying on them, they knew that. On the contrary, he made himself scarce with elaborate tact on these occasions. Bean was just one of those men who seem able to be in two places at once. Dora wondered what his salary was, and why he didn't look for another job. Of course jobs are few and far between, but there must be some other reason. It was probably that he too loved the place, that it was like an exacting mistress to him, impossible to gratify, yet impossible to leave, without tears and a pain too great to be borne.

They arrived at last at what was euphemistically called the Lake. It was really a widening in the little river that flowed through the estate, some fifty yards across. Weeds and rushes were choking it and pulled up at the side, half-full of water, were the rotting remains of a punt. They sat down side by side on a fallen tree, sat for a few minutes in silence. Fish plopped out and blew bubbles, the sun was sinking, a blood-red orb in a bank of mist. Between the trees lights suddenly shone, lights in the cheerful windows of some farmhouse. There were distant voices of children, wholesome, happy sights and sounds. Henry's arm stole round her and they clung tightly together. They felt their hearts beating and did not know why. It was possible that at the back of it all danger lurked in ambush, just as soldiers who went "over the top" knew they might never return. The sun sank lower and lost the battle to the mist that hung like a veil. Dora shivered slightly and clung closer to her lover.

"You're so warm, Harry, and you smell so nice."

It seemed to sum up the whole situation. Harry laughed softly. The tension was broken, but the spell remained.

"You shivered just now, darling," he said, suddenly grave. "If you were to catch cold and die I should never smile again, never pat a dog, never scratch a cat behind the ear. The sun would be darkened and the moon turned to blood. Please don't die!"

Dora jumped to her feet.

"I've no intention of dying; I'm going to live—live!"

She stretched her young arms wide with a sudden gesture, theatrical, but like so many theatrical things, symbolic and real. She embraced the dying sun.

"I suppose," she said, "that we shall squabble like other married people, that you'll reproach me with being a 'fly-by-night,' and a night-club bird, when I was eighteen and the boys were after me, that I shall call you a prig and all the rest of it, but we two, my beloved, are one flesh. Nothing can ever alter that—nothing."

"My darling," he answered after a pause, "do you remember when we went to that Promenade Concert and heard Beethoven's Ninth? I didn't know then what that dying, deaf old man meant by that Scherzo with its sudden terrifying pauses. I know now. I think I know the secret of everything."

"Sweet, darling prig!"

They walked in silence to the house. Against the darkening sky the Gothic arch still pointed its finger heavenward.

"I hope Mrs. Barber has cooked eggs for tea," Dora said and burst into tears. Henry kissed her eyes and tasted the salt and bitterness of them.

"Don't cry, sweetheart," he said, as monotonously as the refrain of a popular song. "Don't cry, sweetheart."

"But I want to cry! Damn it, I'm a woman, and if I want to cry I shall cry. I like it!"

It was all beyond Henry—but Mrs. Barber had cooked eggs for

tea and they ate them, three apiece with quantities of bread and butter.

"In life," Dora said sententiously, "it's the little things that matter. Theologians, philosophers and scientists may argue, but it's the third egg that counts—the third egg."

She dug her spoon deep into the creamy, new-laid shell.

Dinner was well over when Henry got back to Mount Street and went to his grandmother, who was playing patience in the drawing-room. Arabella, being without morals, always got her patience games out somehow. She glanced up as he came in.

"Ah, Henry," was all she said. For a minute or so she cheated her way to success. Henry sat down and watched her. This cheating business always struck him as wrong somehow. Cheat an opponent if you're given that way, but why gammon yourself? It was rather like baiting a mouse-trap and then eating the cheese yourself and feeling you had diddled the mouse.

"Did you enjoy yourself?"

"I had a wonderful day."

"Hm. I trust you did not anticipate the wedding ceremony?"

If Arabella had seen the look of cold hatred that Henry shot at her, she might have ceased to bother about the House of de Birkett and saved herself the necessity of sinning quite as much as she did. He had never thought it possible to dislike his grandmother so much. He choked back his anger and answered with the minimum of indignation.

"Of course not."

"That is as well, as I doubt whether there will be any ceremony to anticipate."

Arabella spoke as if it were the most ordinary thing in the world, and Henry jerked forward in his chair. He had been docile long enough, had taken and obeyed orders as long as he could, but now he was mutinous. Arabella shifted a neat little pack of cards and put them on one side, hardly looking at her grandson.

"What do you mean, Grannie?"

"Just what I say. I am reconsidering the whole question. I had a most unsatisfactory reply to my letter to Sir Creighton Winslow."

Henry felt a chill at his heart.

"What did he say?" he stammered.

"You may read his letter. It is impertinent."

The old lady pushed a letter across the table which Henry mechanically took.

Dear Lady Engleton,

I must thank you for your letter. I have always wanted my girl to marry a man actively employed in some capacity and though I have no objection to your grandson, he does not quite fulfil my wishes in this respect. Doubtless, however, there is yet time to rectify this aspect of the question.

You inquired how much money I was prepared to settle on my daughter on her marriage, and what she might reasonably inherit at my death. My daughter's future is provided for. More than this I am not prepared to say. Etc.—etc.

The letter struck Henry as needlessly terse, but then there was no knowing what Arabella might have said in her prior letter.

"What did you say in your letter?"

"I am not in the habit of being questioned on such things, but I have no objection to telling you on this occasion. I told this man that you and his daughter appeared to be in love with each other and that we were prepared to consider a possible marriage in the future if we could receive suitable guarantees as to settlements and his daughter's expectations."

"'We?' You actually said 'we?'"

"I did. (Ah, there is the ten of spades!) Our interest in this matter is identical, the honour and interest of the Family."

"Good God!"

"I'm sorry if this hurts you, my boy. Calf love is always more real than any other and therefore more easily forgotten. Reality is like that—luckily. I've already instructed Merry to make inquiries as to a suitable wife for you, one who will be well dowered and not too hideous to look at. The de Birketts . . ."

"Damn the de Birketts! Damn the Family!"

Arabella was neither annoyed nor ruffled at this sudden outburst.

"I shall marry Dora!"

"I think not."

"I shall shortly be of age."

"By which time you will have regained your sanity and forgotten this girl."

"I think not!"

"We shall see."

"*We shall!*"

Arabella rang the bell for Caraway and rose to go to bed. She gave Henry her withered cheek to kiss, so different from the sweet young cheek he had kissed only an hour before.

"Don't let us lose our tempers, my dear boy. Good night. My stick, Caraway."

Meanwhile a similar scene was being played out between Dora and her father.

"Don't you trust my judgment, Daddy?"

"In some ways, my dear. But emotions play the devil with the most sensible people. I happen to love you very dearly and I resent that old woman's attitude. There'll be no *droit de Seigneur* exercised in my home."

"But Daddy darling, Henry isn't a bit like the old woman."

"The de Birketts are thoroughly rotten stock, my dear; rotten to the core—always have been. I don't want you to be sacrificed on that altar."

The usually courageous Dora wilted, was thoroughly miserable. She and her father had always been such friends, such complete love and comprehension had united them in the past. She threw back her head with a sudden gesture of defiance.

"Whatever any one may say or do I intend to marry Harry. It's my whole life."

Sir Creighton softened in spite of himself, and he put his arm round her shoulder.

"Heaven knows I want you to be happy," he said. "I've nothing against the boy, but I resent his mercenary attitude. You've seen the letter?"

"I don't believe Henry wrote a word of it, or even knows of it."

Nevertheless Dora wept bitterly that night, saw Henry in the darkness at his worst. He was weak—under Arabella's thumb. The de Birketts *were* rotten, her father was right, in that at least.

There was the horrible business of the Insurance. All the hideous ghosts paraded themselves in front of her sleepless eyes. Arabella had herself chatted gaily about the de Birketts, recounting all the odious scandal. It was puzzling to Dora. After all, she was only nineteen. Then she could only remember her love and bitterly reproached herself. Only that afternoon she had sworn to fight with Henry, had feared some person might intervene, had held him protectively. It was she, not her lover, who was shaken. Suddenly she drove all the ghosts away; a feeling of shame and humility possessed her. Whatever happened, she would marry Henry. She put her arms round a pillow and held it as if it were his head, and was queerly comforted.

Henry slept soundly enough. He had never expected easy victory. To him the issue was clean cut. If Arabella objected to his marrying Dora, then she could put up with the consequences. After all, she could not live for ever, and in any case he would soon be of age and would thereupon inherit the Priory. He had lost his fear of Arabella.

As events proved, this was extremely unwise.

9

BLOOD WILL TELL

Dora and Henry met next day and went for a walk in Hyde Park, making mutual confession of the events of the preceding night. Henry was frankly puzzled at Dora's sense of having been momentarily doubtful.

"It doesn't surprise me at all," he said. "The de Birketts *are* a rotten bunch. Your father is right. But I love you, darling, and there it is. I'll wait, that's all. We've both gained something from this opposition. I've learned to have no fear at all of my grandmother. That's something to the good!"

It was a foggy afternoon and the trees dripped moisture. Passers-by became damp ghosts who appeared for a moment and then were gone.

"And I've learned to be *very* afraid of her," Dora said. "I'm beginning to wonder whether she ever meant us to marry at all, whether her grudging consent wasn't just put up to keep you quiet. She must have known that any one would resent the sort of letter she wrote father. I admit I should have, in his shoes."

Henry pondered this carefully. It seemed too subtle even for Arabella's agile mind. She had only to forbid Henry seeing Dora and, judging from her previous experience of the boy, might quite reasonably have presumed on his instantaneous obedience. Or had she noticed a change in him? It was just possible. More probably she had steered for safety. If Sir Creighton had come to terms—Arabella's terms—all might have been well.

"Which of us is right?" Dora demanded. "I wish to Heaven someone would tell me."

"Perhaps we're both wrong," Henry suggested. "One thing is certain, though, my darling, and that is that I meant every solitary single thing I said yesterday; yes, and a lot more I couldn't put into words."

Dora gave his arm a grateful squeeze.

"Daddy's all right really," she said. "He would like to see you do a job of work."

"So would I," Henry grumbled. "But I can't. I don't know how, and I know that my real job is running the Priory."

"I told daddy about that," Dora said quickly, "but he's the sort that doesn't think running an estate means much. His idea of a job is business or politics. He doesn't understand anything else. He laughed at the idea of you as Gaffer de Birkett."

"If I've got to wait for you, then I must wait. I'll wait for ever, if necessary."

"You'll do nothing of the sort! We must keep our courage up. Talking about 'for evers' is morbid, dear one. No, I think our Arabella is a deep 'un. We must look out. Daddy wants me to go out to parties and things. He thinks it'll keep my mind from brooding. I shall go. . . ."

"I suppose we must chuck some dust about, but it won't make any difference, will it? I hate to think of other men putting their arms round you and capering about, pretending to dance."

"Jealous, dear?"

" 'Fraid so. Sorry!"

"I don't mind. I wouldn't give tuppence for anyone's love who wasn't a wee bit jealous. For all that, Harry, I'm right. We must play up to them a bit."

" 'Spose so."

Henry stared miserably at the darkening grey.

"I want you now, dear," he added. "For keeps. It's all so empty when you're not there."

"Harry darling, we're that odd thing, monogamous moderns. Don't worry, but keep your eye on Grannie. She's not done yet by a long chalk. She's too old to linger long over her plans. We shall soon see what the game is."

Henry was all unconsciously introduced to the game ten minutes after he got in at Mount Street, and had glimmerings of its nature later in the evening. Arabella, having decided that Dora was not sufficiently reliable as a potential financial asset for the House of de Birkett, had quickly got hold of Merry, whom she had already warned. He had presented himself early in the afternoon.

"Henry," Arabella had said, "is broody. His condition is ripe for possible mischief; his visit with this Winslow girl yesterday to the Priory was dangerous. Anything might have happened in that plaintive and romantic atmosphere. My son, fool that he was, once forgot himself there with a girl from the village, and it cost two hundred and fifty pounds to rectify the error. The consequence is, I believe, at Bristol."

"That is so, Lady Engleton," Merry replied with all the brightness he could muster. He had helped to put him there.

"Luckily—I nearly said providentially—both Henry and this girl are prigs, so nothing untoward occurred."

"But I thought, my lady, that you had no objection to this—er —this young woman?"

"I have the strongest objection to impertinence from a mere Foreign Office clerk," she retorted. "Sir Creighton Winslow refused to discuss any settlement or arrangement. The matter is therefore closed."

"How such men get knighthoods is beyond my comprehension," Merry said, with a dutiful sigh. The ancient order of chivalry was at that moment at a very low ebb.

"Have you any rich clients, Merry, with eligible daughters, whose parents will not be squeamish? We have only to introduce Henry to a presentable girl in his present condition, and we may be sure he will soon forget this Winslow child."

Mr. Merry pondered the matter, head on one side; his mouth moving like a hen drinking as he rapidly went through a mental list of rich clients who filled this particular bill.

"I'm afraid the one client I have in mind would hardly meet your ladyship's requirements," he said slowly.

"Is he rich?"

"Extremely well endowed with this world's goods," Merry replied. He disliked a direct answer. "He has an only female child who is his sole heiress and he would without doubt provide for her on her marriage; provide very handsomely indeed."

"Good gracious, my dear man, what a long time you take to say simple truths. What is the objection?"

Merry placed his hands on his knees and leaned forward.

"Trade," he said softly. "Groceries!"

The wave of commerce lapped at the feet of Arabella, a modern and female Canute. Who was she to sweep it back at a word?

"A Merchant King," Merry added, as if the title had been granted by the Herald's College. "A Merchant King. Unfortunately," he went on, "there is little money where there is also breeding. Mr. Peploe's name is a household word in the poorer quarters of our great metropolis, where shops bearing his name abound. He sells foodstuffs of an inferior nature to the working classes."

"Even poor people must eat, Merry," said Arabella, seeking for extenuating circumstances.

"Mr. Peploe would make a large settlement on his daughter Lily, should she marry into the aristocracy. In fact, he has hinted as much."

"Lily!" Arabella moaned. "Lily!"

"Alas, yes. Lily. But indeed a flower amongst girls. She is distinctly pretty and—er—dashing."

"Perhaps," Arabella said, "a dash of plebeian blood might do the de Birketts no harm."

"Indeed no," Merry said, a shade too eagerly to be completely tactful. "The present House of Lords, a fine body of men, is largely composed of noblemen whose mothers have appeared before the footlights."

"Don't talk to me of actresses," Arabella said tartly. "Had the House of Peers been less tainted, they would not be in the ridiculous position to-day in which they find themselves."

"True, my lady, true."

"How much will this feller Peploe give?"

"He might go to fifty thousand as a settlement, not counting testamentary benefits later."

"Why on earth didn't you say so before?" Fifty thousand! This would indeed be a jewel in the crown of her efforts to reinstate the Family. Her own plans seemed puny, Alfred's little bit, the insurances. But at least they were certain, and every farthing counted in the struggle. The sum total might even reach a hundred thousand pounds if she could wangle the Beamishes into making satisfactory Wills! All the same, the idea of trade was repugnant to Arabella; with all her faults, she preserved dignity. It seemed loathsome that the foundations of the revivified Family should be laid on sausages that were sixty per cent stale bread, and butters that were mere hotch-potches of foreign fats. But there! We live in decadent times.

"We can at least give it a trial, Merry," Arabella conceded at last. Thus did Progress and Democracy score a slight skirmish over Reaction and Blood. Merry was pleased at the success of his quickly laid scheme.

"No time like the present," he said. "May I make use of the telephone?"

A few minutes later he announced that Mr. and Mrs. Peploe and daughter were having dinner with him at his house in Fitzjohn's Avenue that evening at eight. By good fortune they were free and had jumped at the bait of a lord being there. Could it be arranged that Henry should dine there as well? Yes, it could—and was.

That is how it came about that when Henry came back from his walk with Dora he was informed that it would be conferring a great favour on Mr. Merry if he could make it convenient to have dinner with him that evening. There were certain matters relative to the mortgages on the Priory (good bait, that!) which required immediate attention. Henry had no valid reason for refusing, especially as his grandmother, when asked, had no objection to losing his company for the evening. It was very nice of her, not to say unselfish.

Merry's house in Fitzjohn's Avenue was large and over-heated. It smelt like Maple's Furniture Department, which was not surprising, seeing that most of its contents had emanated from that admirable spot. It was of mellow late Victorian red-brick, and its opulence bore testimony to the financial benefits of being a solicitor. Nor was there any dust in it visible to the eye, nor any disorder.

Henry had been there once before in years gone by, but the visit had left little impression on him. It seemed odd, however, that Merry who was owner of this semi-magnificence should kow-tow to his grandmother. He wondered if she ever paid her bill of costs. He did not realize that Arabella was a first-rate advertisement for Merry, and was well worth the bother. ("You know, *Merry*—the de Birketts' legal adviser?")

He was greeted with cordiality by Merry and conducted at once into his study and shown the mortgages on the Priory —quite needlessly, it seemed to Henry. Merry explained them briefly and with a knowledgeable air, pointing out quite obvious facts until even Henry, not particularly brilliant, began to wonder what it was all about.

"But enough of dull business," Merry said with a bluff roguishness. "Let us join the others and have a glass of sherry, or perhaps a cocktail. You youngsters like such things, though I confess to being of the old school."

"Thanks," Henry said listlessly.

Merry made his way to the door.

"You must take us as you find us," he said. Henry wondered whether he was going to talk about taking "pot-luck." He didn't, however.

"Just a few friends in to-night. A Mr. Peploe and his wife and daughter. Simple folk, you know. Peploe's a rough diamond. You will forgive him any little eccentricities; a rough diamond, but a Great Brain."

In the drawing-room he was tonelessly received by Mrs. Merry, a tired, faded woman, whose one real occupation was the elimination of dust from her home. Then he was confronted with the Peploes. Peploe himself was not an ill-looking man, might even have been good-looking in a common way in his youth, and might have been a decent, ordinary citizen had he not been lucky in business and thereby persuaded himself that he was one of Britain's Business Brains. He was too stumpy, too overfed, too rich. His arms were over-long and his fingers podgy and nearly all the same short length. A diamond winked at the world from a huge shirt-front. For all that, he was a hearty, good-natured, lecherous old sinner, whose fortunes were grounded in the years of shortage from 1915-1918.

"This is indeed an honour, my lord," he said loudly, proffering a hot, large, damp hand. Henry stared at him, unwittingly playing the part of the exclusive aristocrat, and shook it gingerly. "Meet Mrs. Peploe—my wife, you know. . . ." As if the matter were one of considerable doubt. She was worth meeting, and Henry felt rather as Mahomet must have felt when he met the mountain, providing that the mountain was a large mountain. Henry calculated that it must have taken hundreds of square yards of silk to have covered her, even though it was tightly stretched across the vast bosom, hips and hinder quarters. There was an enormous rope of pea-like pearls dangling from her neck, and her hair rose in tiers, in the fashion of nineteen hundred. Diamonds shone in the coiffure like stars in a henna-ed firmament. She had once been extremely pretty, and one could almost see the be-diamonded hands dragging heartily at beer pumps. She looked like the apotheosis of an Edwardian barmaid, which was precisely what she was. Once Mrs. Peploe had tried to "talk la-di-da," like a newly trained film star, but the acquisition of wealth had put her above such niceties. ("I got the dough, ain't I, Albert? Well—*rot* 'em!") So it was with perfect ease and command of herself that she said:

"Well, this *is* a treat. Glad to know you."

Henry liked her, in spite of the awful waves of scent that blew from her as from some bellows, whenever she moved.

"This is our daughter Lily," she said.

Mr. and Mrs. Peploe stepped on one side, thereby disclosing the said daughter. Merry held his breath. First encounters were important in his estimation, and he watched Henry's face with meticulous care. A decent commission hung on it, anyway. There was no question of it; Lily was absurdly pretty, a platinum blonde, mostly genuine, with a tiptilt nose and a shock of curls. Her parents had taken great pains with her and expensive governesses and Roedean had done their best or worst with her, according to the point of view. Henry made a quick comparison with Dora. This girl seemed to be everything that Dora was *not*. She was a pretty aphrodisiac little thing, whereas Dora had a quiet beauty that soothed and charmed. She was dressed with an expensive lavishness that fascinated, but failed to please, and her full-blown little figure bulged dangerously and left nothing to the imagination. Even at Deauville she had attained a certain notoriety by the complete shamelessness of her beach pyjamas. Lily greeted Henry with calculating cordiality. She had no illusions about this dinner-party, and knew perfectly well what the game was; nor had she any objection to becoming Lady Engleton. Henry, she decided, was "a nice-looking boy, but wanted waking up." She put all the many men she knew into this sort of category. Her A.1 Class, as it were, was "Fierce and Sexy," and the grades descended gradually to "Supposed to be clever, talks about his job, and wears glasses." This was lowest on the list. Henry's category was about fifth; not a bad category either—for a husband. There was a friendly light in the little pagan's eye which made Henry smile cheerfully. Merry was relieved, feeling his task as good as done.

Henry found himself deliberately paired off with Lily. The older quartette drew into itself, leaving youth in glorious isolation and in possession of the cocktails.

"Weak as ditchwater, aren't they?" Lily said ungratefully. "A Manhattan without whisky is like a ram without—well, without horns."

Henry was slightly shocked, but amused and rather fascinated for all that.

"Look at mother," she went on irrelevantly. "Did you ever see anything so fat? I and some of the lads had a sweep once on her weight. Over sixteen stone she turns; a poor devil comes every day and rubs her down, but it doesn't make any difference. You should see her in the altogether! It's as good as a show. I hope I don't get like it, but then I take care of myself. You needn't worry about *that!*" She smoothed her hips with a sensuous self-love. Henry felt slightly warm about the collar. Lily lacked all false modesty, anyway. "Been to any parties?"

"I—I'm afraid not. I'm not asked, even."

"Ferdy Nathan's was pretty warm the other night, but on the whole you don't miss much by not being asked. There's nothing new under the sun nowadays. By the way, what can I call you? I can't go on 'my lording' you."

"My name's Henry; better call me that."

"Sounds a bit prim. What about Harry?"

No! That was blasphemy. Only Dora had ever called him Harry, and only Dora ever should. Dear Dora! Would she be annoyed or amused if she could see him now? At least she would understand the nature of Arabella's game.

"I just don't answer to Harry. I'm sorry—but Henry it is."

"O.K. Well, what do you think of me, Henry?"

Henry looked at her rather blankly, and she flashed a grin at him.

"Oh, it's no good our pretending not to know why we've been pushed together like this," she said. "They are watching us out of the corner of their eyes, wondering if we are going to mate. Well, will I do?" She tilted her head sideways and looked provocative.

Henry was spared the embarrassment of a reply by the announcement that dinner was served. Dinner was a gargantuan affair; there were soups and savouries, fishes and pheasants. Henry hadn't eaten anything like it for years. If only Dora had been at his side and not Lily, though to do Lily justice she rigidly eschewed everything fattening, which was more than could be said for her mother, whose corsage creaked and groaned under the ever-increasing load. Henry felt that he was being watched by Mrs. Peploe (Gladeyes, as her husband called her), picked over and approved. Every now and then she would smile and nod at them, but she spoke but little, her jaws being otherwise occupied. It was Peploe who did the talking, giving the assembled company a sketchy outline of his life and his gradual steps to Parnassus.

Most of the steps struck Henry as being rather dishonourable, but he was fascinated by the man's bumptious good humour. Lily was openly derisive of her parent, giving Henry a little dig on the knee when her sire became peculiarly ungrammatical or too outrageously a self-confessed profiteer and foozler of the poor. Nor did his daughter's derision escape her father's notice. Usually he was afraid of Lily and her superior ways; she was a Frankenstein in a small way of business. He was prepared to pay quite a goodly sum to get her off his hands, provided she was put into titled hands. About her "goings on" he preferred to maintain the proverbial ostrich attitude. Nevertheless he had no intention of being made a fool of before a real lord! Vintage wines and a hot room overcame his habitual feeling of social inferiority. He flushed angrily at a too obvious sneer from his child.

"You may jeer, my girl," he said. "I've been watching you, but where would you have been if I hadn't been a bit fly? Answer me that!"

"Behind a bar pulling beer for the boys, like mother," Lily answered promptly. "Or on the streets," she added, by way of casual afterthought.

"And you wouldn't have cared neither," Peploe retorted, forgetting he wasn't at home.

"'Ush, Albert," his spouse interposed, flourishing a jewelled hand. "What will Lord Engleton think? I was behind a bar all right, and nothing to be ashamed of in that, that I know of."

"Indeed not," Henry said quickly, feeling that something was expected of him. Merry coughed self-consciously, and Mrs. Merry, with an artificial beam of a smile, began to talk vivaciously of the difficulty of getting suitable parlour-maids. This gave Merry his chance of giving Henry his rough-diamond-but-a-good-fellow look. The gathering storm blew over.

"Tact," Lily murmured, "that tact that makes us English what we are, God help us!" In spite of her apparent ease, it was easy to see that she resented her parents. Luckily the long meal was nearly over and it was only a few minutes before the three men were left alone over the port and brandy. Awkwardness was still in the air, and Henry dreaded that old Peploe would go back over it. He did, with promptitude.

"Things have come to a pretty pass," he said, glancing at the port. "A pretty pass!"

"Youthful high spirits and that glorious feeling of independence," Merry said harshly and with meaning. He did not want Henry choked off early in the negotiations. "A charming, sweet girl, really."

"Eh?" Peploe asked, looking at him with sudden comprehension. "Dare say you're right, Merry. In the right 'ands she'd be all right. My 'ands don't seem right. My fingers is all thumbs when it comes to 'andling that girl."

"She's certainly very good-looking," Henry said.

"She's that all right. Take after her mother *and* me if it comes to that, though I says it as shouldn't. When I was a youngster I wasn't bad-looking. I remember once . . ."

Apparently old Peploe still fancied himself with the girls. It was dreary to listen to. At last they went back to the drawing-room, where Henry saw to his dismay that a bridge table had been put out.

"Dear me," Merry said with pretended surprise. "I'm afraid there are too many of us for a rubber. I'm sorry, as I know how much you like taking a hand, Mrs. Peploe."

"I like a round o' bridge, too," Peploe grumbled. And indeed, strange as it may seem, he played a very good hand.

"Don't bother about it," Lily said. "I hate cards—except a spot of poker, and then not much."

"And I'm sorry to say I don't play at all," Henry added.

Mr. Merry had a Great Idea.

"Would you young people care to see my new billiard table?" he said. "I'm sure you both play billiards." There was a pressing enthusiasm about him which didn't encourage refusal.

"I'm afraid I . . ." Henry began honestly, when Lily cut him short.

"If you don't play, Lord Engleton, I'll teach you." She took his arm and began to pilot him to the door.

"Have a little sense," she whispered. "They mean us to be alone—somehow and somewhere. No use fighting."

The billiard-room was more for show than for use. Merry had done admirable business over the green field of its table, which was all uncovered ready for use. Everything was being worked according to plan. Lily sat on the table, waving exuberant legs.

"Turn on the gramophone," she said in order to give the shy Henry something to do. "Have they got 'Salut d'Amour?' That seems appropriate."

Henry turned over some records which lay at the side of the opulent machine. They seemed new and untouched.

"This one's called 'Fruity Cutie,'" he said doubtfully.

"Specially bought for me! More suitable still. What's on the other side?"

"'Poppa's got the Heebie-jeebies,'" Henry announced reluctantly.

"They've thought of everything! Put it on."

Henry obeyed, and Lily's shoulders swayed automatically to the obvious rhythm of "Fruity Cutie."

"They're not what you'd call subtle, are they?"

"Perhaps you're imagining it," Henry said, but not believing himself. Lily laughed scornfully.

"Do you mean to say you didn't get full instructions? I was informed all about it this afternoon."

"I didn't even know I was going to meet you."

"Otherwise you wouldn't have come, eh?"

"I didn't say that, Miss Peploe."

"Lily to *you*. But you meant it. This is a great day for my lousy parents. They've fattened me up for the last ten years for this minute; sent me to snobby schools. Now, I'm all decked out with parsley for a real, live lord."

She lit a cigarette and looked at him sideways out of her pretty blue eyes. Henry was revolted and rather annoyed at his grandmother's ambush. Merry was a contemptible lick-spittle, a pimp, and other rude things. But try as he would, he couldn't help liking this impudent, cynical little bundle of curls. In spite of himself he grinned. The gramophone stopped, gave a sort of gulp, and swallowed the record, depositing it in an automatic stomach at the side.

"What are you going to do?" she asked. "Pick the goods over? Better have a look at my legs now."

She thrust out a long stretch of silk-covered leg. Henry had no idea that stockings were made so long and far-reaching.

"They're not bad, are they? Feel 'em if you like. Go on. I've no shame."

"Don't be so cynical. It's not a bit like you."

"I was waiting for you to say that. It's exactly like me. And what's wrong with it? Why should you buy a pig in a poke? Fair's fair."

Henry suddenly felt a wave of anger.

"Do you seriously mean to tell me that they told you that—that——"

"That I was to be your future wife? That's right, and gave me all the details of the purchase price. They fixed it all up this afternoon."

"What did you say?"

"I said, 'What's the poor boy done?'"

Henry made an impatient gesture.

"Well, what else *was* there to say?"

"I could have thought of lots of things."

"They wouldn't have been any use. Better give in now. Those guys wear you down in time. Anyhow, it doesn't matter much."

"Marriage doesn't matter?" Henry was genuinely aghast.

"You've said it."

"I don't believe you mean what you say."

"Perhaps not all of it. But most of it."

There was a pause during which Henry simmered. Then he gave a half-laugh and slumped bewildered into a chair. Lily eyed him curiously but not unkindly. She definitely liked this strange, serious young man.

"By the way," she asked, stubbing her cigarette out on the sacred edge of the billiard table, "did you really mean what you said about not knowing that I was here on show? Prime meat up for inspection?"

"Of course I didn't know."

"I like you for that, which isn't a bad start. I suppose I was a bit of a mug to take it lying down, but then I always was; brought up like it."

Henry jumped to his feet with sudden resolution and straightened his tie, a look of battle in his eye.

"What are you going to do, Henry?"

"I'm going in to tell Merry and the whole boiling of 'em what I think of their filthy, dirty behaviour."

Lily jumped off the table in genuine alarm.

"For God's sake don't do that!"

"For God's sake, I will!"

"No, please don't. They'll give me hell if you do. Say it was because I was smart over dinner. I'll never hear the end of it."

"I don't care a hoot!"

For all that he paused, thus giving time and opportunity for Lily to insinuate herself between him and the door. Her lips were pouted, she tossed back her mop of fair curls.

"Be a sport," she said eagerly. "Be a sport. Let's pretend, anyway. You don't know what it means."

"No!"

Henry made a determined step towards the door and to his amazement Lily opened her arms as he advanced and put them round his neck. He felt her warm young body pressed to him; her lips on his mouth. He kissed her in return. Slowly her lips left his and she hung limply on him like a coat on hooks; he could feel her quick breathing. Henry was no Samson, but this girl was quite definitely a Delilah. The thought rushed through his head that she was desirable, to be replaced at once by his adoration —real adoration—of Dora. Sorry as he was for this pseudo-sophisticated pretty thing, he knew it was all wrong—silly and meretricious in the strictest sense of the word.

"Ask me to marry you," she murmured. "Get it over. I don't mind. After all, it might be worse."

"I'm in love with someone else!"

The declaration gave him sudden comfort and happiness.

"I shan't be particular."

The complaisance horrified Henry; he was priggish, but quite genuinely sorry for her.

"You—you poor little—wretch!"

It was the only word he could think of. The next moment he was feeling the side of his face, having received his first experience of an angry girl in the shape of a slap.

"That's for yourself! I don't want your perishing pity. Nor your beastly patronage. Lord, are you? Lord, my foot!"

For a wild moment Henry had an almost ungovernable impulse to subdue her, to make her eat dirt.

"Now go and tell them all about it," she cried, shrilly reminiscent of her mother. "Tell 'em I smacked your face, and I'll tell 'em why! I'll say you tried funny business. *Now* then!"

Henry floundered, hopelessly out of his depth, his head still singing from the smack. For a second his eyes blazed, something in his de Birkett nature flamed, but for a second only; he just was not made that way.

"I'm sorry," he said humbly. "Heaven knows I didn't mean to be patronizing."

"I'll call myself all the names I like," Lily said fiercely, "and a few I *don't* like, but I won't have *you* doing it."

Then, astonishingly enough, she burst into tears all over the billiard table, supremely disregarding the fact that most of her underclothing was thus demonstrated before Henry's chaste gaze. It was all very bothering. Why couldn't people leave him alone; let him marry his Dora and live at pleasant and passionate peace? It wasn't much to ask.

"Don't cry, Lily," he said feebly.

"*Shall* cry if I want to! My tears, aren't they? Leave me alone!"

He left her alone and sat awkwardly clearing his throat at quarter-minute intervals, and wondering whether his cheek showed red. He even thought of getting up and having a look in the glass, but reflected that such an action might be construed as being in the worst possible taste.

It was thus that Merry found them about a quarter of a minute later. The rubber was over, perhaps it was time that they were getting home, Mr. and Mrs. Peploe thought. Merry, of course, had observed Lily's reddened eyes and the flush on Henry's cheek. Something had happened, he thought. What it was, he didn't know, but suspected Henry of the worst, even as Lily had threatened. Blood will tell!

10

YOUNG GIRLS' FANCIES

Henry told Dora all about it the next day. Yes! Down to details, even to the kissing episode, frankly and withholding nothing.

"You do believe me, darling, don't you?" he asked over the phone. Dora made a supreme effort and swallowed twice before replying.

"Yes," she said, "I believe you, but for all that I should like to box that girl's ears."

Henry's first impulse was to defend Lily, but he was wise enough to resist the impulse. There was no need to throw fat in the fire. There was an awkward and constrained little pause. After all, they were only human—very human.

"Let's meet," he said; "have a stroll in the park after tea."

"Harry, darling, I'm awfully sorry but I can't. I'm going out."

"Who with?"

There was a jealous sting to his voice.

"Monty Jackson."

"What?"

"There's no need to shout, Harry."

"That gambling womanizer!"

"You've never met him, Harry. Be reasonable."

"I've *heard* of him. I object!"

"I met him last night and he asked me to go and dance at the Rochester. He's quite fun in his way."

"Fun? He's a blackguard."

"I'm capable of looking after myself, which seems to be more than *you* are!"

"Dora, my sweet, don't let's quarrel. Have you forgotten the Priory?"

But the line was blank; Dora had rung off in a sudden huff. For a moment Henry tried to get the number back, and then with sudden retaliatory temper, asked for Lily's number, which she had taken care to give him on the previous night.

"That you, Lily?"

"Sure. Is that my up-stage, belted peer?"

"It's Henry, anyhow. Doing anything this afternoon?"

"Nothing that can't wait."

"Have tea with me at the Rochester."

"Have tea with you? Are you serious?"

"Yes."

"Then sure I will!"

First blood to Arabella. Henry went in search of her directly she returned from her morning walk with Caraway. The old lady smiled when they met, though she was in none too good a temper. The weather had turned cold and she had had to call on Hamish for a prescription for her chilblains. The result had been a bottle of liniment, though Hamish had reiterated the fact that he knew nothing about chilblains and cared less.

"Then you can't expect a fee for your ignorance, my dear Hamish."

Hamish had handed her a prescription, however.

"Don't drink it, my dear Great Aunt, or you'll turn up your toes. Soak your hands in it."

It was something for nothing in Arabella's opinion, and she had already had a telephone conversation with Merry, via Caraway, as to the success of last evening's introduction. Merry had been detailed and hoped for immediate results.

"It gave me great joy to effect such an altogether delightful introduction. A handsome, gay couple. They took to each other like ... like ..."

"Tell him a Tom and Tabby on the Tiles, Caraway."

"Her Ladyship says 'A Tom and Tabby on the Tiles,'" Caraway repeated obediently. Good-natured and hearty laughter from Merry who, after explaining that Mr. and Mrs. Peploe had more than approved of Henry and that, if anything came of it, they were prepared to "give the young couple a start in life," incontinently rang off. More than that, Merry would not say. Arabella had not as yet met Henry, and therefore greeted him with an arch smile.

"Ah, my dear boy, did you enjoy yourself last night?"

"Quite, thanks, Grannie. Can I have a pound, please?"

Arabella stiffened; she had not foreseen that all this would entail an outlay. Her smile was not quite so beatific as she replied:

"What do you want a pound for?"

"I'm taking a girl out to tea, and I haven't enough money." He spoke hardly and coldly. This was a "come back" for which he had not bargained any more than had Arabella. It gave him a delicious satisfaction to make Grannie pay the piper.

"What girl?"

"The girl you and Merry arranged for me to meet and marry. She told me herself."

"I don't like your tone, my boy. We thought you wanted cheering up."

"I'm afraid it'll cost a bit of money."

Arabella considered the question for a second or two, and then gave a sigh of satisfaction.

"Give his lordship a pound from my cashbox, Caraway. We shall have to save it somewhere in the housekeeping." It was going to be a puzzle to find out where any further economy in the Mount Street budget could possibly be effected. In fact, it just couldn't be done, and Arabella had only said that with the idea of impressing Henry with the knowledge that he must manage without money on such a scale. Caraway went away obediently. "Don't let this establish a precedent," Arabella said. "You can't hurl money about. You already have two pounds a week instead of the customary one pound."

"But, Grannie, if you want me to run after this girl I shall have to spend a bit. A sprat to catch a herring."

"She'll say snip to your snap any time," Arabella grumbled.

"I'm sorry, but I can't do it on nothing. Modern girls, especially rich ones, expect presents, and then of course there'll be the ring."

Henry almost laughed in her face, but only his eyes twinkled.

"I'll see that Merry makes you an advance on Alfred's legacy," she said.

Caraway came back with the pound note, and Henry, with a curt and quite ungrateful "thank you," took his departure, leaving Arabella to brood darkly. Uncle Alfred's wretched nine thousand wouldn't go far, she reflected. They must not waste the substance for the shadow. There was a rebellious restlessness about her grandson and it was time he was settled, time the money came in, whether as dowry or insurance mattered little. A sprat to catch a herring? He was taking a dangerously calm view of his separation from Dora. For all that he was taking this vulgar little Lily thing out. That was excellent. Her thoughts were brought back to earth by the sound of Caraway's voice making light conversation: why couldn't the fool keep silent?

"I think Miss Winslow is *so* pretty—*most* suitable in every way. . . ."

"His Lordship has changed his mind about Miss Winslow."

"But, my lady, they seem so much in love, so sweet to watch!"

"Don't talk like a dog breeder."

"I feel sure Lord Engleton still loves her."

"That's as may be. I don't wish to have the matter mentioned again. They will *not* marry. I don't wish it." She spoke in the usual bullying voice she had used to Caraway for years past. "Get me my patience cards."

Caraway fetched them from the bureau where they usually resided and put the baize table in front of the old woman.

"My lady," she said, as Arabella began dealing out the cards, "I once promised Lord Engleton to do all I could for him at any time. . . ."

"That was very forward of you."

"I feel it my duty to ask you to reconsider your decision. I'm sure he's unhappy."

Arabella regarded her in frank amazement.

"Are you pleading for 'Love's Young Dream?'" she asked.

"Yes, m'lady!"

"Then don't. Don't you muddle in Eugenics. There's only one thing that matters, Caraway, and that is the Family. The Family needs money at all costs. I don't think of my grandson as a human being but as a destiny, therefore he must marry money. Most people think these things, my good woman, but don't say so. Now get on with your knitting."

Arabella bent over her cards, but Caraway's knitting lay unheeded in her lap. Her meek hands trembled ever so slightly. Love's Young Dream was a romantic reality to her, one which actually happened to people. Her dream, she had hoped, was to be lived by proxy. Henry was to realize it.

"It seems so dreadful," she said, her voice shaking.

"Nothing's dreadful."

Caraway girded herself for a supreme effort.

"Not even squeezing a sponge of water into a dying man's mouth?" she asked.

"The Jack—Queen—King—Ace," Arabella said evenly, and then added: "No, not even squeezing water into a dying man's mouth. I always guessed you looked through keyholes, Caraway; it accounts for your bloodshot eyes. Trying to blackmail me, are you?"

"No, my lady!" Caraway was genuinely shocked at the suggestion. "Only hoping to influence your decision."

"Well, you won't. Understand that!"

There was a pause during which Arabella, quite unperturbed, went on with her everlasting patience. Caraway had the unpleasant knowledge that her bombshell had failed to explode.

"Am I to leave your service, m'lady?"

"Not unless you want to, and frankly, I'd rather you didn't. You're used to my little ways, how I like the sponge kept and hot-water bottles. No, you can stop."

It was all wrong, and Caraway felt she had been cheated out of her dramatic climax. Arabella seemed impossible to corner, or even to ruffle.

"Aren't you afraid that I—that——"

"That you might tell? Lord bless you, no! No one would believe you if you did, and you'd only land yourself in trouble. No, my dear woman, you can forget all that. And if you think you're in danger yourself you need have no fears. You aren't worth powder and shot. Besides, who would look after my rice pudding, my lozenges and my lemonade every night?"

Who, indeed!

"I beg your pardon, my lady."

"I'll overlook it this time. But don't let it happen again."

"I'm sure I hope it won't, my lady."

"And I think, my dear Caraway, that we can dispense with all forms of impertinence. When I'm dead you can say what you like about me, if you think it will assist Lord Engleton; till then, kindly keep a still tongue in your head and refrain from keyhole prying!"

Henry hung about the vestibule of the Rochester that afternoon with definite trepidation. He paced up and down flicking cigarette-ash about and had almost forgotten that he was there for the express purpose of meeting Lily. Somewhere inside there was Dora, having tea and dancing with the loathsome Monty Jackson. Desperately he longed to see her, and yet almost dreaded the moment when they should meet face to face. The muffled thud and thump of a jazz band was in the near distance. This made him think of Lily and wonder what sort of attitude to adopt. Then he remembered last night and determined, if possible, that he would not let her know that he knew Dora. That might mean another smacked face for all he knew. But, good Lord, if he did that, Dora might think he was there just to snub. Oh, hell! Why on earth had he come? That just showed how dangerous it was to act on impulse—for him, at any rate. He almost contemplated flight when he espied Lily approaching him; she was dressed almost completely in scarlet which set off her mop of curls and her blonde, film star beauty. There was no doubt of her being attractive, even if she were just a little—well, just a leetle bit——

"You think I look too flash?" she asked at once, voicing his doubts. "I think it's cute as a rig-out, myself."

"I think you look absolutely delightful," he answered. It was true enough, but there was just a shade too much jewellery. However, Lily smiled gratefully, and Henry wondered whether he wasn't after all a bit of a frump—frowsy, too critical and finnicky.

"I hate this place," she said frankly. "It's full of people I don't want to meet in daytime. What made you pitch on it?"

"First place that came into my head."

"I was too surprised at being asked at all to argue. I thought you wouldn't want to gratify your grandmother and my two darlings. They've named the first baby already—Albert, after father."

She prattled away, but Henry noticed that she glanced anxiously at him to see how he was taking it. In spite of her pertness there was something plaintive about her, though he hardly dared admit it, even to himself. They were making their way to a table, Henry trying to appear nonchalant and unconcerned as he anxiously raked the tables for a sign of Dora.

"Forgiven me for smacking your clock?"

"Absolutely and unconditionally."

There she was! Over on the extreme left. The fleshy man opposite must be Jackson. He wondered whether she would see him, and what she would do. The brilliance of Lily's frock brought all eyes in her direction, so the chances of escaping notice were not great and diminished as they travelled closer and closer to Dora's table. Henry felt his heart contract as Dora looked up; never before had he loved her half as much as he did at this ridiculous minute. She was his! Damn Monty *and* Lily! Damn 'em all! Dora bowed to him in what she imagined was a cold manner, though the sudden flush in her cheeks gave it the lie. Then one of those odd things happened for which not even Arabella had made provision. Monty caught sight of Lily and broke into a broad and welcoming grin.

"There's Monty Jackson," she said, shouting down the band. "Come along and talk to him. He's O.K. One of the lads."

Lily, without waiting for Henry's assent, began to hurry over to Monty and Dora.

"Consider the Lily how she dresses herself," Monty cried. "Who's the latest lucky boy friend?"

Henry felt himself colouring under Dora's steady stare which he felt rather than saw. Lily introduced him.

"This is Lord Engleton," she said with a slight proprietary air. Dora could have slapped her.

"This is Miss Winslow," Monty remarked, remembering his few manners, "Lily Peploe and Lord Engleton."

Dora acknowledged the introduction.

"Lord Engleton and I have already met," she said coldly, her poor heart beating wildly.

Monty swept them all into one party with overbearing heartiness. He wasn't a bad sort; spent too much money on horses and women, but that's a common complaint. He liked, too, to pretend to be Americanized on the strength of once having taken a horse to Boston for marital purposes. This was irritating and led to misunderstandings all round, and only conferred denationalization on him. He was good company all the same, and he and Lily did pretty well all the talking, no easy task to the accompaniment of hot music. Henry and Dora maintained acid silence, too obvious not to be noticeable. Lily and Monty talked incessantly of horses and parties and people the others didn't know, people with strange nicknames characteristic of human foibles moral, mental and physical. Henry stole a glance at Dora and noticed with joy that she was breathing too rapidly. At last Lily turned irritably on Henry.

"You're not what I should call chatty," she said snappily.

"I don't feel chatty," Henry replied.

"Children! Children!" Monty intervened with fat tact. He turned to Lily. "None of your tantrums," he said. "Come on—fling a leg!"

Lily rose and soon she and Monty were lost among the dancers. Dora turned to Henry with an impassive face.

"Nice girl," she said. "Very pretty and clean-looking."

"I came here deliberately to see you, Dora."

"And to show me your new fancy?"

"She's not my fancy."

Poor silly children; hearts aching, tragedy brewing, and all because of a scheming old woman and a pandering solicitor.

"And anyhow, what about this fat-faced, horsey individual?"

"Give me credit for having better taste than that!"

"Just playing him up, I suppose?"

"I'm not contemplating marrying him for money, anyway."

The band thumped and wailed, adding to their miserable irritation. Henry could see the scarlet Lily bobbing in and out of the dancers.

"We neither of us mean a word of what we are saying," he said. "Not a word. We love each other. . . ."

"Do we?"

"Yes."

He turned on her with violence, a well-bred, rather juvenile violence . . . but violence nevertheless, a good sign in these days.

"For God's sake," he said, gripping her knee with iron vigour, "don't let's waste time or behave like fools. I adore you, d'you hear? Adore you! They'll never separate us—never! They're having a damned good try, but they're not going to bring it off. Understand that now and for ever!"

Dora turned a pathetic face to him.

"I do love you, Henry. I'm jealous and I'm an ass."

"You're not. You're a darling. You're mine! That girl means nothing to me, but I've got to play up to this silliness for a bit, and so have you. It's disgusting, but there it is."

"Forgive me, Harry. I've done the preaching and now I've let you down."

"You haven't. It's my grandmother who's at the bottom of it."

"Look out! They're coming back."

"Go on, darling, dance with Monty. It'll do me good; make me rage and make me sensible."

That hurried conversation, the result of Arabella's machinations, crystallized the romantic love of those two, strengthened it better possibly than anything else could have done; they adored each other more than ever. Two smiling, miraculously transformed faces greeted the return of the dancers. Lily, like all physically inclined people, had a keen sense for any form of amorous atmosphere; "the smell of monkeys," as she elegantly termed it. She was puzzled by Dora, but half-guessed the truth. She felt a sudden pang and realized that this marrying a lord was going to be no such unpleasant duty. Lily reached her decisions, especially erotic decisions, with astonishing rapidity. She would conceive a "crush" at sight and in an hour's time be violently in love. She had nothing else much to do. Henry was different from the usual run of her friends. She could think of none of them who, if asked, would have declined to examine her legs, or, indeed, as much of her as possible. She reseated herself and made instant use of her powder-puff, dabbing carefully at any little patch that might have become shiny. Monty was more frank and wiped his baldish head openly.

"Not the man I was," he said. "Get puffed as blazes."

"It's something to know you're not the man you were. Any change is for the better."

The band struck up again almost at once, and Lily rose ready for the fray.

"What? Not again?" Monty groaned.

"Not at any price. It's Henry's turn, anyway."

"But, Lily, I don't dance."

"Then I'm going to teach you. Walk in time to the tune and hold my hand tight."

It wasn't so difficult, and Henry managed sufficiently well. Lily had her own method of dancing, a method which she had found very efficacious in the past.

"Yes, my lad," she whispered softly, "I'm going to teach you lots of things, more than you ever dreamed of!"

Henry smiled down at her with supreme confidence. Let her do her worst! If Lily chose to become his grandmother's ally, she had backed the wrong horse. The fact that the girl was really falling in love with him never entered his head.

II

THE FINGER OF GOD

Mellingham Parva, or at least that section of it that came under the immediate sway of the Beamishes, was all of a flutter. Arabella had written to Miss Vera hinting more than clearly that she would be pleased to return the visit that the Misses Beamish and Major Hugh had paid her. This was about two months after the death of Uncle Alfred. Arabella had not exactly invited herself, but had laid herself open to invitation. She had dictated the letter to Caraway, eyeing that unfortunate woman with impish amusement as she ladled out fulsome untruths. She had, she said, so much enjoyed having them to stay at Mount Street, and would feel herself under an eternal obligation to them for their consideration to their nephew, about whom she expected there would soon be a very interesting announcement. She felt that his aunts should be told privately and not see the bald announcement in the *Morning Post*. How pleased our dear Helen would have been! It was warm for the time of year and she thanked them for the sweet little crochet doyleys they had sent her for Christmas, that sweet season of mutual goodwill ("Silly rubbish! Throw 'em away."). How was dear Major Hugh?

"There," said Vera, "I knew it would be a good thing to send those doyleys to Lady Engleton rather than to the Sale of Work."

"And how interesting about dear Henry. It must mean that he's engaged to be married. I wonder who the girl is? How nice of her to think of consulting us," Sophie chimed in.

"Consulting *me*, Sophie. I thought she would respect me for making a stand about that jewellery."

Sophie said nothing. She still thought her sister had not behaved in a strictly honourable manner on that point. Once she had had the temerity to say so and had never been allowed to forget it. Vera had maintained that there had been no question of morality involved, had even persuaded herself by dint of hard talking that the set of garnets actually *had* belonged to Helen. Now the fact that Arabella wanted to visit them effectually clinched the argument.

"Perhaps you're right, dear."

It was easier to agree with Vera and be done with it, and Sophie had discovered this fact many years before.

"We must invite her to stay, and perhaps if we do it at once we can get her to open the Sale of Work!"

"But we've no accommodation. She'll have that nice, refined companion to look after her."

"Hugh must invite her."

And Hugh did. Perhaps the County would now be less exclusive, would recognize his existence as a man of birth and noble connections, a fact which hitherto had been rather overlooked! Hugh gobbled like a turkey when he thought of his treatment at the hands of the County, and fully approved Vera's idea of getting Lady Engleton to open the Sale of Work.

"I'll sit on the platform too," he boomed. "That'll teach the Tontines a lesson."

It was an understood thing that a certain Lady Tontine always opened the Sale of Work. Sir Julius Tontine was only a knight, and a party funds knight at that, at least so the Major insisted.

"Hadn't we better ask the Vicar first?" Sophie asked timidly.

Her interruption was regarded by the others as in bad taste and therefore ignored. Arabella should be invited down to stay at The Grange (the official name of the Big House) and the Vicar was to be informed of this on arrival, when the whole thing was a *fait accompli*. The invitation to stay with the Major was accordingly sent and accepted. Caraway was, of course, to come as well. It was arranged that Arabella was to stay the night at the Bell Hotel, in Norwich, thence to proceed the following day by hired car. It was a long journey for an old lady of eighty-three, but presented no terrors to Arabella. The de Birkett Family demanded her services!

Major Hugh set about getting a room ready and the sisters rushed down to bullyrag the Vicar.

When, years previously, Old Man Beamish had to all intents and purposes committed *felo de se* by living on his own health foods and leaving nothing, the outlook for the children would have been bad, had Hugh not inherited The Grange and an income of nearly a thousand a year from an uncle.

The Grange was a largish, ugly, early Victorian house, which lay incongruously in the Norfolk village. Travellers always described it as an eyesore. They were right. It was, however, comfortable and Hugh had also inherited an enormous number of sporting guns, his uncle having not much else to do except shoot birds on the marshes. Hugh did likewise and carried on the tradition. To do Hugh justice, he could shoot straight.

His prowess in India "after pig" and shooting tigers was quite remarkable, and The Grange was littered with trophies of the chase. Tigers lay about the floors. There were no less than three in the drawing-room alone. Two of them looked as if steam rollers had passed over them, so flat were they, and so tightly pressed into a sort of scolloped shadow of felt. The third, the most noble of the trio ("Man-eater, gobbled up three native women and a bearer!"), had also suffered the steam roller in every part of him save his head, which bared its teeth and rolled glass eyes, and over which every one tripped. There was also a profusion of stuffed birds, recent victims of Hugh's ubiquitous gun and deadly aim, owls and one enormous cormorant with spread wings. These creatures and ponderous Victorian furniture served

Hugh for a home. At first it had served Vera and Sophie as well, but that didn't last long. Vera was not the sort that is easy to live with and Hugh insisted on being boss in his own house. Vera had regarded his every action with goggle-eyed, fat disapproval, had tried to stop him smoking in the drawing-room, had driven the servants distracted and been a general nuisance. One day Vera had tripped over the tiger's head and great had been the fall of her. Her insistence on the instant relegation of the tiger to the lumber room had been the last straw. There had been a fearful row and they had separated. The Major had not ungenerously rented a large cottage and allowed them £300 a year. Sophie had trailed along with Vera, glad to exchange one tyrant for two, for neither of them had shown any consideration for Sophie. No one ever did, somehow.

Hugh determined that that "grand old lady," for so he described Arabella at a distance, should have the best his hospitality could run to. He hadn't liked Arabella at all when he had met her on rare occasions during his life. Claude de Birkett had been his friend, and had died a hero's death. It had not been Claude's fault that he had been no military genius. Alas, wars are not won by physical bravery alone! But Arabella was his friend's mother and her grandchild his nephew. Besides this, it was one up against the Tontines, and anyway, Arabella was a "grand old lady" to be well received and made much of. Hugh even turned out of his own bedroom, a dismal, large room with a huge mahogany bed in it, and a little dressing-room adjoining. This little room was to serve for Caraway. He turned out of it voluntarily and moved into the spare bedroom ... the room that had once contained Vera, but had lain fallow ever since. The noble tiger was moved up to Arabella's room—"nice for the old lady's feet."

The Major enjoyed his preparations for Arabella's visit; he boomed and brayed at the small staff and shot quantities of seasonable fowl on the marshes. He even burrowed about in the small wine cellar, searching for treasure left by his late uncle, and what's more, found a bottle or two. The Major didn't drink wines. "Frenchified stuff! Give me a burra peg or some beer!" He added beer out of habit and because it sounded English, but his real love was Scottish—"burra pegs." No, Major Hugh Beamish,

late of the Indian Army, was not a bad man, unless one counts
uselessness and badness as synonyms. True, he was a petty tyrant
and unpopular in the village, and counted a bore, but he was hospitable, believed in the great destiny of England, and was physically courageous.

During these preparations, Vera had spread the news of the
forthcoming noble visit, and had broken the news to the Vicar
that "Her Ladyship would most certainly expect to open the Sale
of Work on the Monday," thereby putting the good man and his
wife in a fearful quandary, and leaving them to break the news to
Lady Tontine, who was to have done so. The Vicar's wife had all
been for defiance of the Beamishes; she was younger and more
spirited than her spouse; but finally the Beamishes had prevailed.
It was not mentioned that, as yet, Arabella Lady Engleton knew
nothing whatsoever of the arrangement.

The great day came, a Friday, and Arabella drove up, in
company with Caraway, to the gates of The Grange, the Beamishes being drawn up to greet her. Arabella was glad enough to
leave the ancient hired Renault which had done sixteen miles
from Norwich, but her heart sank at the sight of Vera. The Major
was more or less an unknown quantity, but Vera was a menace
to any woman. Arabella was received with shrill cries and deep
booms of welcome, and immediately retired to her mausoleum-
like room. She rather liked it, ponderous and dreary furnishing
being to her taste. It was opulent and spelt riches. She enjoyed,
too, watching Caraway trip repeatedly over the tiger's head.
Instant refreshment was served her with instructions (humble,
supplicatory instructions) not to descend until dinner-time,
at seven. Caraway unpacked and hung clothes in the wardrobe
while Arabella took stock of the place. She peered from the
windows out over the rather cheerless Norfolk marshlands, wondering how much The Grange would fetch in the open market,
and why anyone had ever elected to live in such an out-of-the-way
spot. The heavy portraits of defunct Beamishes were examined
to discover if any of them were "real"; that is, by any painter of
commercial value. She was amused, too, by Caraway's shocked
discovery of a quantity of evil-smelling literature in the drawer
of the dressing-table, which the Major had forgotten to remove.

French novels of incredible antiquity, "Maria Monk" and American Art Publications and photographic deminudes "for artists and draughtsmen only." She insisted on Caraway going through them. Arabella tormented this hapless woman more than ever since her victory, torment to which Caraway submitted with ever-increasing docility.

"Have a look at this one, Caraway," she said, adjusting her glasses. It was a portrait, a back view photograph of a girl holding a glass globe in the air and staring into space. It was labelled "The Mystic." The photography was fuzzy, which gave it an "art" appearance. The girl seemed to have no other worldly possession but the glass globe. Caraway hastily averted her eyes.

"I'd rather not look, m'lady."

"Makes you feel hot, eh?" Arabella studied the picture more closely. "That girl can't have been very warm—not even a wisp of tulle! Hm! Well, it's an interesting sidelight on our host. He must have bought these things when he was staying at Mount Street."

"It's shocking, m'lady, dreadful to think such things are allowed."

"Bah—actresses!"

She went on chuckling, however, and laughing heartily at "Maria Monk." Arabella was in a puckish mood. Something was in the wind!

The Major's dinner was a reproach to Mount Street. No hashed mutton about him! He carved with gusto, heaping up plates and keeping up a running flow of village small talk.

"I'm afraid, Lady Engleton," he said, "you'll find us quiet folk here, just country mice. . . ."

Vera struck Arabella as being rather a plump mouse, a mouse that shovelled in food voraciously.

"But we have our little amusements, though a bit different from the old Simla days. More wine?"

Vera was chewing rapidly to clear her over-filled mouth; she was about to give tongue. The pause was tactfully filled by the Major replenishing glasses.

"Our dear Vicar—such a good Evangelical—was most anxious that you should open the Sale of Work on Monday. I accepted in your name, as I felt sure you would be only too pleased to confer such an honour on our humble little village."

Arabella turned a fishlike eye on the speaker. If she were "only too pleased," she hardly looked it. Vera scented danger, and added:

"I had no time to write to you and the notices had to be printed. Pray excuse me."

For a moment or so the social fate of the Beamishes hung in the balance. Arabella had no views about the two women, didn't care a rap about annoying them, but the Major was different. He had money and no heir, that is, except these two "mice." She saw to her surprise that he was as anxious for her compliance as were the others. That rather altered matters.

"If your great age . . ." Vera began.

"My great age, as you call it, has nothing to do with the matter."

"The Sale is in aid of our local Girls' Friendly Society," the Major said. "A worthy object, and it would be a shame to disappoint the Vicar. Good feller, the Vicar. Dashed good feller, if I may say so!"

Arabella looked at the Major with a spice of malice.

"Girls' Friendly? Do you ever give them lectures, Major?"

"Er—me? No, I can't say I do, though I once gave an address on Pig-Sticking in the Parish Hall."

"It was not well attended," said Sophie the tactless.

"I have often thought," Arabella said, "that it might be interesting to reverse the usual method at these meetings for the betterment of young girls. Some clergyman always tells them what they ought to do, how they ought to behave. It would be a good plan sometimes to tell them what *not* to do, to describe the exact nature of the moral pitfalls. You could do that with ease, Major. I'll bet the Hall would be crammed."

The Major turned a covert glance at the old lady. She was laughing at him. Good Lord, had she . . . ? Those books . . . ? Had he forgotten to shift them? Heavens, if Vera were to find out! The very idea gave him a nasty sinking sensation in the pit of his stomach. He covered his growing uneasiness with a boisterous laugh.

"Jolly good! Jolly good!" ("After all, the old girl's a sport, won't give me away.")

Arabella, after a little more shilly-shallying, gave her gracious consent to open the Sale of Work. The Vicar, it appeared, was coming to dine at The Grange tomorrow, Saturday, with his wife to meet her ladyship (Decent fellar, the Vicar), and they would have a little music. Arabella had a ghastly vision of Sophie singing *Juanita* again. Arabella felt she must do something to justify being uprooted and coming into the wilds. But what? What? She had not come to Norfolk for fun. That dirty literature might give her a pull on the Major . . . that was a providential find . . . a gift straight from Heaven. The Lord was looking after His own—perhaps!

After dinner they sat in the drawing-room, Arabella in an enormous arm-chair decked around with cushions as if in a mould. The Major had helped himself to a double "burra peg" and was waxing talkative, mostly about himself. Vera was aching to ask questions about Henry and the interesting news, but she never had a look in when Hugh was well away. He was living in a miasma of reminiscence, a fog that obscured all else.

"That chap upstairs, Lady Engleton," he said, referring to the feline remains that glared from the floor and constituted a trap for the unwary, "was a man-eater. Terrible business, created a panic. It was at Clamgooli, I recall; gobbled up native women like oysters when they went out to get water of an evening—just gobbled 'em up!"

"Must have been a member of the Girls' Friendly," Arabella murmured. "Go on, Major," as he turned an uncomprehending eye, "most interesting!"

"They sent for *me*, you know. Send for Beamish, he can shoot straight. The whole village was chattering. It was 'sahib' this and 'sahib' the other, don't you know. Macklin was with me. 'What a fuss about a few girls,' he said. Cynical feller, Macklin. The trouble was bait . . ."

"Bait?" Arabella asked curiously.

The Major buried his inflamed, kindly old nose in his tumbler.

"That's right," he said, coming up for air; "bait. Tiger didn't fancy anything but man meat."

Vera yawned quietly but ostentatiously; she had heard this story countless times.

"And the British Government discourages using natives as bait, does it?" Arabella asked. The Major found it difficult to settle whether his noble guest were joking or not. He was sensitive about having his leg pulled, but happily very impervious. There was a curious note of genuine inquisitiveness in the old lady's voice.

"I always booted the beggars," he said with honest, bluff simplicity, "but usin' 'em as bait's out of the question. Boot 'em, yes."

"Unless they are native princes." The remark came unexpectedly from Caraway. All heads were turned coldly in her direction and she resumed her knitting, colouring guiltily. Companions should be seen and not heard. Caraway's sense of loyalty had been outraged. Kicking princes, even black-blooded princes, seemed a fearful thing.

"Where was I?" the Major asked plaintively.

"Booting blacks," Arabella prompted.

"Yes, and you and Captain Macklin shot the tiger and all the village danced and you were both heroes," Sophie said, finishing the story for him.

"I wish you'd let me tell my story in my own way, Sophie. I never told you about the trap and how the tiger was tempted by a kid—an animal, you know, not a child."

"I'm sure Lady Engleton doesn't want to hear it," Vera said, and the Major looked sulky. "It's a very dull story, Hugh."

"Perhaps Lady Engleton is tired," Sophie ventured, seeing the blood slowly mounting to her brother's head.

"I think, Major Beamish, that you must be a very brave man," Arabella said. The Major looked grateful and the colour began to subside. There was no question of it; Arabella was a fine old girl!

"I wouldn't say that, Lady Engleton," he said modestly, pulling at his moustache as if he were trying to root up a weed.

"I'm quite sure you wouldn't."

The Major forgave all possible leg-pulling. He was not conceited and did not really think much of his bravery, but he was human and liked flattery. He took another pull at his drink to cover his blushes.

"The other two I shot at Chindraputra," he said, "I'll tell you about 'em when we are by ourselves," he added nastily and for Vera's benefit. "Tiger shootin' is very excitin' and you feel you're doin' the natives a real kindness, especially when they're man-eaters—er—the tigers, that is. And I'll show you my guns—wonderful collection, though I say so."

"I should very much like to see them."

"I'll show 'em to you before lunch to-morrow."

"But Lady Engleton is coming to lunch with *us* tomorrow." This quickly from Vera.

"No, she's not. She's my guest and she's stoppin' here. Now then!"

Truly the Major had had just two too many pegs. His latent and permanent dislike of Vera was let loose.

"But, Hugh, we arranged it all yesterday."

"I don't mind what you arranged."

"The extra food!" Vera's voice got shrill.

"Let it go mouldy."

Vera trembled with passion. She dared not explode before Arabella, but equally dared not set the evil precedent of giving Hugh best without a struggle. But what can one lone Vera do against a whole host of mixed drinks? Vera drew in her breath with a loud hissing sound which boded ill for Hugh. It was very vulgar and Arabella's aristocratic gorge rose in revolt. She was glad that they were not de Birketts. A de Birkett might commit a crime, but not a *gaucherie*.

"Caraway, help me up. I think, if you don't mind, I'll go to bed."

"You see, Hugh, you've tired Lady Engleton out," Vera said unkindly.

The Major ignored his sister and gallantly helped Arabella to her feet.

"You must pardon my sister," he explained genially, "but she is over-excited. I trust you will find your room comfortable. The milk pudding, made of rice, and the weak lemonade have not been forgotten."

It was courtly in tone but the effect rather marred by a sudden loud hiccup which everyone affected not to have heard. The

Major was inured against whisky, but the introduction of French alcoholic allies into his internal workings had created chaos.

"Pardon," the Major said softly. "I trust you will sleep well in a strange bed," he added loudly, to cover his confusion.

"I expect so; I am tired; but if not, Caraway will read to me."

The Major became all concern at once.

"A book!" he cried. "A book! Would you like a book, a Bible or something?"

"No, thank you," Arabella said. "I've read that. There was a book—several, in fact—already in my room. You had thoughtfully left them."

"Eh?" said the Major, a cold chill striking his heart. Perhaps, after all, he *had* forgotten his literature "for gentlemen only." "What book?"

"Don't bother her ladyship about such things," Vera cried.

"Dean Farrar's *Life of Christ*," Arabella replied at once, thinking of the dullest tome she knew. This confirmed the Major's worst fears. He knew right well that there was no copy of that monumental work in the house. He lit the way up for Arabella sobered and thoughtful, to return a few minutes later to face Vera. Should his sister ever discover the facts of his private library she would become more formidable than any tiger at Clamgooli or anywhere else! He went down to find her denunciatory and angry at having been made to look a fool. The obvious retort was no remedy, and he sank down gratefully when his sisters had gone to have a last and final peg before bed—"just to put my stomach right." Farrar's *Life of Christ* indeed!

Upstairs, Arabella lay back in the mahogany bed. Everything was complete, as her host had said. A fire burned cheerfully in the grate. Whether it was the strange bed or the wind that whined over the flats, or her own broodings, sleep was denied Arabella. She could hear Caraway disrobing in the adjoining dressing-room and summoned her. It was the first time she had seen her companion decked out for slumber, and she eyed the phenomenon curiously. Caraway waited for orders, longing for the peace of her bed.

"Those curlers don't become you," Arabella said. "Not that it matters."

Caraway said nothing—just waited.

"Since you tried to blackmail me," Arabella went on, "I suppose you watch me like a cat and wonder why I have come down to this God-forsaken marsh."

"It's not my place to wonder, my lady."

"True, but I dare say you forget your place. I don't quite know myself what has induced me to walk amongst savages. But I'll find a reason, never fear. I think all the Beamishes deserve to die."

With pleasure Arabella noted the alarm that flitted over Caraway's face.

"The Major is a licentious, ill-mannered hog. Vera is a shrew and unpleasant in every way, and the other woman is a fool. Yes, they'd all be better dead."

Caraway pulled her thin frame to its full height, rather as a very timid martyr might have done before Diocletian in a playful mood.

"It is not for us," she declared, "to question the workings of the Almighty, or to hasten His plans."

"Tcha!" Arabella said impatiently. "Have you never thought that the assassin might be the Finger of God? Might be divinely ordained?"

"With all reverence, there are things Almighty God cannot do. He cannot sin or break His own laws."

But Arabella didn't seem to hear. Her eyes were alight, her thin fingers clawed at the counterpane.

"The Finger of God!" she whispered. "Perhaps *I* am the Finger of God!"

Caraway trembled at the blasphemy.

"Oh, Lady Engleton, how can you say such things?"

Arabella relaxed her tense position slowly and the light in her eye gradually dimmed.

"Ah, well," she said at last, "I don't hold with such nonsense, anyway. Herbert Spencer knocked all *that* on the head. Come on: read to me."

"Read to you, my lady?"

"Yes, yes, that's what I said."

"Read *what*, my lady?"

"'The Awful Disclosures of Maria Monk,' of course!"

"Please excuse me, my lady. I beg you . . ."

"Nonsense! Do you good. Pick out the saucy bits. . . ."

So poor Caraway read on, shivering with horror. Arabella chuckled maliciously till her eyes closed and Caraway heard her regular breathing. The woman's voice died away. There was no sound but the whining of the wind.

12

THE "FEET"

Major Beamish awoke the next morning with a feeling that all had not gone well the previous evening. He surveyed the yellow tinge in his eyes with nausea and quickly went in search of that essential hair of the dog that had bitten him. He needed it. His liver had been the scene of civil disturbance and why, oh, why, had he been so careless about his light reading?

Arabella had, of course, had her breakfast in bed, and it was getting on for midday before she made a ceremonial appearance on Caraway's arm. A bath chair had been imported from Norwich (on hire at five shillings a week, plus carriage) for it was understood that Her Ladyship expected to be gently propelled for an hour before luncheon. It was also to be used to convey her about the village, and there it stood in the hall with a bearskin rug (one of the Major's trophies) ready to receive its precious though temporary burden.

The Major greeted Arabella effusively and with boisterous good humour, rather marred by his yellow and bloodshot eyes. She was gracious in return and announced that she had slept well, been *most* comfortable. So far, so good. If she had been offended by his slight lapse of the previous evening or by discovering his taste in reading, the Major decided that she was at least "a sport" and volunteered personally to push the bath chair should she decide to take a little outing. So a little later they slowly paraded the bleak garden: Arabella completely covered with the bearskin, over the edge of which her face peered, surmounted by her enormous bonnet. The Major pointed out the places where the beauties were in summer and showed her rows of vegetables, roots and rather evil-smelling winter greens. Arabella nodded cheerfully and said "very nice" at intervals. Her attitude cheered the Major and the gentle exercise cheered his liver, which Heaven knows needed it. They came to a halt in a patch of sunshine which, though wintry, was yet warm and encouraging. The Major came round from the back and took his stand at Arabella's side.

"It's a pity, Major," she said, "that you have no son and heir to carry on after you, to look after your good work." She spoke as if she expected the row of greens to make a bow.

"I never had time for marriage, Lady Engleton."

"And yet you must have loved."

The Major coughed. He had done that all right, but didn't want to talk about it.

"My dear son Claude often used to wonder whether or not to appoint you guardian of his son, the present Lord Engleton. I could have wished he had, at times. Henry has been a grave responsibility for an old woman."

Claude had never said such a thing in his life, but as he was not there to contradict, it made no difference. She spoke so winningly that the Major almost wished it, too.

"A fine lad, I thought," he said, "a true de Birkett; a true son too, of my dear sister. Does you credit, Lady Engleton, does you credit."

"Thank you, Major, but yet a man's helping hand would have been an asset. Of course you have your weaknesses, Major, but we all have a chink in the armour."

"Quite, quite . . ."

He wondered what was coming next.

"I could have wished my dear grandson to have had the benefit of your masculine bravery, the traces of which cover your floors, though perhaps not of your taste in literature."

The Major felt himself getting red and kept his face resolutely averted from Arabella.

"I was never much of a one for reading . . ."

"Just for looking at pictures, eh? There, bless the man, I'm not blaming you."

"I always had an eye for the artistic."

"Yes, I know. They call the nude that nowadays, though goodness knows why. My husband was just the same, though he had not got the advantage of photography. Don't you worry, I won't tell and I'll persuade Miss Caraway—if I can."

"Good Heavens! Did she see 'em?"

"Naturally, but I'll try and persuade her not to tell your sisters. She's a goody-goody person and thinks they *should* be told."

It was a gross libel on the unfortunate absentee, who blushed at the very thought of the artistic literature and had hidden it carefully.

"My sisters have no eye for the beautiful," the Major said, sticking to his artistic leanings.

"No, nor for good books like 'Maria Monk' . . ."

"Makes one glad one's C. of E., eh?" the Major said piteously. He was getting out of it nicely. There was a pause, during which they both scanned the horizon as if searching for inspiration.

"I suppose when you die that your sisters will inherit this beautiful spot—or is it entailed?"

"No, there's no entail—and they've no claim." His many grievances against Vera welled to the surface. "I can do what I like with it, and so I shall, by Jove!" It was a pleasing thought that Vera should find that she had nothing when he died. He would have given something to see her face.

"You were very kind to allow yourself to be insured for our dear boy's advantage. Thank you, Major."

"That was nothing. Only too pleased. And I'll do more for him yet."

Arabella's hand came out from under the bearskin and she held it out to him. They solemnly shook hands.

"You'll find Henry, your own blood nephew, a worthy heir. Again I thank you, Major Beamish."

It wasn't quite what the Major had meant, but why not?

After all, she had been very nice about the pictures, but for all that he was quite surprised at finding his nephew his heir.

"I've done quite a lot for my sisters. Settled money on 'em. Even if I die before 'em, they'd only leave my estate to a Cats' Home. I'll see that my nephew inherits, Lady Engleton; my dear sister's son and the son of my old and gallant friend."

He found himself getting quite lyrical about it, and added untruthfully:

"I've often thought about it, Lady Engleton, but somehow one puts off making a Will."

"Not a wise thing to put off. Making a Will doesn't help one to die. If that were so, I'd have died fifty years ago."

"I'll do it this afternoon, dashed if I don't."

"I'll help you, Major, and I'll see that Miss Caraway keeps her mouth shut. I can quite believe that your sisters don't appreciate Beauty. It wouldn't do at all. . . ."

That afternoon Arabella and Major Hugh Beamish drew out the latter's last Will and Testament, and Henry became the potential owner of another substantial sum of money, including real estate. Arabella was in such good humour that she was affable even to the two sisters when they arrived that evening in company with the Vicar and his wife. The little party was an immense success. Sophie sang and played a duet with Vera. The Vicar sang; nearly everyone sang. Even the Major! He sang defiantly as if he were doing Vera a bad turn, no more than a half-truth, for besides having no eye for beauty, she equally had no ear for music. In fact, it was a typical "evening," as indulged in by those who live near the soil but not on it. The Vicar and even his wife thought Arabella "a dear old soul," in spite of the fact that Lady Tontine had expressed distant displeasure at having been superseded in the office of opening the Sale of Work. Yes, it was almost a riotous evening, and did not break up till nearly eleven o'clock, when the Vicar reluctantly announced the fact that to-morrow being Sunday, he had duties to perform, early service, and so forth. He was a conscientious man and strove mightily to do his bounden duty.

The party re-met the following day at Divine Service at eleven, and one of them at least prayed with all the intensity of her being. That was Caraway. She prayed for her employer, prayed for those around her to be spared from the arrow that flies by day and the terror that stalks at night, prayed for forgiveness and guidance. On the way home to The Grange, Arabella informed Caraway that though she had no objection to private devotions, she considered it ill-timed and ostentatious to behave like a hen drinking.

The rest of the Sabbath passed quietly enough. The usual large joint, and afternoon naps for all. The sisters kept away, which was a relief for everybody. After tea, Major Hugh once more referred to his Last Will and Testament. He was glad, he said, that he had thought of bequeathing all his goods and filthy lucre to his dear nephew, and expressed a wish that the boy would come down "for a bit of shooting," and to inspect his future inheritance. Not that the Major had any intention of dying! Oh, dear, no! Far from it! Then he looked grave and thoughtful as he made the highly original observation that in the midst of life they were in death. He knew a chap once in India, bitten by a snake, dead in half an hour. One never knew, did one? This called for more Indian reminiscences and further accounts of tiger slaying.

Arabella, after years of experience, had acquired the trick of being able to think of other things while appearing to listen. She had, therefore, always been popular with bores. On this occasion she devised ways and means of keeping her grandson in ignorance of the fact that he was his uncle's heir—the boy was so pernickety he might object—and then made a mental valuation of the goods and furniture around her. It didn't amount to much, but every little helps. She heard the Major waxing enthusiastic about his collection of guns—the finest in East Anglia bar none. It appeared he had guns of every make and description and nationality—a veritable armoury. It was the fact that he stressed unduly the monetary value of this collection that caused Arabella to express a wish to see it. Eagerly he took the old lady to the gun-room and showed his treasures. If anything, he had understated the case. His uncle Beamish had had a quantity of ancient weapons, flintlocks and a blunderbuss.

"Dangerous thing," the Major said, handling the latter, and speaking as if the rest of the collection were completely harmless. "Dangerous thing, a blunderbuss. Stuff this bell thing full of slugs and rubbish and blow half the house away, don't you know."

Major Beamish was in his element. There was every kind of gun, from a rook rifle to a miniature howitzer for destroying elephants, and each one had a story. There were also war relics —a real, live Mills bomb, bayonets and different sorts of tin hats. They were his pride and the joy of his childless life. And Arabella listened and flattered, making notes for future reference. She noted, for example, that he had a habit of looking down the barrels.

"It's been very interesting," she said. "Interesting and instructive. . . ."

"I'm glad they'll all be Henry's," he said. "Not much good them falling into Vera's lap—except perhaps the jolly old Mills bomb," he added as a pious afterthought.

Thus passed the Sabbath, in peace and quiet as was fitting.

2

The following day Arabella went down to lunch with Vera and Sophie, a gracious concession on the Major's part. From thence they were to go to the Parish Hall, where at four-thirty the Sale of Work (known locally as "The Feet") was to be opened with proper pomp by Lady Engleton. Vera had gone so far as to ask Hugh to lunch as well, but he had declined flatly and bluntly.

When the bath chair hove in sight, Vera and Sophie were drawn up as a guard of honour to meet it, Noreen, their servant, discreetly in the background.

Vera stepped forward with a bland smile.

"Welcome to our modest little cottage," she said, and took over the control of the bath chair from Caraway, rather in the manner of a pilot bringing in a Cunarder. There was a great taking of rugs and giving of helping hands, and at last Arabella was installed in the chair of honour in the overcrowded sitting-room.

"You must forgive the smell of cooking," Vera said, "but our poverty does not enable us to live as we could wish."

Sophie disappeared into the back with Noreen, leaving Vera in possession. Sophie did the cooking herself, Noreen did the housework, and Vera found fault with them, going around finding dust and writing her name in it, an amiable trick.

"We have done our little best to make the place habitable," Vera explained to Arabella. "Our brother was not easy to live with, and it was the best our limited resources could aspire to."

The truth was it was a charming sixteenth century cottage

built in flints in the Norfolk fashion and heavily thatched. There were five rooms, at least four rooms and an attic in which Noreen slept. This did not count a kitchen and a wash-house at the back. Vera's "little best to make it habitable" had been to cover up the beams that stretched across the ceiling and spanned the walls with flowered wallpaper, and to festoon the dismal furniture with antimacassars as plentiful as leaves in autumn. Even Arabella thought it ugly, and she was no judge. A small cat thrust its head into the room, and Vera clapped at it noisily. The head was hastily withdrawn.

"My sister's pet," she explained to the startled Arabella. "I dislike the creatures and only permit it because I suppose they are necessary for the destruction of mice, but I *will not* have it in the drawing-room."

The whole house was a network of things Vera would not have, mostly things to do with Noreen, to whom practically all pleasures were denied, including singing, whistling, humming, staying out after seven, and any attentions from tradesmen. She explained at length to Arabella how difficult it was to keep servants even in Mellingham Parva, where the depressed state of agriculture had struck heavy blows at the local inhabitants and made "service" an essential for unproductive daughters.

"I don't believe Noreen would stay had her father not been out of work for months," she said vehemently. Neither did Arabella. "But come what may, even in these wicked times, when the working-classes are pampered and spoiled, I—will—not—have disrespect. One owes a duty to one's social inferiors, I admit that. If I did not keep a perpetual eye on that girl, Heaven alone knows what disaster might not occur. Mellingham Parva is not a moral village."

She added this regretfully and shook a heavy head, a head that seemed to say: "I could tell you such things—*such* things—but just as Jonas saved Nineveh so do I save Mellingham Parva." At that moment, however, Noreen put a red but comely visage into the room and said briefly:

"On the table!"—disappearing before Vera could rebuke her.

And so it was—a rabbit roasted like a hare, with red currant jelly (home-made by Sophie) and stuffing. Arabella ate judiciously, praising the cook, but her praises were somewhat marred by biting the shot that had laid the rabbit low and nearly ruining her denture.

"It's providential you didn't swallow it," Sophie said, when the confusion had abated. "Lead is poisonous, and I have already extracted three pellets."

"Hugh's rabbits always seem to contain more shot than others," Vera said ungratefully looking a gift rabbit in the face as it were, and congenially blaming her brother at the same time.

This contretemps and the fact that Noreen had to be rebuked no less than twice for bursting into song in the adjoining kitchen were the only ripples on the sea of an otherwise calm lunch. It had been arranged that, subsequent to the meal, Arabella should rest in state in the sitting-room while Vera and Sophie dressed in beautiful garments for the Sale of Work, but before they rose from the board Sophie gave a little cluck like a hen and announced that Her Ladyship *really must taste her homemade wine*, even reminding Arabella of the fact that she had promised to do so in London.

"We had a glut of red currants this year," she cried happily, and Arabella shuddered in anticipation. Four large port glasses were placed on the table and hospitably filled to the brim by the eager Sophie, who skittishly raised hers to the financial success of the Sale of Work and the Girls' Friendly. Arabella sipped hers gingerly.

"There's no doubt about it being red currant," she said. "No doubt at all."

"Very nice," Caraway murmured. "Very nice indeed."

She was genuine too, and had her glass refilled. Arabella excused herself on the ground that she would need all her wits about her to face the ordeal of speech making.

"Do you make much wine?" Arabella inquired of Sophie, wondering how to cure a suddenly furred tongue.

"A great deal!" Sophie answered eagerly. "Wine, pickles, preserves, chutney, all the good old-fashioned recipes. At the moment I am making home-made whisky. Barley, raisins and yeast. Not *real* whisky, of course!"

"Very strong and doesn't have to mature," Vera said.

"I am selling some of last year's wine on our stall this afternoon," Sophie went on. "I do every year. Last year Lady Tontine bought some of my orange and added quinine to it and gave it away to the poor as a medicine. Tonic, you know! I must give you some for dear Henry."

"And speaking of Henry, Lady Engleton," Vera said, as if prompted by the word "tonic," "please tell us about his engagement—the interesting announcement, you know. Who is she?" Vera looked as roguish as is possible to one whose resemblance to a hippopotamus is little short of a misfortune.

"It's a secret as yet," Arabella said. "But she is a sweet girl, the daughter of a—of a well-known merchant. He has said nothing to me yet, but it's easy to see which way the wind is blowing. They are always out together. I only thought it right that you, as his aunts, should be amongst the first to know."

"How very kind of you," Sophie said. "You must taste my parsnip."

Arabella looked puzzled, and then remembered the wine. Sophie once on her hobbyhorse was not easily dismounted, and would not be satisfied till Arabella had gone into the wash-house and inspected the whisky. This necessitated passing through the kitchen, where Noreen was slouching huddled over the remnants of her meal (cold mutton) and a hastily concealed novelette.

"Not gone yet, Noreen?" Vera asked angrily.

"I was waitin' to wash up," Noreen replied sulkily.

"Wash up? I told you to go at once to the Parish Hall and help set out the stall. Wash up indeed!"

She spoke of washing up as if it were some subtle breaking of a Commandment. Noreen departed muttering.

"The girl is little less than a Bolshevik!"

She trembled with indignation for some few minutes, even while Sophie demonstrated the manufacture of whisky. Half a dozen slightly fermenting bottles of liquid reposed in a large tin pan and were, Sophie explained, fed and filled up from a small jug. It was nearly ready now, nearly finished.

"To-morrow I shall cork it down. It's nearly done working, and in a week's time we two lone women will sample it. It's the first time I've ever attempted it, but I'm told by old Mrs. Clayton that it is most delicious."

Arabella stooped and sniffed at the unappetizing-looking stuff.

"I can't think what girls are coming to," Vera said, still trembling. "I can understand the decay of the towns, what with cinemas and ritualism, but here, in God's good country——"

"You put the barley and raisins together with the brown sugar..."

"One thing leads to another. The girl must be confirmed as soon as possible..."

"The yeast—just a trifle—floats on a piece of dry toast..."

"Disobedience to employers leads to breaking the Ten Commandments..."

"And you let the whole mass work for a fortnight."

"... and Free Love is the result. Abominable. I shall speak to Mrs. Ramsbottom..."

"... and then bottle it down. I'll give you the recipe."

"Noreen's mother, you know."

"Yes," said Arabella. "Very nice, I quite agree."

They let it go at that, and the sisters retired upstairs to dress. Arabella and Caraway were left facing each other over the sitting-room fire. Arabella said nothing, and Caraway said nothing unless first spoken to, which was rare enough. So silence reigned supreme, and whether it was the warm fire or the red currant wine or the interaction of each, Caraway began to nod. As a rule, Arabella used to talk or find something for the woman to do if she detected any signs of somnolence, but on this occasion she said nothing, did nothing, but kept her sharp old eyes riveted on the dozing woman. Caraway was not beautiful awake, and even less so asleep, but it was a welcome sight for Arabella. The untidy head rolled on one side, and the mouth sagged. Arabella noticed with distaste that the woman's false teeth fitted badly. Caraway began to snore, a hissing sound followed by a little pop.

The knuckles on Arabella's hands showed increasingly white. She was eighty-three, and the effort required to heave herself out of a chair without help and soundlessly was considerable. At last she tottered to her feet. Quietly she reached for her handbag and listened. Upstairs she dimly heard a drawer being opened and shut, and the dull rumble of Vera's complaining voice—Noreen's downward progress on the broad way that leads to Perdition was being gone through in advance. Caraway had made no movement.

Slowly and cautiously the old lady made her way across the untidy kitchen into the wash-house—Sophie's Distillery. Through the open pantry door Arabella could see a cat, the one that had been clapped at, furtively and greedily drinking the remnants of a boiled custard. The creature looked up and for a second or two Arabella and the cat eyed each other. The cat had large unblinking yellow eyes.

"You've copped me thieving," he seemed to say. "But if I'm a thief, what the devil are *you* up to, eh? What are you doing with that whisky?" He resumed his illicit custard drinking. "Carry on. I won't tell. . . ."

Ten minutes later, Caraway woke with a start. Arabella was in her chair watching her with an amused smile.

"You sleep and snore and rend apparel out," she quoted.

"I'm sorry, m'lady. That red currant wine; I'm not used to it. It was very delicious."

"There's no explanation of a depraved palate, but personally I can hardly imagine anyone ever becoming inured to such an abomination."

"Oh, my lady, I thought it most palatable."

"I should try methylated spirit; you'll find it doesn't fur the tongue or dry the tonsils. By the way, you were snoring and your false teeth don't fit properly."

"I'm sorry, m'lady. . . ."

A few minutes later Vera and Sophie came downstairs. Their arrival was heralded by Vera's voice saying:

"Put that brooch higher. You are showing too much chest."

To Arabella's amazement, the sisters were dressed in what they imagined was Old English costume. Tightly fitting brown bodices made of casement cloth, laced in down the front, and full skirts showing thick ankles. Each wore an immense mob cap and a green scarf.

"Good gracious me," Arabella gasped. "Why on earth are you dressed as waitresses?"

"Didn't we tell you?" Sophie asked. "The Sale of Work is being given as an Old English Fair, and as many of us as can are going in costume. It attracts the country people, you know. We made these ourselves."

It seemed impossible that Vera would not burst or boil over, as it were. Her face and the V at her neck glowed scarlet like red-hot coals, and the mob cap gave her a supremely comic yet vindictive look. It had been a tight fit getting into the bodice and the seams were none too good. Arabella felt that she had been polite long enough, and cackled with mirth.

"You'll have all the men after you," she said.

Vera didn't like the tone of the laughter but kept her temper. This was her moment of triumph among local society and she wasn't going to spoil it. She must pay the price of snobbery.

"It was a question," she said, "whether we would have set the Bazaar in the East. 'Arabian Nights' Bazaar,' you know. But it was too expensive."

"We may do that next year," said Sophie.

"I'll come down and open it," said Arabella, "if you promise me to appear as Nautch Girls or Odalisques. Trousers and transparent skirts!"

Caraway was helping the old lady on with her coat and bonnet and steering her to the bath chair.

"The nicest Odalisque I ever saw," said Sophie, "was the one in Windsor Park erected, I believe, to the memory of the late Duke of Cumberland."

Arabella cackled again.

"You two girls'll be the death of me," she said, "or I'll be the death of you!"

Vera thought the remark ill-timed!

3

The Parish Hall had once been an immense Dutch barn and had been converted to its present use as a social centre by the enterprise of the Vicar, who had begged the small sum necessary for the purpose from every conceivable source, both diocesan and private.

As Arabella approached the Hall she was greeted by an illuminated hand-done streamer stretching across the door.

YE OLDE ENGLISHE FAYRE
Admission 6d.   After 7, 3d.   (Children, 1d.)
WALKE UPPE.   WALKE UPPE.

"Shall we have to pay?" Arabella asked anxiously.

Sophie looked awkward. It was usual for distinguished patrons to spend quite lavishly, and Arabella's question didn't sound hopeful.

"I have the requisite entrance money," she said, coldly for her. She was still a little hurt at being laughed at.

"Good," said Arabella.

There was a certain difficulty in getting the bath chair up the steps into the barn, but this was soon overcome by stalwart arms lifting the whole thing, Arabella included, and propelling it in. The place was already full and buzzed like a genteel beehive. The atmosphere was stuffy and redolent of hot tea-urns. The Major was there, and accompanied by the Vicar, brayed a loud welcome. At that early hour there were only local gentry present; the commonalty waited till after seven and paid threepence.

Everything was got up to be "Olde Englishe." Festoons of coloured paper with dangling bells, shrubs, holly and colour-washed stalls almost completely effacing the huge beams and lofty roof. Arabella was pushed up the centre and towards the platform, shedding Vera and Sophie *en route*. This annoyed them intensely, as Arabella was their property. They had hoped she would remain at their stall, "Fancye Worke," and attract a crowd. In fact, Vera showed signs of having another trembling fit, especially when Lady Tontine bustled forward and swooped on Arabella, greeting her as if she had known her for years.

The Vicar's wife, in despair at offending Lady Tontine, had gone to her and made a clean breast of the whole affair, putting the blame where it belonged; that is, on Vera's ample shoulders. Lady Tontine, a hawk-nosed, bony woman, had taken it in good part, exonerated the Vicar, but registered a grim determination to take it out of Miss V. Beamish. And this was the method—a fairly easy one, as she had no particular stall to mind.

"How are you, my dear Lady Engleton? This is, indeed, an honour. Let me take you round."

And take her round she did! Caraway found herself gently but quite firmly dislodged from the bath chair and Lady Tontine, grabbing the handle, started on a grand tour, leaving everyone else behind.

There seemed no end to the stalls. There was "Ye Olde Dainties," supervised by Lady Tontine's own daughter Juliana. There were cheap sweets, bought wholesale cheaper still, and made in Poland. A few toffee apples gave the necessary old English atmosphere.

"What are you going to buy?" Lady Tontine asked. This was a bit of a poser for Arabella, who was bewildered by this large, hearty woman, and it took her at least three seconds to formulate a plan.

"I'm afraid, Lady Tontine," she said, "I've left my bag at home." As it happened, she was sitting on it. "Please write my purchases down on a piece of paper and I'll send the Vicar a cheque for the grand total."

Lady Tontine found this rather disappointing, but there was nothing else to be done. Arabella thereupon made purchases at each stall, usually giving them back to be resold, and the price was entered on a sheet of paper to be paid later by cheque. The cheque, of course, was never sent. Old ladies are very forgetful!

It was like a bad dream to Arabella, and she found herself committed to credit expenditure of nearly five pounds before she had completed the tour of the stalls. Her generosity in handing the goods back was loudly applauded, and she adhered to this principle rigidly except in Vera's case, where, remembering how she had been diddled over the garnets, she diddled back by taking two lace pillow slips priced at five shillings each, and sticking to them. Lady Tontine pushed the chair to the foot of the platform on to which it was again lifted, and Arabella found herself the centre of a crescent, consisting of the Vicar and his wife, Sir Julian and Lady Tontine, the Major, and Captain Champneys. There was an instant hush, broken only by the ineffectual efforts of Vera to reach the platform and sit on it. She was hushed, and in a few well-chosen and flattering words the Vicar introduced Lady Engleton.

They must all feel honoured, he said, to welcome amongst them this grand old lady. He hoped he didn't speak disrespectfully; one who had seen the end of a great era and had welcomed in a new one, whose interest in the welfare of her fellow Christians had rightly gained for her a place in contemporary life. He called on Lady Engleton to declare their Sale of Work—for which they had all worked so hard and hoped so much—open!

This palaver gave Arabella breathing space and she was grateful.

"My friends," she said, "I trust you'll forgive me calling you friends, but I seem to know you all from the accounts given to me by my kinsfolk. I know you will understand my not rising. I am an old, old woman. (Here the Vicar smiled and made a deprecating gesture.) Oh, yes, I am! You have yourself said so, and rightly. An old, old woman. This makes it all the more fitting that I should openly associate myself with a work devoted to young girls. (Hear, hear!) A work in which my good kinsman, Major Beamish (mild clapping) and his sisters (milder clapping) are so keenly interested. I have read Major Beamish's literature on the subject and heard him speak. I can assure you he has the interest of young girls ever before him. (Here the Major blushed and examined his boots, an action mistaken for modesty.) No less is the interest of his sisters, who are constantly discussing the grave problem of unemployment and morality as it affects young people. (Here Noreen was heard to mutter something that sounded like "Lousy old cats.") As some of you know, my son died fighting for his country, but his son lives on, and I in my small way have fought for him, to make him worthy to occupy the position that his birth has thrust upon him, to make him a credit to the great name he bears."

For an instant the old woman stiffened and her eyes flashed. It seemed she scarcely realized she had an audience. Then once more she wilted.

"I declare this Sale of Work, this 'Olde Englishe Fayre'—as it is so appropriately called—open."

Instant loud applause, led vociferously by Lady Tontine, who lost nothing in prestige thereby. Captain Champneys began to sing "For she's a jolly good fellow," in which he was joined by the Major, who had already had a couple. No one else joined in much, but that was because the villagers had not yet turned up. It served, however, as music to get Arabella off the platform. She was instantly pounced on by the indignant Vera, in no degree mollified by Arabella's soft platform soap.

"I'll come to your stall in a minute, Vera," Arabella said testily. "Just now I'm talking to Lady Tontine."

"Absurd the woman looks in that get-up," she added to Lady Tontine, taking her seemingly into her confidence. She didn't really like Lady Tontine, but felt a grudging admiration for the manner in which she had routed the Beamish women. Anyhow, she had an ulterior motive.

"I can't say I'd care to risk those sort of clothes myself," Lady Tontine said.

"Of course not," Arabella said promptly. "You're a sensible woman. By the way, is there any chance of getting a glass of something stronger than water?"

"Surely," said Lady Tontine, seeing light. "Give me a chance."

She manœuvred the bath chair towards "Ye Olde Dainties" stall, which was set at an angle in the corner, and skilfully getting it out of the glare of the light, pushed it into the corner, behind the stall. Here they found Sir Julian and Captain Champneys opening a bottle of champagne and unpacking caviare sandwiches. It was satisfactory from every point of view, and Arabella spent a thoroughly agreeable half-hour drinking admirable champagne and eating at someone else's expense. The din in the hall grew louder as the village arrived, the men primed with beer and the women with the chance of picking up a bargain, and the children in the hope of pinching something. When it was rumoured that the Vicar was searching high and low for her, Arabella felt it would be a breach of hospitality to remain and thereby expose the Tontines' private provisions to possible clerical depredations. It was a long time, however, before Caraway could be found. She was found at last, and, once again harnessed to the bath chair, pushed over to Vera's stall by request.

"Isn't it time we went home?" Arabella asked the sisters. Sophie stared blankly. This was an unforeseen problem. No one had thought that Arabella might want to go home! Both the

Beamish residences were shut up and the staffs (under supervision) allowed to make merry. Vera lost her temper. It was the last straw; the Sale was proving a failure as far as she was concerned. Her stall was not proving an attraction; she had seen people grinning at her clothes and she had been publicly slighted.

"There's no one at home," said Sophie timidly, "and we've only just begun. The concert will start in a minute or two and the Vicar will be hurt if you go."

"I'm tired," said Arabella.

"Give me back my pillow slips," Vera burst out, her grievances welling to the surface in one tense phrase.

"What on earth does the woman mean?" Arabella faced her with stony composure, and they spoke in fierce undertones.

"I mean I want my pillow slips."

"I've already bought them."

"Where's the money?"

"Ssh! Vera! Ssh!"

"Kindly don't shush at *me*, Sophie."

"Push the chair away, Caraway, and relieve me of this creature's presence. She is as impertinent as she is plain."

An awkward situation was saved by the arrival of the Vicar.

"Come, Lady Engleton," he cried. "I have kept a place for you at the front. The concert is just about to begin. We're waiting for you."

So for once Arabella bowed before the inevitable. The Bazaar beat her, when all else had failed.

The concert went on, seemingly interminable to Arabella. The Vicar sang his usual jolly songs, Captain Champneys gave a humorous recitation, the one about the Fire Brigade that played on the slate at a public house, a thin woman played the piano, a boy sang *Fly, White Butterfly*, and another woman recited *If.* Then followed the *pièce de résistance.* Three skinny women and three idiotic-looking men appeared on the scanty stage in strange garments, from which ribbons hung. The school-master thumped the piano and they capered about, banging sticks together, picking up handkerchiefs and slapping each other's hands. It was a contingent of the local Folk Dancing Society, and it purported to be Morris Dancing. "Ye Olde Englishe Dancinge!" Ruder members of the audience openly jeered from the obscurity of the back.

At last it was over, and the scrambling over the rubbish heap broke out with renewed vigour. The Major bawled louder than ever. Arabella plucked angrily at Caraway.

"If you don't take me away," she said, "I'll scream, old as I am." And she meant it, too.

It took some time to make the matter clear to the heated Major, but at last Caraway was successful and the idea that Arabella had to go percolated through. He regretted his inability to leave the Bran Tub, but managed to secure one of his staff, who was to make suitable arrangements at the darkened Grange. In any case, a ginger-headed member of the Sewing Guild had thrown him a meaning glance—an advantage he meant to pursue.

Arabella left without saying good-bye to anyone.

At The Grange there was no fire, no milk pudding, no weak lemonade, and Arabella sat in the bath chair until the defects had been at least partially remedied, glowering in silent rage, refusing to be moved. But at last a fire crackled in the bedroom grate, milk was warmed and lemonade prepared, and Arabella was safely put to bed by her exhausted companion. There she lay and made uncomplimentary remarks about the Beamishes, not even the sight of the pillow slips affording much comfort.

"Five shillings, indeed! Shoddy rubbish!"

4

"Where is your chilblain lotion, m'lady?"

"Mind your own business and let me sleep."

"I can't find it . . ."

"I upset it . . ."

"It was a green bottle with a red poison label, wasn't it?"

"For goodness' sake stop chattering and let me sleep."

"Good night, m'lady."

"Be quiet, woman!"

5

To sleep, but not for long. About an hour later the Major returned, to have a "final" with Captain Champneys. Their loud voices made the night hideous. But they were drunk, and so stand partially excused by the world; but not by Arabella, who snapped her eyes savagely in the darkness as she listened. She heard the Major's voice, forsaking politics, passing into the drawing-room.

"That little piece with the ginger hair has got a coming-on manner, ole boy . . ." Bump!

The voices became muffled as the door closed. This was the last straw, and it was without a pang that the following day Arabella shot Major Hugh Beamish dead.

13

EXIT THE MAJOR

Arabella had let the sun go down on her wrath, and the sunrise found it in no way abated; in fact, if anything, the matter had gathered force. She gave no sign of it, however, when she went in search of the Major in the gun-room. She was cold and rather aristocratically distant as befitted offended and aged dignity.

The Major had, of course, been well and truly apprised of Vera's lapse from grace and was ponderously apologetic. Arabella found him gloomily cleaning a rook rifle, surrounded by bits of rag and oil cans.

"Words fail me, Lady Engleton," he said: "words fail me. My sister completely forgot herself. Small wonder she is so disliked in the village. But there, words fail me! Sophie told me. Lucky it wasn't public, and all because she couldn't put her great behind on the platform. Beg your pardon," he added quickly, realizing his impropriety.

"You may take a walk, Caraway," Arabella said. "Don't hover about. I shan't be going out."

Caraway, thus dismissed, withdrew, leaving Arabella and the Major in privacy.

"Words fail me," the Major repeated, fascinated by the phrase, and fell to cleaning the barrel.

"Don't concern yourself too much, Major." Arabella said with studied kindness. "I confess I was horrified at your sister's conduct, which naturally makes it impossible for me to remain here any longer."

"Don't say that! Don't say that!"

"I have no choice in the matter. I came down here to Mellingham Parva with the sole purpose of trying to patch up an unfortunate difference of opinion I had with your sister about some garnets, of trying to understand her better, of bearing an olive branch. I have failed."

"She told me about that. Cheap and silly I thought it—unworthy of a Beamish. I told her so!"

"But I am delighted to have got to know *you* better."

"Silver lining to every cloud, eh?"

"Indeed, yes. And your conduct towards your nephew has been most generous."

"That's all right, Lady Engleton. Jolly glad you suggested it—at least—er—that I thought of it. But I'm sorry you want to cut your visit short."

"I'm sorry, too. I hope you understand, Major."

"Yes, I understand, but it's yoo-miliating . . . that's what it is . . . yoo-miliating."

Truly the stars in their courses fought that morning for Arabella. The Major picked up his rook rifle, opened the breech and closed it again, thus giving a gratuitous demonstration of its very simple mechanism. Arabella knew enough about guns to know that you put in a cartridge and pulled the trigger with distressing results for anything that happened to be at the business end of the muzzle.

"Vera's a dreadful woman—dreadful!" he said.

"I confess," Arabella remarked coldly, "that the very thought of last night makes me feel faint."

This aroused the Major's hospitable instincts, as indeed was the intention.

"Will you take anything?" he asked solicitously. "I feel the need of a peg myself—just a couple of fingers. Do have a glass of sherry wine or a spot of brandy."

The Major had risen to his feet and looked like a dog ready to retrieve a thrown ball.

"I rarely drink in the morning, but perhaps just a tiny glass of brandy would not come amiss. . . ."

"Indeed, yes."

The Major hurried out. There was the rook rifle, there were the cartridges. The box had been well broken into and one would not be detected were it removed. Where was the risk? Should Major Beamish discover the cartridge which Arabella hastily slipped into the breech she would easily explain it away and no harm done. She glanced out of the window, which was over-hung by creeper. No one could see in and there was no one in sight even. She sensed the fact that in spite of his foolish habit of peering into the barrels of guns, the Major would instinctively refrain from pointing a weapon at anyone, even inadvertently. He was too old a bird for that. Where he had acquired his bad habit no one knew—but there it was. Presently he returned, bearing a generous brandy for Arabella and an immense peg for himself; he also radiated the aura of a recently deceased peg.

"Drink it down," said Arabella kindly. "You'll feel all the better for it."

It was kind of her not to deprive him of his last comfort. Even the poor wretch ready shorn for the guillotine may drink his fill. Major Beamish didn't wait for a second bidding and Arabella watched the muscles of his throat moving like a fish's gills with a certain fascination. The Finger of God was about to move!

"I've been examining your gun," Arabella said. "Old as I am, firearms still fascinate me."

"Pretty bit o' work . . ."

"Indeed, yes, but what is that wad of cotton wool for in the muzzle?"

"Cotton wool? There oughtn't to be any cotton wool. How the devil did that get there?"

Her comment acted just as she had thought it would. The

Major swung the rifle round, rested the butt on the bench and peered into the muzzle.

"I don't see anything," said the Major, puzzled but still peering. "Let me show you . . ."

Arabella leaned forward and shot him neatly. The bullet tore its small way through the brain. It seemed to Arabella absurdly simple. She had only needed just to touch the trigger. . . . She saw a look of blank surprise on his face before he rolled over on the floor, still staring at her. It wasn't a pleasant sight, that flame-licked face with a shattered eye from which blood oozed. Arabella felt no remorse, only physical sickness. Uncle Alfred had been simple, would probably have died in any case. . . . She gasped, and feeling faint, drank the brandy which the dead man had provided with unconscious forethought.

The shot had been heard and a few minutes later Arabella was taken to her room by Caraway in a state of collapse. A doctor was sent for—and the police; but what was the good of them? A clean case of an unfortunate accident. The fine old lady bore her terrible ordeal with fortitude. They had been talking—the Major had fetched her some brandy—and had had whisky himself—rather too much whisky. He was cleaning the rook rifle when . . . It was terrible . . . terrible. . . .

2

Sophie was prostrate with grief, incoherent and quite incapable. It was grief that was conventional and to a degree heartfelt. Was not Hugh, with all his faults, her brother? And such a dreadful death. . . .

Vera was made of sterner stuff. It was a judgment on him, she declared, for his drinking habits. God was not mocked. She came and took charge. There was to be an inquest, and much to be done. Vera knew where her duty lay. It was she who sent the wire that summoned Henry from London.

"I shall do my duty both by my poor dead brother and by Lady Engleton, though they have both treated me disgracefully. . . ."

3

Henry and Dora had made the most of Arabella's absence and for days had been together as much as possible. Arabella had been quite taken in by their minor deception, quite sure in her own mind that they had bowed to her decree and put all thoughts of each other out of their minds. This had been one of Arabella's prime mistakes, results of her growing megalomania. They had both felt rather guilty about Lily, but Lily was not the sort of person who invited either consideration or pity. In any case, people who are violently in love develop unscrupulous instincts. Lily, Henry argued, regarded the projected marriage coldly and purely as a social step; he had told her the facts of the case, though not very strenuously. Lily's attitude towards love was very callous; at least, she pretended it was. Having adopted what she was pleased to think was a "modern" attitude, she felt obliged to stick to it, out of sheer pride.

"I don't mind your being in love with other women, even after we're married. Why should I? We're all polygamous, and golly, don't I know it!"

Henry didn't attempt to argue, though he felt very differently himself. His whole life seemed bounded by Dora; infidelity seemed unthinkable and bad-mannered, anyway. He was like that. Nor did he realize that Lily talked for the sake of talking, for the sake of justifying her rather grubby little life. The truth was that Lily hated the very thought of Dora and pattered along about freedom and so forth in the hope of winning him by displaying a lack of jealous instincts.

"Personally," said Henry, "I wouldn't give tuppence for the love of anyone who wasn't a trifle jealous."

Life was crammed with sexual skirmishes for all of them, and they all three found it quite enjoyable, though Lily less so than the others. But, she told herself, she had riches and flair on her side, which in the long run are irresistible.

Henry received Vera's wire about midday on the Wednesday morning.

Major Beamish met fatal accident. Lady Engleton prostrate. Your presence essential.

VERA BEAMISH.

He was sitting with the open wire in his hand, wondering what to do next, when the telephone rang. It was Lily, a Lily plaintive with neglect. Would he, at least, take her out to lunch?

"I'm sorry, Lily, but there's been some sort of serious trouble in Norfolk. I'm afraid I must get there as soon as possible. Major Beamish is dead, apparently, and my grandmother upset by it all."

"I don't see that's your affair," Lily said. "Your dear grannie's got her companion. But I suppose you must go. *Noblesse oblige* and all that. Seems silly to me! Where is this place?"

"Near Norwich. Heaven knows how you get there."

"Tell you what—I'll take you in the Bug! Give me something to do."

"The Bug," was Lily's Bugatti, painted all scarlet to match her clothes. To do her justice, she drove it extremely well, excessively fast, and with no regard whatsoever for the convenience of anyone else on the road.

"I wouldn't dream of bothering you."

"Stow it! I'll be round in an hour's time."

"But . . ."

But Lily had rung off. She'd show him! Here was a trick that his namby-pamby Dora couldn't do. And really, from Henry's point of view, it seemed the best possible method of getting to Mellingham Parva comparatively quickly. He rang up Dora and asked her advice.

"Of course you must go," she said, "but I wish there was some other way than Lily's Bug. You be careful, my darling."

"You can trust me with Lily, sweet. We've had that all out."

"It's not your virtue that worries me, dear. It's your neck."

"Lily's a good driver."

"So they say. I wish *I* could drive."

"So do I."

"Well, God bless you, Harry. So sorry you've more troubles, dear."

"They'll end some day."

"Only with your grandmother."

Henry informed the household and dashed upstairs to pack a bag. An hour and a half later he was speeding noisily northward at Lily's side, a telegram having been previously dispatched to announce his coming by road. It was a chill day, the sun hanging a red ball in the sky in a bank of mist. Gradually it increased in size as it sank lower, and dusk was on them almost as they entered Cambridge. There was no question of it; Lily was a good driver. They had roared up the North road, hardly seeming to slow down for the towns on the way. Henry found it thrilling if rather cold, and did not object to Lily's suggestion in Cambridge that "a nice hot cup of tea would do them no harm."

Skilfully she swung the Bugatti into the parking place in the market behind Great St. Mary's, snatching off her beret and shaking out her mass of curls. The street lamps were beginning to indulge in their daily struggle with the setting sun.

"First stage over, laddie," Lily said. "And now for some tea!"

"What about the 'Bull?'"

Lily made a face.

"Not too keen on the 'Bull,'" she answered. "Wasn't there some bloke in a Dickens novel that couldn't go down streets because he owed so much money, and had to walk a couple of miles to go a hundred yards?"

"Dick Swiveller!"

"That's the chap."

She took his arm and leaned ever so slightly against him, warm even through her leather coat. Her eyes seemed to glow in the half-light.

"Cambridge is rather like that for me. Not that I owe money, but I might be recognized."

"How do you mean?"

"I've had too many adventures in Cambridge. You can cut the 'Bull' out. Last time I was there I was Mrs. Joshua Robinson of Catford."

Henry looked puzzled.

"Mrs. Joshua Robinson?"

"I don't know what made us think of that name."

They began to wander down the little passage that connects

the Market Place with King's Parade. The turrets of the glorious chapel stuck up into the growing gloom, mysterious and mist-enshrouded.

"But why on earth should you want to be Mrs. What's-it Robinson?"

Lily snuggled closer. Her leg was touching her companion's even as they walked, and well she knew that her face was obscured from him. What she had to say just had to be said.

"I sometimes wonder," she said lightly, "whether you are so innocent as you pretend to be. Haven't you ever been to a hotel with a girl as Mr. Smith?"

Henry felt as if a stream of cold water had been dropped down his spine. He had always known that Lily was unconventional, gay if you like, but he had never dreamed that she . . .

"No," he said firmly. "I've never done that."

Lily laughed rather bitterly and adopted what is supposed to be the Nonconformist-conscience-voice in reply.

"What, nevah? Well, *hardly* evah!" Then her voice became hard and callous. "If you can't take a hint, I spent a week-end at the 'Bull' with a man. Think of *that!*"

There was an underlying note of anxiety in her casual tones. She had determined, however, to tell Henry the worst before others did it for her. Some of her male friends, she reflected bitterly, were of the kiss-and-tell variety, and the kissing lost nothing in the telling, you may be sure. Henry felt a strange numb sensation; he suddenly realized that though he was in love once and for all with Dora, yet he was curiously fond of this pretty golden creature. He intensely disliked the idea of her being anyone's "bit." They halted before a shop in Trinity Street that looked cosy and from which there came an inviting scent of toast and hot tea cakes.

"Shall we go in here?" he asked.

Lily didn't reply but just walked in.

"I could do with a couple of poached eggs on toast," she said, when the waitress appeared, sucking an interrogative pencil. For a second or two neither of them spoke, then Lily regarded him with anxious, large blue eyes.

"I suppose you're shocked," she said.

Henry laughed uneasily.

"Oh, no," he said in what he imagined was a broad-minded voice, rather like a curate telling a *risqué* story just to show he knew what was what. "I suppose I'm a bit of a prig, that I haven't moved with the times, but I'm not shocked."

"I went what you'd call 'wrong' on my seventeenth birthday, if you want to know," Lily said defiantly. "It was after a party and I wasn't very sober. He came into my room and badgered me. . . . It didn't seem to matter much. I'm made that way. I wish I hadn't now."

Henry noticed, rather to his alarm, that her full, pretty lips were quivering and that she kept her eyes averted. He noticed, too, that Lily was an object of interest to a tableful of undergrads near-by—and small wonder, really. She was ridiculously flamboyant and pretty.

"But I'm not sorry now," she added. "I'm not—*really*."

Henry longed to say something comforting, pleasant and understanding, but for the life of him could not formulate the words.

"For the Lord's sake, say something," Lily said suddenly. "Do you believe me?"

"Yes, of course I believe you. Why shouldn't I? Poor kid."

"I hate you when you get patronizing and pity me."

"Believe me, I don't mean to pity you or to be patronizing. I really *am* sorry."

"Why?"

"Well—just because you seem sorry yourself, I suppose."

There was a pause, during which the waitress brought the poached eggs and the tea. Lily allowed her eyes to wander round the tea shop.

"Nice-lookin' boy, that one with the crinkly hair," she said, the ghost of a smile hovering on her lips. She frowned suddenly as she realized that her smile was being returned with interest, and attacked the eggs.

"I'm sorry if I got catty, Henry," she said penitently. "I know you're what's called good and it's not fair to rake up my past. I don't suppose you've got a past, have you?"

Henry grinned. The conversation seemed to be in safer channels.

"No, I'm bound to confess I haven't," he replied.

"Haven't you ever looked at a girl in the Tube or somewhere and just wanted her, without having heard her voice even?"

"I've thought strange girls pretty and attractive . . ."

"That's not what I mean. I mean wanted them physically, then and there? *I* have—frequently."

There was a pause.

"I suppose I'm a bit cracked," she added, "but I don't suppose people like you—good people—understand what a few drinks and an evening of jazzing about will do for a gutter rat like me, with too much money."

"Eat your eggs," said Henry, "and cut out all that about my being good."

"I'm eating my eggs——" Poor Lily nearly added that she was eating her heart as well.

"When shall we get to Mellingham?" Henry asked.

"God knows, but I'll do it as quickly as Malcolm Campbell, my lad . . ."

But Lily had not reckoned with the mist that gathered thicker as they sped over those dreary, marshy miles that lie between Cambridge and Ely. The mist was fast developing into a patchy fog. Fingers of mist clutched at them like ghosts, momentarily obscuring the road and dropping a thick curtain over the headlights. Even Lily had to decrease speed. The roads are narrow and dangerous and for many miles bounded by a river that is perilously easy to run into headlong. They nearly came to grief over a narrow bridge.

"Easy!" Henry cried, seriously alarmed as they scraped the wall.

The fog looked at them with blank, white unseeing eyes. It was eerie and cruel. Lily kept on swearing under her breath.

"What are we going to do?" Henry asked as they pulled up.

"Bust me if I know! I'll fix the fog screens."

She jumped out and made Henry help her to fix rubber, amber-tinted caps over the headlights. They certainly afforded a slight help, and by fixing a beam on the edge of the road they managed to crawl into the noble city of Ely, set like a fortress in the fens. Not that they saw much of Ely, as the fog was then dense. There was no question of going any farther, and Lily was insistent on the fact that she must have a double Scotch or die before they even thought of anything else. They were lucky to have got there at all. They ran the car up to the entrance of a hospitable-looking hotel. Scotch was ordered in largish quantities and they sat down gratefully by the fire.

"What are we going to do?" Henry asked again. "I wonder if there are any trains."

"Don't be an ass," Lily said shortly. She seemed quite cheerful now that she was nursing a large whisky. "Just like a book, isn't it? I'm the compromised heroine, but you don't look a bit like the wicked seducer who has tampered with the engine. And *I* haven't, I swear!"

"We can't go on, that's a cert. I'd better phone through to Mellingham, though I don't think The Grange is on the phone."

"Get the post office, tell them you're Lord Engleton; and they'll take a message wherever you like. Everyone'll do anything for a lord."

It was a good idea and Henry acted on it. The office had long been shut (it was after half-past eight), but the exchange put a message through to the Vicar, who said he would personally convey it to Lady Engleton. Yes, she was better, my lord, but still feeling the shock. Your lordship doesn't yet know anything of the terrible accident? His lordship didn't. It appeared that Major Beamish had met his death actually in Lady Engleton's presence. Very dreadful! Very sad! Indeed it was, very sad indeed, and that was therefore that, and with many "good night, sirs" and "my lordings" receivers were re-hung.

On returning to the hotel lounge, Henry found that Lily had made herself very comfortable with a further supply of Scotch. An admiring little group was round her, discoursing vehemently on the evils of fog. At least they were pretending to. In reality they were buzzing round blonde curls and an impudent smile. Henry briefly informed Lily that the message would be delivered to his grandmother by the Vicar, and that the old lady was better —"bearing up wonderfully well."

Lily had ordered dinner and they were to have it in twenty minutes' time. Steaks had to be grilled, it seemed. They were not particularly good steaks, but they were healthily hungry. Lily seemed rather unnaturally elated; perhaps it was the whisky, which she fortified with brandy later. She regarded her companion rather as a lion might regard a young gazelle.

"Seems to me," she said deliberately and with a flickering smile, "that we'd better put up here. It seems a decent place."

Henry wondered what was coming next.

"Perhaps," he said, "I'd better go and find a room somewhere else. I'm not particular."

Lily laughed.

"Depends what you mean by particular. You're just like a romantic Victorian hero. Haven't I told you enough to convince you that you can't hurt my reputation? Oh, Lavinia!" she cried, with a mock Victorian throwing up of hands and casting down of eyes. "To think of it. I had to sleep alone in an hotel. You may be sure I placed a chair against my door. Speak no more of it, but hand me my smelling salts. Go on, you silly mutt. Go and register. Mr. and Mrs. Joshua Robinson. Buck up!"

"I do wish you'd be serious, Lily. This is a damned awkward situation."

"It seems to me a present straight from Heaven, my dear. We're entitled to a cuddle after all that fog." She laughed suddenly. "I wish you could see your face."

Poor Henry! He certainly felt like a male Susannah and wondered what that lady would have done if benighted in a provincial hotel. Lily had clearly had a shade too much to drink, so he wisely refrained from arguing. He wished he didn't like Lily! But he wished even more that the fog hadn't fallen. Lily leaned forward, bringing her face closer to Henry's. He noticed the dilation of her pretty little nostrils; she caught hold of his arm.

"You remember what I told you about looking at people in the Tube? Well, I feel like that now."

"I remember what you said about girls and a few drinks equally well, Lily dear."

"Go on! Go and register!"

Henry felt a slight trembling; a catch at his heart. Yes, they had two rooms. Lord Engleton and Miss Lily Peploe. Rooms eight and nine. Most unfortunate, this fog. Charles, take the bags out of the Bugatti! Push the car into the garage. The leather suitcase into Room Eight and the red one in Room Nine. Thank you.

"I'll go up and have a look at the room," said Lily. "I don't trust 'em. I'll see that the bed's aired properly and lay out your pyjamas. Not that you'll—well, never mind."

Henry noticed her use of the singular.

"Rooms," he said, rolling the S. "Beds."

Lily looked at him for a second or two.

"Serious?" she asked.

"Dead serious!"

The girl's eyes dropped and she seemed to contract in size. She extinguished the stub of her cigarette viciously.

"My God!" she said. "You *are* an insulting swine!"

Her breath came quicker and Henry could see she was on the point of having one of her little outbursts. He compromised quickly.

"It wouldn't have been tactful," he said. "No good asking for trouble."

"Trouble, do you call it? You've turned me down, damn you. That's not happened to me before. You'll have to whistle for another chance. I wish to God I'd left you on the road."

"Lily, you really must see reason!"

"I wonder what room that lad with the ginger hair and plus fours has got."

"Don't be nasty . . ."

"You make me feel physically sick!"

Lily chose to sulk for the next hour. True, they played Pin-ball and she ogled the said lad with the ginger hair, but the minutes passed slowly and uncomfortably. The bar gradually cleared and the inevitable minute of bedtime came. They ascended the ancient staircase and found themselves outside Rooms Eight and Nine. Lily had been alloted Number Nine.

"Good night, Lily. Sleep well!"

"Good night, but if you think I shall sleep much, you're an optimist."

He heard her door close. Slowly Henry undressed and got into bed. A fire had been lit and flickered cheerfully. It was very cosy and pleasant. What a nuisance all that silliness with Lily had been!

He wished she hadn't talked like that, as he was only human and Lily's attraction was very real . . . very real indeed. He wondered what he would have done if he had not been so desperately in love with Dora, if . . . if . . . Oh, a thousand damnable "ifs"! He saw Lily's point of view. If she had been genuine when she offered herself to him, it was hardly surprising that she was in a temper. Drat the girl! She had been genuine enough; no good trying to get out of it that way. Why the dickens didn't they let him marry Dora and put an end to all this humiliating nonsense!

He was half-asleep when suddenly he was aware that the door had opened and shut quickly, and he heard Lily's voice ask:

"Are you asleep?"

"No. What do you want?"

It was a silly question which he regretted almost before it was uttered. He had spoken it automatically.

"Ssh!" she said. "Keep your voice quiet. Don't shout. You needn't worry. I'm not Mrs. Potiphar making a desperate effort. I'm just lonely and miserable."

She sat on the edge of his bed, the inevitable cigarette in her mouth. She was in her nightdress, such as it was, covered with a wisp of dressing-gown. Henry heaved himself up on his elbow and blinked sleepily. The red glow of the fire illuminated Lily's face and turned her tousled hair into an aureole.

"I'm sorry I was sulky in the lounge," she whispered. "I always seem to be apologizing to you. You were quite right."

"That doesn't matter, Lily. For all that, I don't think this is very discreet."

"You needn't worry about that. Everyone's gone to bed. I gave them time."

"Aren't you cold?"

"Yes, but it's not my fault, is it? Oh, Henry, my dear, I'm so sorry!"

"Sorry?"

"Yes, sorry for all my dirtiness. One little slip and it haunts you. I wish I was—was clean, my dear."

"You are, Lily."

"If you only loved me you wouldn't say that. It's always the way. I suppose you'll chuck my silly past at me when it suits you.

I don't blame you. It hasn't been much fun. I nearly told you the details to-day."

"There was no reason to tell me anything."

"Yes, there was. Every reason."

She leaned towards him and the flickering firelight caught her glistening eyes.

"Why don't you love me, Henry?"

Henry was silent.

"Aren't I attractive?"

"Very attractive, Lily . . ."

"I love you, Henry. Yes, I do! God! I wish I didn't! I love you so much I could kill you. I've never cared tuppence about those others—not really. Let *me* do the talking. Let me talk sense for a change. I've got rid of enough fool talk in my time."

"I'm dreadfully sorry, Lily, but I'm in love with Dora. I've never pretended otherwise."

"No, you've been straight. Go on! Marry your Dora if you must. Perhaps you won't want to—to-morrow!"

"I shall always want to marry Dora. I just can't marry you, Lily . . ."

"I'm not asking you to marry me. Just love me. Take me, my darling. I want to lie in your arms. Forget all that dirt! Take me! I don't care a hoot if you don't want to marry me. But you will! You will! I just can't bear living unless you do. Just once!"

She put her cigarette down on the tray.

"Lily! Please—for God's sake!"

"I've never asked a man to take me before. They've never needed any asking."

Henry turned away from her. He was afraid, he had only to hold out his arms for her. Dora? He could never look at her again. His love for Dora was stronger than his desire.

"Look at me, Henry! Look at me!" he heard Lily say.

He turned a rather miserable face towards her and with a sudden movement she slipped out of her dressing-gown. The nightdress didn't count for much and well Lily knew it.

Henry caught his breath; he had never been faced with passionate exuberance before. She seemed to radiate light, and conscious of it, held her arms wide.

"Lily, you're not playing fair . . ."

"Yes, I am. Anything's fair!"

"Go away, for the Lord's sake. You're being beastly."

The minute he had spoken Henry wished he had not.

Lily's outstretched arms fell to her sides; her lamp of life was extinguished. In the half-light he heard her give a bitter little sob of humiliation, and with a sudden movement she grabbed the still glowing end of the cigarette and jabbed it firmly on her thigh. She gave a gasp of agony.

"I'm a prig. I'm a cad," Henry whispered. "Forgive me, Lily."

Lily made swiftly for the door; he could hear her suppressed sobs.

"Go to hell!" she said.

The door closed softly behind her. In spite of the warmth of the room Henry shivered and in spite of his shiver he flung open the windows. Outside the cold mist dripped miserably from the eaves. There was no breath of wind, and he faced a blank wall of thick whiteness. There was no comfort in that, and he felt a wave of loneliness.

"Dora! Oh, my dear, what cruelties loving you make me say —and do!"

He listened, but there was no sound. Almost it might have been some odd dream. Then his eye fell on the little wispy wrap and he picked it up. It was still warm. With a certain reverence he folded it up and put it away carefully.

In the adjoining room Lily sat on the edge of her bed and treated her burn with face cream.

"Damn him!" she muttered. "Rot him! And—oh, hell! I've left my dressing-gown behind!"

14

DEAD MAN'S FINGERS

The Vicar had delivered Henry's message within a quarter of an hour. His lordship and a Miss Peploe, who was driving him down, had been benighted in the fog and had been obliged to stop at Ely. This news Arabella found highly satisfactory, though naturally she expressed public concern to Vera, Sophie and Caraway. If the young lady possessed half the qualities that Merry had discreetly hinted at, Henry's marriage was as good as accomplished. The fact that Henry might resist Lily's blandishments didn't enter her calculations. The de Birketts, with all their faults, could hardly be described as eunuchs. In any case, the girl was, with any luck, compromised, and Henry's sense of honour would be a useful asset. It was decidedly good news.

Arabella had spent most of the time since the Major's untimely end recovering from the shock in her room. For a while she had been worried about the Major's will, and had told Caraway to keep an eye on Vera. True, she had seen it properly witnessed and put away in the desk, but if Vera got nosing round and found it she didn't trust her not to put it in the fire. She would have done so herself under similar circumstances, and had no reason to think Vera above reproach. Sophie just didn't count; she was a fool and in any case spent her time weeping bitterly over her dead brother's relics—his pipes were objects of especial veneration and tears.

Arabella need not have worried, however, as Vera had a great idea that "nothing must be touched" till after the funeral and the reading of the will. She had a secret weakness for detective fiction and had been adamant on the point, even blaming the doctor and Saunders, the gardener, for having shifted the body before the police had arrived. She went so far as to rebuke Sophie for fingering the dead man's pipes, some vague notion about finger-prints stirring her strange brain.

The inquest had been fixed for Thursday morning. No jury had been summoned. Clearly the matter was a sad misadventure. Everyone was agreed on that. The police had even been willing to take Arabella's evidence on commission, but this she had vetoed. She knew her duty to the State and to justice. Arabella would be there, despite the early hour and her shattered nerves! A certain Mr. Griffin, a solicitor from Norwich, had arrived that afternoon and been presented to her. He had had charge of the Major's affairs and acted for him now and again. Vera had taken a dislike to him; he was a young man who had succeeded his father in the well-established legal business, and had been rather casual and unfeeling about it all.

"It is not," she said to Sophie, "that young Griffin has *said* anything, but he does not seem to realize that we have sustained A Great Loss. *Old* Griffin would have been different."

However, young Griffin had bowed to her wish that nothing must be touched, but only up to a point. He had insisted on going through the Major's papers. There might be something which would "throw light." As if the Major might possibly have taken his own life and left a vulgar letter. He would never have done anything so wicked. Griffin nevertheless went through the desk, much to Arabella's gratification and relief. Vera did inquire, however, whether he had "found anything." Yes, there was a will and all was in order, which Vera considered highly satisfactory. The future, she declared, would see changes at The Grange. The cottage days were over. Never for one second did she imagine that her late brother could have done other than recognize her devotion and general virtue. Arabella watched this attitude with a strange sense of elation and jolly anticipation of the moment when young Griffin would make interesting disclosures.

The inquest was a mere formality and had been over some hours when Henry arrived at Mellingham Parva in the company of Lily Peploe. The journey from Ely had not been very exhilarating for Henry. The remnants of the mist had fought the sunshine for the most part successfully, and Lily had preserved an aloof cordiality which was more embarrassing than open hostility, nor could Henry discover what thoughts were occupying her long silences. During a short stop in the course of the journey, Henry had handed her a small parcel containing the dressing-gown, with just a tactful and non-committal "I think you forgot this, Lily."

"Thanks," said Lily. "History reverses itself. On this occasion Mrs. Potiphar left her coat with Joseph!"

Henry preserved silence and stared down his nose.

"You can keep it as a memento. A memento of how you triumphed over the allurements of a tart."

Not a nice thing to say, and Henry did not want it as a memento. Such mementoes are difficult to explain away and, mixing the metaphor frantically, come home to roost like one o'clock.

"I'd rather you had it, Lily."

She took the clumsily made parcel and with a superb gesture flung ten guineas'-worth of silken allurement at the nearest hedge.

"I hope some milkmaid finds it and uses it for the benefit of Jarge the cowman," was her only comment.

Beyond that she made no reference to the previous night; just set her face and drove like the devil.

On arrival they were taken at once to the Presence. Arabella received them graciously and was more than pleasant to Lily. Henry was solicitous and just a shade too eager to explain the fearful density of the fog.

"I may be old-fashioned," Arabella said softly, "but 'different times, different customs.'"

"We couldn't help the fog," Henry said.

"Of course not, my dear boy. Of course not."

There was a pause and they both felt that no excuse could possibly have any weight with Arabella. She began to treat Lily as a daughter; asked after her father and mother with solicitude and made everyone (even Lily) feel uncomfortable.

"How did the inquest go?" Henry asked, changing the subject.

"The coroner was most considerate; behaved in every way as a gentleman should. Just asked me a few questions and apologized. In fact, he thanked me for being present under the distressing circumstances."

"What was the verdict?"

"Death by misadventure, I think it was called. Poor Hugh! He was telling me about shooting a tiger in some place with an absurd name ..." Arabella shuddered. "It was terrible, but I hardly remember anything. I felt so faint and ill."

"Naturally ..."

"The Major was most particular about his guns. How the cartridge came to be in the horrible thing is, and I'm afraid always will be, a complete mystery."

"It's very horrible," Henry said sincerely. "I hardly met Uncle Hugh, but he seemed an agreeable old boy."

"He was very fond of *you*, Henry. He told me what an instant liking he had taken to you. He liked your frankness over the question of the insurance."

"I'd forgotten that ..."

"One doesn't think of such things at tragic moments like this. I'm so sorry for the sisters. Vera I can't profess to like personally, but I hope I am broad-minded enough not to let my charitable instincts become obscured by personal feelings. The other one, Sophie, is a good-natured creature." Sophie was always referred to as a "creature."

Lily had sat rather downcast during this talk. Arabella looked at her with a sudden smile.

"It's very sad, my dear," she said, "to drag one so young and so pretty into a house of sorrow."

"I'm afraid I've brought no black dress," Lily said characteristically, "but I'll borrow something off one of the servants. They always have black frocks."

"How truly democratic!" Arabella said. "You delight me, my child. I wonder if you would gratify an old woman by giving her a kiss? Not an unnatural request under the circumstances."

What circumstances? Henry shuffled his feet uneasily as Lily gave the old lady a very platonic kiss, rather as if she were kissing a very fragile piece of china, or the burnt side of a bun.

"And now, Henry," Arabella continued when the rite had been performed, "it would be a fitting attention if you went and sat with your aunts for a while. They are in need of comfort, and in any case I should like to have a little chat with Lily."

Henry was at a complete loss; he simply did not know how

to tell Arabella that there was no question of any engagement between Lily and himself, nor ever could be. She seemed to assume it, seemed in some subtle unvocal way to assume that he and Lily were irrevocably bound by having spent the night in utter chastity at Ely. Even Lily looked a trifle scared and glanced pleadingly at Henry.

"Shall I bore you?" Arabella asked, noticing the glance.

"Not at all," Lily answered. "Only too pleased, I'm sure."

There was nothing for Henry to do but to set out on his paracletic errand.

"Now, my dear," Arabella said to Lily when the door had shut behind him, "let me take a good look at you."

Lily, for the first time in her life, felt embarrassed. Men had looked at her and mentally undressed her, but this old woman seemed to strip her to the bone.

"You're very pretty, and your figure is of the old-fashioned variety. I can't stand these girls who look like ham-bones with frills around them."

Lily smiled awkwardly.

"I'm glad you approve, Lady Engleton."

"I hardly knew what to say when Henry first told me about you. The de Birketts are an ancient and honourable family with great and glorious traditions. I reserved judgment. But now, having seen you, I can only say how delighted I am to welcome you as the future Lady Engleton, to know that one day you will stand in my shoes."

Lily suddenly saw Arabella for what she was; her mind was simple and therefore in some ways acute. All this talk was gammon; and she hated the old gargoyle. She had nothing to lose, nothing to fear.

"That's quite nice hearing, Lady Engleton, but my dad's spilled the beans," Lily said. "He told me that it was on the cards that he and Merry were going to fix something up. Henry's title against—how much was it?"

Arabella rather appreciated such candour. In any case, it was a trick of hers to agree and steal thunder.

"When you get to my age, my dear child," she said affably, "you will know that the marriage of convenience is the best sort of marriage. It is wisdom and experience as against juvenile and sometimes disgusting emotions. Henry is a good, clean-living young man with wonderful traditions behind him. You will learn to love him. Everyone does."

"You needn't bother about that. I love him already."

"Then what on earth are you complaining about?"

"I don't think I've complained once. But there won't be any marriage. You can take that as certain."

"Why will there be no marriage?"

"Because Henry doesn't care a tuppenny damn about *me* . . . that's why."

"I can't believe that. Would you accept him if he were to ask you?"

"You can bet your life I would. I've told you I love him, badly as he's treated me."

Arabella rapped on the chair before her and asked eagerly:

"Did he treat you badly—at Ely—last night? Answer frankly. I'm not a fool or a puritan."

Lily grinned impishly in spite of herself.

"Very badly indeed," she said. "I could hardly believe it of any man, and I've known a few; I just don't know how to meet his eye this morning. I'm only a young girl, Lady Engleton."

Arabella sniffed incredulously.

"There's no need to be facetious, my dear. Young girls nowadays know everything, and a bit more. When I married I knew absolutely nothing about the facts of life, and a good job too! My grandson has compromised you and I'll see that he marries you. I won't have the honour of the de Birketts tarnished."

"Sounds O.K. But I don't want a man who doesn't want me . . ."

"You were foolish, my dear child, to experiment. Never mind. It's just as well— We'll see."

2

All this time Henry had been comforting his aunts, helped by Mr. Griffin and a bottle of the late Major's whisky. The comfort didn't amount to much, as Vera wasn't in need of it and Sophie, like Rachel, refused to be comforted. For a while they all four sat in silence, broken by Sophie's sniffs. Vera ritualistically dabbed at her nose. Sophie's poor nose was swollen to a huge size.

"I think," Vera said at last, "that it is time you controlled yourself, Sophie; especially in front of dear Henry. Our brother has met an untimely end. Those that take the sword shall perish by it. I always disapproved of all those guns, and shall take an early opportunity of clearing them all out."

Griffin looked up quickly, having already read the terms of the late Major's will.

"Eh?" he asked. "Clear 'em all out?"

"Certainly," Vera replied. "Certainly, and dispose of that ridiculous tiger's head. All the tigers!" she added, with the sudden desperation of a national dictator. "*All* the tigers."

"They were so dear to him," Sophie sniffed. "He'd never forgive us."

"He has gone to a Higher Tribunal," Vera said severely, "where no thought is taken of tigers' heads or, indeed, skins. I shall also have this room repapered and whitewashed. It smells of stale tobacco smoke."

Griffin hastily put out his cigarette. It was a shock to him to realize that Vera laboured under the impression that she was a legatee. He said nothing about it, however; he lacked the courage and apologized for an absent-mindedly lit gasper.

"I'm sorry, Miss Beamish. I lit a cigarette without thinking. I'm sure I'm . . . very sorry . . ."

"Manners have died since the Great War."

Silence fell on them again. Griffin tried to find an opportunity of winking at Henry, but the latter avoided meeting his eye, so Griffin poured himself out some more whisky.

"I think," he said, going on a new tack, "that Lady Engleton faced the ordeal of the inquest this morning with remarkable fortitude."

He smiled at everyone, feeling rather proud of the phrase, which he had translated mentally from "thought the old girl showed guts."

"We of the old school," Vera said, "have iron self-control."

"But you're not as old as Lady Engleton, are you?" Griffin asked, sincerely interested. He was no tactician.

"Certainly not, but I was bred in the same tradition. I hope that whisky is to your liking?"

Griffin put the bottle, which he had just taken up, down again hastily. He was beginning to look forward to reading the will to-morrow when the obsequies were completed. He'd get a bit of his own back vicariously.

Henry's contribution to the work of comforting his aunts had, up to date, amounted to just nothing at all. He had the ordinary sensitive person's dislike of courting a snub and in any case his mind was filled with wonderings about Lily and his grandmother. He trusted neither of them; they were both, it seemed, utterly unscrupulous as to gaining their own ends. As a combination they might be formidable indeed. Please Heaven, Lily might commit some *gaucherie* and antagonize Arabella. But a large dowry is an excellent antidote for feminine indiscretions of all sorts. Nothing would induce him to marry Lily; that was definite. After all, they couldn't wed and bed him without his free consent—not even Arabella, who seemed able to move mountains by sheer effort of will.

"It was very good of you to respond so quickly to my tele-gram, Lord Engleton," Vera said. "It was a grave responsibility to have her ladyship on my hands, especially during my great sorrow."

"I could do no less. It was a pleasure—er—at least—" His voice trailed away as he felt he was somehow saying the wrong thing.

"I understand what you mean—perfectly."

That was all to the good, anyway.

"It must have been a great shock," Henry said politely, feeling an idiot at the solecism.

"We were just preparing tea," Sophie interposed, "when the —the—terrible news was brought to us. I hardly lived through the next ten minutes."

"We were only told after an interval of nearly three hours—an unpardonable delay—and then by a mere constable." This was another grievance. The truth of the matter was that the doctor's one thought had been to get Arabella to bed, and to tend the living after certifying the dead. Everyone else had frankly funked the task of telling the sisters, even when they had thought of it, leaving it to the police at the last. The constable had disposed of the inquest in advance when he had said:

"Bad news, 'fraid, ladies. Major Beamish has had an accident. He's dead—shot."

But the fact that there had been delay rankled with Vera. She should have been sent for at once—*at once!* Was she not his nearest relative? Abominable!

Vera was well under way, enlarging on this enormity, when the door opened and Lily came in, hot from her interview with Arabella. This was the first time that the Misses Beamish had seen Lily and they fell into a miniature flutter, a flutter chastened by the nearness of death. Lily, puzzled and yet rather elated from her interview, reverted to type, forgot her careful upbringing and awkwardly greeted the women with a pair of "Pleased to meet you's" ("So this was dear Henry's intended." "Such a pretty girl." "So unaffected."). Arabella, it appeared, would be glad if Henry could spare her a few minutes. For the first time in many weeks Henry went gladly. Better a match-making Arabella than Sophie and Vera!

3

Henry found his grandmother alone in the gaunt room, huddled over the fire and the grinning tiger's head.

"You wanted to see me?" he asked with cold courtesy.

"Yes, Henry. I have been talking to this young Peploe girl. She has beauty, physical health and a large fortune, and though I could wish she had also birth and breeding, one cannot expect everything."

Keyed up for action, Henry joined issue at once.

"I think, Grannie," he said, "that it would save a lot of unnecessary talk if I said right away that I've no intention whatever of marrying Lily."

There was a grim silence and Arabella, leaning back in her chair, regarded him coldly.

"Do my ears deceive me?" she asked.

"I hope not," Henry said flippantly, "but in case they did, I'll repeat it. I have no intention whatever of . . ."

"I heard you first time. I only hoped that I had not. You will marry this girl as soon as possible. That is my last word."

"It's not mine!"

"This is unlike you, Henry. Must I remind you that I brought you up from infancy and expect your love and respect?"

"I'm more than grateful for all you've done for me, but even that doesn't give you the right to dispose of my manhood, especially over such an important matter as my marriage."

This was the first occasion on which Arabella had ever known her grandson to revolt openly.

"It's hardly fair to attack me in this way," she said feebly, "especially as I'm a semi-invalid and have suffered an appalling shock."

Henry was instantly penitent, as she well knew he would be.

"I'm terribly sorry," he said gently, "and perhaps we should have selected some other time to discuss it. It hardly seems decent with a dead man under the roof."

"You yourself," she said, "have made the question a matter of urgency, I think. It is none of my doing."

"How have I done that?"

"Have you forgotten last night?"

Henry shivered at the recollection.

"No," he said, and foolishly added: "I'm not likely to, either."

The remark confirmed Arabella in her certainty of unchaste conduct.

"Lily is in love with you. She has told me—about yesterday."

"Told you what?"

"You cannot expect me to answer that question delicately."

"Whatever Lily has told you, Grannie, I assure you that—that —well, that nothing happened."

Arabella smiled incredulously.

"I could hardly expect you to say anything else," she said, "though your manner scarcely bears out your words. In any case, I have never known or even heard of a de Birkett who would miss an opportunity of that nature. No! Not even your Uncle Alfred!"

Henry made an impatient gesture.

"I assure you on my honour—" he began.

"I think," said Arabella, "that we may leave honour out of this;

if you persist, that is to say, in your refusal to right the wrong you have done this girl."

"I've done her no wrong," Henry cried indignantly. "None at all."

"Even if what you say is correct, that you have done no technical wrong, you have ruined this girl, spoiled her chance in the marriage market."

"Good Heavens," Henry said irritably, "we are talking like Victorian songs. ''E dun me wrong.' There's nothing in it at all."

"The girl thinks differently. So much so that I have written to her father telling him not to worry, and to get into touch with Merry about the settlements."

"How could you! The letter mustn't be sent."

"The letter has already been dispatched. I sent Caraway with it at once!"

"If Caraway has any conscience and knows what's in it, she'll throw it away!"

"I provided against any outbreak of that kind by instructing her to register the letter and bring me the receipt."

"How dared you do such a thing, Grannie?"

It was a genuine question, not an outbreak of temper.

"I dare do anything, my boy, when the honour and welfare of the de Birketts is at stake."

"Especially welfare," Henry said bitterly. "I think you brood about the de Birketts too much, Grannie. It's becoming an obsession. Everything has to be subordinated to some fantastic abstraction called the de Birketts."

Arabella touched the rings on her thin fingers, smoothed them and caressed them.

"I consider—I *know*," she said quietly, "that the future of England and therefore of the world rests on the de Birketts and others like them. You are the only real de Birkett left."

She spoke absolutely sincerely and evenly, like an oracle.

"Poor England! Poor wretched, miserable world," Henry muttered. There was something awe-inspiring about his Delphic grandmother, something that made outrageous words and deeds take on sweet reason.

"You may say," she went on, "that England is not what it was.

That is because the de Birkett Family is not what it was."

Q.E.D.!

Henry disentangled his mind from the web in which Arabella was folding it, and clung to his point.

"Anyhow," he said, "I am not going to marry Lily."

"I venture to disagree. I presume that you are still thinking of the Winslow girl. You must forget her, Henry."

"I never shall, nor can, nor wish to forget her."

"Henry, I'm an old woman near my grave. I have worked unceasingly for the Family and for you. I implore you not to betray my trust nor to nullify my life work."

"Oh, Grannie, you put me in an impossible position."

"Were the Winslow girl dead or non-existent, would you marry Lily?"

Dora dead! The idea was too horrible, too dreadful!

"I can't answer such a question."

"I insist on it."

"I shouldn't care much what happened. I love her, Grannie. She means everything on earth or in heaven to me."

"You should have thought of that yesterday."

Henry turned on her in exasperation.

"But I've already told you that Lily was not compromised. In any case, she's not just out of a convent."

"You must marry her within three months from now, Henry."

"Why the hurry? Why three months?"

"Should there be natural consequences of last night's indiscretion, they will be sufficiently obvious in three months' time to arouse comment amongst sniggering reporters or town gossips."

As her meaning gradually dawned on Henry, he was divided between a desire to smash things and to howl like the dog that ran through the city.

"Well, I'm damned!" he said, and it was the first time he had ever sworn before Arabella. "Utterly and completely damned. Oh, it's no use talking in circles; we get no farther. I must talk to Lily about this. Good night, Grannie."

"Aren't you going to kiss me?"

"Yes, I suppose so . . ."

He gave her a perfunctory kiss.

"Good night, my dear boy."

4

Owing to the arrival of Henry and Lily at The Grange, the sisters were that night sleeping at their own cottage, and when Henry returned to the drawing-room were on the point of departure. This was a great and obvious relief to Lily and Griffin, who had been exchanging covert winks and secret signs about the whisky.

"Good night, Henry," Vera said. "Good night, dear Miss Peploe. I expect we shall see you to-morrow at lunch, after the funeral. Lady Engleton, of course, will not be present at the sad ceremony, and I expect you will keep her company."

"Naturally, Miss Beamish. Good night."

"Good night, Mr. Griffin." Vera changed her tone and said stiffly: "I take it you will hold a formal reading of my brother's will after lunch?"

"Before lunch, if you don't mind. I must get back to Norwich, and the trains are very few and slow, as you know."

"As you wish, of course."

"Good night, Miss Sophie."

"Good night."

"Good night!"

Directly they had gone Lily heaved a great sigh of relief.

"Thank God!" she said shrilly. "Now for that drink. Pour me out a stiff 'un, Griffin."

Lily always addressed men by their surnames on short acquaintance. Griffin obeyed with a will, and helped himself as well.

"Lord Engleton?" he asked, with bottle poised.

"Please."

Lily sprawled herself in Vera's vacated chair.

"My Gawd!" she said. "My Gawd, what a couple! What a dragon that fat one is, eh? She makes me feel I want to make low-life signs."

She made a few, much to Griffin's delight. Henry looked on with what he felt to be rather an inane smile.

"Your grandmother's sharp, too. Knows her way about."

"Yes," Henry said abruptly. "She is. I want to talk to you about it."

"Not now," Lily said. "I just couldn't bear it. D'you know any good stories, Griffin?"

The pre-War whisky and the horror of Vera had made Griffin a trifle less discreet than usual.

"No," he said, "only the usual ones. But I found some stuff in the Major's desk that I'm going to cart away. Wouldn't do to leave it about; poor old chap's dead after all. I'll cart it away, unless you'd care for it?" he added, for Henry's benefit.

"What sort of stuff?"

"Hot books?" Lily asked eagerly. "I've got one or two that take a bit of beating. Let's have a look."

"No." Henry interposed. "Please not."

Griffin remembered himself.

"Of course not," he said, jumping up. "Sorry I mentioned it. But it just shows that you never know people. My old dad told me once about what he found in a clergyman's drawer when he was dead. Surprising! Well, I'm for bed."

He drank up and, after bidding them both good night, left them tactfully to their own devices.

"Pour me out another," Lily ordered. "I need it."

"Haven't you had enough?"

"No. I haven't had anything yet, and what the hell's it got to do with you, anyway?"

Henry poured her out the required drink, watching it carefully as if he were dispensing a medicine, and not bothering to answer the purely rhetorical question. Lily was dangling her legs over the arms of the chair with a certain defiance.

"Lily!"

"Uh-huh?"

"Why did you tell my grandmother that—that we—that last night we slept together?"

Lily swung her legs clear and stood up to him.

"I didn't tell her that. S'welp me God, I didn't."

"She thinks it, anyway."

"She assumed it with me, too. I didn't say Yes or No; just let her get on with it."

"You should have denied it at once, like I did."

"Why should I? I don't mind, one way or the other."

"That's not fair. She's written to your father."

Lily broke into a quick smile.

"Has she? Now there'll be a dust-up. You see, Henry, you might just as well have gone the whole hog yesterday as not."

"I've told you I'm in love with Dora Winslow and I'm going to marry her."

"Perhaps she won't want to, after this story gets around. I'll put it about myself, just to see."

"This is serious, Lily."

"Oh, everything's serious with you. That's what's wrong with you. You make a mountain of everything."

She got up wearily.

"I'm going to bed, and I won't knock on your door to-night. By the way, which is Griffin's room? He seems a sport."

"I wish to God you wouldn't talk like that."

Lily laughed.

"That's why I do it. Oh, Henry, my dear, what am *I* going to do? Tell me that. You don't want me, because I'm soiled goods."

"It isn't that."

"Not altogether, but partly it is. I've been a fool, my dear. I suppose I've got an attack of the Real Thing." She smiled rather ruefully. "I'm sorry for all my silliness, and now I'm either going to be a nun or any damn' man can have me who likes. . . . Good night."

"Good night, Lily. I'm sorry, too."

"There you go again. Show me my room and leave me alone. I'm tired. . . ."

"So tired," she said to herself a few minutes later, as she surveyed the gaunt Victorian bed prepared for her, "that I could sleep alone—even in that thing. Oh, damn *all* men!"

5

The funeral could hardly be described as a success. To start with, the undertakers had arrived too soon and being local men had known how to evade the licensing laws even at that early hour. It is a definite drawback to an undertaker's mute to have that nature that wears a fatuous smile after only a few drinks. The horses were black enough as far as the hearse went, but the others could only be described as being shades of black, and the tails were very obviously donned for the occasion.

There were three carriages (excluding the hearse) and five mourners to sort into them. The two sisters, Henry, Griffin and Caraway. Caraway was grand deputy for Arabella. The undertaker's idea was that the first two carriages should contain a sister, each accompanied by one of the gentlemen, and the last the odd lady.

He laboured hard to bring this about, but both the gentlemen managed to evade him until at last it became obvious to the meanest intelligence that neither of them meant to travel with Vera even the short distance to Mellingham Parva churchyard. The situation was finally solved by putting the sisters together.

The announcement in *The Times* had asked for "No flowers by request." "He would not have wished for them" Vera had said. Why he would have wished for no flowers was difficult to ascertain, but it saved expense and bother, and anyhow, where could one get flowers in Mellingham Parva at the end of a cold January?

It was a nasty day and the Vicar's surplice kept on blowing up and showing his legs (he wore no cassock) with subsequent loss of dignity. A few old men stood round the grave, for the Major had stood a pint or two of beer to the less fortunate.

The Tontines turned up and Captain Champneys, but to Vera's relief, they declined her lukewarm invitation to "come back to the house." There was only one cold boiled chicken and limited ham.

Noreen was there, and to Vera's indignation and surprise, was asked to return to the house by Griffin as an interested party in the Major's Will.

It is safe to say that the only people who enjoyed themselves were Noreen and Caraway, to whom it meant temporary freedom from their respective task-mistresses. They both cried. Sophie did not so much cry as "break down" all over Griffin, who was fearfully embarrassed. But it didn't take long. The sky-cracking words were spoken reverently enough and "our brother" was committed to the earth.

At The Grange the cold collation and Lady Engleton and Lily awaited their return. The mourners had an immediate glass of sherry to revive them sufficiently for what was to follow and Vera was nothing loth when Griffin suggested an immediate reading of the Last Will and Testament.

Henry, being thoroughly sick of Last Wills, tried to excuse himself, but Griffin was insistent. He, too, was, much to his surprise, an interested party.

Vera opened her goggle eyes a bit at this, but had no inkling or suspicion that she was not (perhaps with Sophie) possessor of all her brother's goods. Some little gift, perhaps, a gun or some such. She was puzzled by Noreen; could it be that ... that Hugh and Noreen ... ? Unthinkable!

They all sat down in the drawing-room. The card table had been provided for Griffin, to act as an altar on which to rest the Last Will. Arabella was there by courtesy; she just came and no one said her nay. Lily was there out of curiosity; she wasn't going to miss a bit of novel fun like this!

Noreen was provided with a hard chair near the door and sat on the edge of it.

Griffin bowed formally and put on his glasses.

"The Will of the late Major Beamish is quite simple," he said, "and is strangely enough only dated a few days ago. I have no other Will. In fact, I think this is the only Will in existence."

"It is providential that he thought of it," Vera said. "It would have been a great pity had he not done so."

"Quite," Griffin said shortly. "As you say, Miss Vera, most fortunate. Death duties are higher in cases of intestacy. The will is quite in order, properly signed and witnessed. Perhaps I'd better read it. After the usual provisions for just debts and funeral expenses, I am appointed executor and trustee."

"Surely there is no need for a trustee?" Vera asked.

"If you will allow me to read the document, Miss Beamish, you will learn that the provision for a trustee is quite in order."

Vera turned pink. She had been snubbed and, worse still, had her first inkling that all was not well as far as she was concerned.

"Go on," she snapped. "Your remark was uncalled-for."

Griffin swallowed his annoyance and read:

"To the girl Noreen Ramsbottom, I give and bequeath the sum of five pounds as some slight compensation for having been in the service of my sister Vera for the last six months. I am sorry for her."

"Lawk!" Noreen squealed. "Do I get five pounds for myself?"

"That's it," said Griffin with a smile.

"Ooray!"

"Monstrous," said Vera. She had grown purple under the posthumous insult. "I believe there is some other and more sinister reason for this disgusting bequest. Hugh's rudeness to me is typical and not unexpected."

Griffin went on reading.

"To the men who dug my grave one quart of mild and bitter beer each. This is to be regarded as funeral expenses and paid at once."

Griffin looked up.

"I've already attended to this very human and rather touching bequest," he said. Vera sniffed, and Lily began to wish she had met the late Major Beamish.

"To my sister Adelaide Charlotte Sophia the sum of twenty-five pounds and the freehold of the cottage now occupied by my sisters, known as Woodfulls."

Everyone turned and looked at little Sophie.

"Are all those names really yours?" Lily asked. "Adelaide and all that?"

Sophie blushed an acknowledgment.

"Bless us!" said Lily. "Who'd have thought it?"

Vera glanced at Sophie ferociously.

"But the freehold was already mine—ours, I should say."

"No, Miss Beamish. Your brother charged you no rent, but the covenants and deed (I have them here) are in your brother's name."

Vera snorted angrily.

"Rubbish!" she snapped. "Rubbish! I'll look into the matter. Go on," she added ferociously.

"The sum of three hundred pounds per annum which I have

allowed my sisters is to be paid, as before, from the estate for their use and during the lifetime of either or both of them. It is then to revert to the estate."

"But that money was *settled* on us. It was an unconditional gift," Vera cried loudly, now thoroughly alarmed.

"There is no trace of it," Griffin said.

"There soon will be! I'll have a real solicitor to look into this." She laughed bitterly and mirthlessly.

"Really, Miss Beamish! I must protest!"

"Protest away. Only wait, Mr. Griffin!"

Arabella was trying hard not to look triumphant, not to chuckle. It was a grand minute for her. Even Henry was avoiding Lily's eye.

Griffin flicked the sheet of foolscap before him angrily and went on with a certain relish.

"To my sister Ethel Caroline Vera the bottle of Lysol which was the cause of a certain quarrel between us which will be found in the bathroom cupboard; my wish being that she should do with it as I asked her at the time of the said dispute."

Everyone looked at Vera this time. Her face resembled nothing so much now as a map of the world—a large green patch for Russia, a blue patch for the United States, all seamed over by the frequent red patches of the British Empire. It then turned into a map that marked mountains and the depth of the sea, mostly white but with smudges and blue bits. Lily tittered and so restored sanity to the assembly; she liked the Major more and more. There was a flavour of Rabelais about him.

"What did he tell you to do with it?" she asked. She had read the directions on Lysol bottles, so her curiosity was more than natural.

"Drink it!" Vera said in a sepulchral voice. "Drink it!"

"But it's poison," Lily said, and then added after a pause: "Oh, I see. I get you! I thought p'raps—well, it don't matter!"

Griffin was anxious to get it all over, so went on rapidly before Vera had recovered sufficiently to butt in.

"The rest of my property, cash in hand, Life Insurance, securities, real estate, my guns and indeed all my personal possessions to my nephew, Henry, Baron Engleton."

Griffin cleared his throat and then added:

"That is all."

"*All!*" Vera cried, her voice rising in intensity. "*All!* I should hope so. I have been made a fool of! Who witnessed that outrageous document? Who witnessed it? I demand to know!"

"I have no objection to telling you," Griffin said easily. "It is witnessed by Arabella, Lady Engleton, and George Saunders—the gardener, I believe."

Vera turned on Arabella and let loose the full flood of her wrath.

"So it was you," she thundered. "I might have guessed it."

"One minute, *please.*" Arabella held up a restraining and imperious hand. "Your brother told me that he wished to leave his property to his nephew, his nearest male relative. He told me how you had treated him in the past, and I confess I was not surprised at his wish. He had been intending to take this step for some time past."

Henry had been too flabbergasted to say anything; this question of suddenly inheriting from newly made Wills was rather bewildering, not to say frightening.

"Good Heavens," he said. "This is all a complete surprise to me. I knew about the Life Insurance, but—I never dreamed that Uncle Hugh intended leaving me anything more. I'm not sure that . . ."

"It's quite natural, my lord. You were the Major's only male relative," Griffin said. "Think it over!"

Henry subsided, not sure what to say or do. Had the dispossessed been anyone else but Vera he would have tried to renounce the bequest, but something about Vera made him think twice about it.

"I shall contest that Will," Vera said. "There *is* such a thing as a man being mad, and what is called undue influence. That outrageous and abominable document doesn't sound like Hugh!"

"No," said Sophie. "Hugh was never very funny!"

Vera turned on her with such ferocity that Sophie cowered and Henry rose in alarm.

"Funny, do you think it? Funny! Very funny indeed. Dispossessed of a rightful heritage! Thrown like beggars into the street! Funny!"

She laughed with elephantine hysteria and then stopped abruptly. It was a fascinating though somewhat terrible experience to watch her. Her eyes goggled, her throat and bosom worked alternately, and her nose became purple as her face became white. Henry remained poised, half-standing. Even Arabella was appalled. Then slowly Vera became normal once more, outwardly at least. The convolutions ceased. How great the fierce spiritual conflict which had raged within had been only the Recording Angel could say.

"Shall I get you a glass of water?" Henry asked.

Vera waved him away.

"I *know*," Vera said, "who is at the bottom of all this. I *know!* You're a very wicked woman, Lady Engleton! I shall contest this Will!"

"I think you'll be ill-advised," Griffin said.

"You *would* think that. A fact which gives me encouragement. I shall fight you all! Come, Sophie."

Vera made a majestic progress to the door. Sophie seemed anxious, not unnaturally, to remain with the others. Her scared, birdlike face looked from one to the other, asking for help.

As Vera approached the door Noreen, who had never taken her eyes from her mistress since the Great Crisis, backed away in a semi-circle, still keeping her gaze fixed upon her. It is rather in the same way, as we are told by naturalists, that the deer is fascinated by the python. Vera stopped and frightened the girl still further.

"You, Noreen," she said ominously, "will go back to the cottage at once."

Noreen gave a squeak of apprehension.

"No!" she said. "Never again, miss. Never again! I'll send father round for my box."

"Your tin box shall never leave my house without a legal struggle."

"Then my mother won't send back the washing."

The beginnings of Vendetta in Norfolk. The situation was fast becoming Corsican. Vera once more gave her scornful laugh, forerunner of evil, and passed from amongst them, Sophie in her train. The survivors of the typhoon relaxed and Griffin mopped his forehead.

"Poor woman," Arabella said softly. "Poor demented creature!"

"You'd never believe it unless the eyes had seen it, would you?" Griffin murmured.

"I thought those things only happened in stories," Lily said.

Henry heaved a monumental sigh.

"I feel very badly about it all," he said. "I didn't want the old boy's money. Don't you think we'd better come to some arrangement with her? I'm sorry for poor Aunt Sophie."

Arabella had feared this and glanced up sharply. It was Griffin who spoke, however.

"Certainly not," he said sharply. "If Miss Vera had behaved reasonably we might have thought of it. As it is, I strongly deprecate the idea. They are both well provided for and Miss Sophie is fully protected."

"Has that woman any grounds for legal action?" Arabella asked casually. "Real grounds, I mean."

"I should say none whatever."

"Ah . . . !"

"She may start an action if she can get any lawyer foolish enough to take it up. She'll have to look sharp about it, as I shall apply for probate at once, and she must enter a caveat within ten days."

Vera didn't enter a caveat, for the very simple reason that within ten days she had entered the Valley of the Shadow of Death. Griffin wasn't to know that, however. It was only Arabella who had any information on that point.

Griffin looked at his watch and made strange noises with his teeth.

"What a bother. I've missed the train for Norwich."

"I'll run you in," Lily said. "I've got to get home to-day."

"There's no hurry, my dear child," Arabella interposed. "None whatever."

But there was for Lily, who was heartily sick of Mellingham Parva and all its ways. In any case, a trip with the gallant Griffin offered possibilities of escape from all this hullabaloo, offered a temporary anodyne for her aching and humiliated heart.

"I think, too," Arabella went on, "that we might have some lunch."

So they sat down to the cold boiled fowl and ham ordered by Vera as the final episode in Hugh's career.

Henry was hungry, and ate it, though it seemed, in a queer way, cannibalistic.

15

MEN OF THE WORLD

Henry wandered amongst the cabbage stumps and desolation of his new estate, the same vista that had thrilled Arabella sufficiently to make her tackle Hugh on the great question of his heir to such beauty. He stared at it and found it unlovely. Lily and Griffin had departed in a whirl of back-firing for Norwich, and Arabella was resting after the excitements of the fantastic Will-reading. Noreen had rushed off to the village to spread the good news of Vera's disappointment and of her own novel position as a legatee. She had now a dowry and was making the most of it with the boys of Mellingham.

Henry had examined the Grange in detail, made a tour of the desolate and half-empty rooms. It was gaunt and grim. The gun room especially gave him the shivers. That long row of shining barrels should be disposed of as quickly as possible. In fact, the whole place had better go in the market according to Griffin, and Henry was inclined to agree. It was a dispiriting occupation, and Henry felt morally bankrupt at the end of his stock-taking. He was profoundly uneasy, and remembered Dora's remark about founding the House on dead bodies, or words to that effect. The bodies seemed to pile up.

Why had Uncle Alfred altered his Will under such strange conditions? Why had Uncle Hugh left him a stiver? There was no answer, except something that he dared not think of. And that something was too vague to formulate. Arabella? Arabella figured in it somewhere and was assuming a somewhat displeasing position in his muddled head. Disconsolate, he wandered into the village and arranged for a car to convey Arabella and the rest of them to Norwich the following day.

On his return he found his grandmother engaged in her perennial self-cheat at the game of "Miss Milligan."

"I've arranged for the car to-morrow," he said.

"I shall be glad to return home. This visit has been a tragic experience," Arabella said, sweeping up a sequence of cards. "Most tragic. I doubt if I shall ever get over it."

"I feel rather guilty about Aunt Vera."

"There is no occasion, my dear boy. As Mr. Griffin so correctly observed, ample provision has been made for her. Your uncle disliked her. He told me as much. Why should he leave her his money?"

"I'm scarcely surprised at his dislike. But I was afraid she might burst something or take to drink."

"Take to drink? That might indeed be a solution." She bent over the table once more, shifting the little packs of cards. "I have had a reply to my Communication to Mr. Peploe."

"A reply?" Henry sat up and took notice.

"A wire. You may see it."

She pushed a telegram over, which Henry opened. It was very lengthy and must have cost old Peploe a small fortune:

Mr. Peploe presents his compliments to Lady Engleton and begs to thank her for her esteemed communication Stop Can't think what young people are coming to Stop Agrees that marriage only solution Stop Lady Engleton will not find Mr. Peploe ungenerous under distressing circs Stop Demands amends in name of decency Stop Have honour to remain Peploe

"Somewhat muddled," Arabella said, when Henry threw the thing on one side, "and confusing as to grammar. The purport is obvious, though. It cost him four shillings and fourpence, an even clearer indication of his anxiety and grief than the words themselves."

Henry was too weary to argue the point, and, truth to tell, too frightened. His grandmother had a way of winning arguments, so he contented himself by preserving a moody silence.

Arabella smiled to herself. She was not accustomed to losing her games of patience, and, as we have seen, was not scrupulous as to her methods of victory. One can always juggle the cards.

2

"Now it ain't no good shilly-shallying, or prevaricating. Did you or did you not sleep with his lordship?"

"You can ring up the hotel and find out!"

Lily had arrived home to find her father ready for battle and waiting. She faced him fiercely, but he had her at a disadvantage. She was tired, and he was roasting his hindquarters at the fire after a good dinner.

"You can't diddle me like that, my girl," old Peploe said with infinite cunning. "I've rung 'em up already."

"Well, then?"

"True you occupied different rooms. But that don't signify. Rooms 'as doors an' doors 'as 'andles." He added this as one who has discovered a great natural secret. "There is such a thing as creeping about. Did 'e creep?"

"No. Henry's a gentleman."

"Even gents creeps."

Lily tore off her beret and flung it on the sofa.

"You make me sick," she cried. "You've got a dirty mind. You and your creeping! You ought to know."

"I don't want none of your cheek. For the last time, did you or did you not——"

"No!" Lily shouted suddenly. "No, I didn't."

Even old Peploe was a trifle taken aback by her vehemence.

"You'd 'ave to say that any'ow," he mumbled. "You owe it to yourself!"

"Oh, *do* I?" Lily said with heavy sarcasm. "*Do* I? I shall damn' well sleep with whom I like, so there!"

"Not in this house you won't."

"There isn't anyone in this house I want to sleep with," Lily retorted. "Unless it's Jennings," she added as an afterthought. Jennings was a good-looking chauffeur who propelled the Peploe Rolls.

"Ter think," old Peploe said with pathos, appealing to Heaven to be his witness, "ter think it should come to this! With a lord, too! After all the cash I've spent 'aving you educated."

"Shut it," said Lily wearily.

"Ruined by a lord! Never mind. Right's right, and lord or no lord, 'e'll 'ave to do the right thing."

"Do you—or do you not," Lily said in dramatic imitation of her august father—"do you—or do you not—think I'm a virgin?"

Peploe blew out his cheeks and sucked them in again.

"Well!" he said, outraged. "Well!"

"Do you—or do you not——"

"Course I do! You oughtn't to talk like that."

"Well, guess again!"

"That's an admission, that is." Peploe pointed a stubby, minatory finger at Lily and proceeded to waggle it.

"Stow it!" Lily shouted. "Pipe down! You've got no business to talk, anyway, not if half what the girls in the wholesale say is true. What about that Gwendoline?"

"None o' that, my girl!"

"Well, you had to pay her a hundred pounds. *Why?*"

"To save scandal and stop a lot o' parrots from chattering!"

"Sez you!"

"It'll cost more'n hundred to 'ush all this up!"

"Bah!" It wasn't exactly that that Lily said, but near enough.

"Look at yer pore mother now—just see what you've done!"

Odd as it may appear, Mrs. Peploe seemed to have been overlooked, and she was certainly not a sight to be lightly disregarded. Picture to yourself an infant hippopotamus seated in an arm-chair in a distressed state with a triple tiara of wax-like hair, and you have a faint idea of Mrs. Peploe. She was still swathed in tightly-stretched silk—she had an idea that she looked thinner in silk. A small handkerchief was pressed to her eyes and at intervals the body gave a jump like a hiccup. Lily let her eye dwell on her mother for a second or two.

"If I'd done anything," Lily said, "I could understand her behaving like that."

Mrs. Peploe looked up.

"I'm sure you don't get it from me," she said. "When I was

behind the bar lots of lords tried to have a cut at me. Even a vizz-count. But I always kept my pride and kept——"

"Myself *to* myself," Lily finished for her.

"That's right." Mrs. Peploe seemed surprised at her daughter's ability to read her thoughts. "Your father even tried hard, but . . ." She stopped, aware that she was blundering. "And," she went on, "I've forgiven your father over that Gwendoline—*and* the other two."

Mr. Peploe glared at his spouse.

"Go on," he said bitterly. "Go on. I paid that 'undred to save the name of Peploe from stinking."

"It's the only thing that you saved," Lily retorted. "The eggs stink, the marge stinks, the bacon stinks, and the tea tastes of road sweepings."

"You shouldn't say such things, Lily," Mrs. Peploe said reproachfully. "I've had worse tea than your father's 2/4. The others don't seem to draw much, I'll admit . . ."

"Look 'ere," old Peploe bawled. "Which side are you on, Gladeyes? 'Ers or mine?"

"Yours, of course," Mrs. Peploe answered, surprised that her loyalty should be doubted. "That's why I've been crying. Because Lily's been sinful, not because of being on your side."

"For Gawd's sake go on crying then!"

Mrs. Peploe obeyed at once.

"As for you, my girl," Peploe went on, "I 'ardly know what to say, and that's a fack."

"Hold your jaw, then."

"You've got a damn' cheek. Ungrateful little 'orror, stinging of the bosom that's warmed you. Never mind! I've seen Merry, and you'll marry this young rip or I'll know the reason why."

"*Will* you?" Lily said. "You can lead a horse to the mare, but you can't make 'em marry!"

"There ain't no call to be indelicate. Do you like 'im?"

"Yes, I do."

"Then what are you making all this fuss for?"

"Who's making a fuss?"

"You are!"

"I'm not. . . ."

"Then you ought to be makin' a fuss. You've been sedooced and you be'ave as if you just 'ad a cup o' tea! But lord or no lord, he's got to marry you. You can bring an action against a man for seduction."

"I haven't been seduced."

"Well, your good name's gone, any'ow. 'Er ladyship as good as says so."

"She's after your money."

This was so obvious that Mr. Peploe ignored it.

"You're a disgrace, my girl. After all the money I've spent on you! I might just as well have poured it down the sink or—or——"

"Given it to that Gwendoline!"

"Don't you so much as breathe that name again. Before your mother too! Can't think who told you."

"Mother told me," Lily said with relish. "Mother told me."

Mrs. Peploe put her handkerchief away.

"Oh, Lily," she moaned, "'ow can you? I'm sure I've always tried to keep you pure. Once let a man be familiar, I said, and there's no stopping him, and when there's no stopping him— well, you never know what might happen, I said."

This was Mrs. Peploe's sole contribution to the great problem of sex education. Peploe was annoyed with his wife and transferred his attentions from Lily.

"'Ow dare you tell Lily a lot o' nonsense about me?" he bawled.

"The girl 'erself said . . ."

"Girls say anything!"

"But you 'ad to admit you 'ad that private room."

"When my girls is in trouble, they come to me for 'elp. She pulled a bit o' blackmail. I never touched 'er."

"A hundred pounds is mingy, anyway," Lily chimed in.

"Who's in trouble, me or Lily?" Peploe snorted indignantly. "By the way you talk you'd think it was *me* who'd been sleepin' with a lord. I'm 'ere to say what's going to be, not to be ticked off."

Lily jumped to her feet.

"Look here, Dad," she said decisively, "you dry up. I'm not in trouble, and for the hundredth and last time, I didn't sleep with a lord. That's *that!*"

"Nice thing if you start 'aving a child."

Lily raised her hand.

"One more word, and I'll smack your face!"

Peploe saw the light in her eye and refrained from pursuing the subject.

"Well, we'll 'ope it won't come to that."

Lily turned on her heel and slammed the door behind her.

"If she were a bit younger," Peploe said, "I'd turn her over my knee and give 'er a good hiding. Never mind! Right's right!" He felt he had scored a moral victory.

Lily cried herself to sleep that night, torturing herself with visions of her lurid little past. She had one determination firmly embedded in her heart when she woke. If she could win Henry by her own methods, she would. That was fair hunting. But she would under no circumstances have him bullied into matrimony. She happened to love him too much for that.

3

Arabella had made an error when she thought that Henry's unwillingness to discuss the Lily situation was due to a growing complaisance. He had quite definitely avoided mentioning Lily since Mellingham Parva had been left behind. It would therefore have surprised her to learn that he was waiting for Mr. Merry at his office the very morning after the return. Merry greeted him with lawyer-like cordiality. He had already had an interview with Peploe and was expecting another.

"Glad to see you, Henry," he said heartily, thrusting out a hand which Henry ignored. "Come in. Come in." He waved a hand towards a chair. "May I congratulate you," he said, "on your new heritage? Major Beamish's death was very sad, very tragic, of course, but I'm glad you've come in to the estate. Let me congratulate you."

"No, thanks," Henry said coldly. "I'm in two minds as to whether or not to refuse the legacy."

"Come, come!"

"In any case, Mr. Merry, I've come to see you about a different matter."

Merry looked concerned, pretending ignorance of the gist of the remark. Then a flash of enlightenment passed over his face and he looked waggish.

"Ah," he said, "I presume you refer to the settlement with Mr. Peploe. Quite a romance! I'm happy to have been the unconscious instrument in bringing it about. Very charming girl! You may safely leave the business side of it to me."

Merry had heard all about the Ely affair from both Peploe and Arabella, but it was no business of his to refer to it; he had also vaguely gathered that Henry was being what is called "difficult."

"I'll thank you, Mr. Merry, not to interfere in my affairs at all. There is no romance, no settlement, and no marriage!"

Merry leaned back in his chair and appeared thunderstruck.

"Good heavens," he murmured, "you surprise and, if I may say so, shock me, my boy."

Henry jumped to his feet and leaned forward over the desk.

"Look here, Mr. Merry," he said quietly, "you and I may as well understand one another. You and my grandmother and Mr. Peploe entered into a conspiracy, an indecent conspiracy, to force me into marriage with Lily. Nothing doing!"

"I resent that word 'conspiracy.'"

"I don't withdraw it."

Merry gasped with astonished indignation.

"This doesn't sound like you, Lord Engleton. I can barely credit my hearing."

"No one ever seems able to believe their ears if I speak the truth. I am growing up, Mr. Merry. Living with my grandmother has made me precocious. I'm refusing to be ordered about any more!"

"You force me to refer to a disagreeable episode. I gather both from Lady Engleton and from Mr. Peploe that you and his daughter spent the night together at a hotel at Ely. As a man of honour . . ."

"If you speak of honour, Mr. Merry, you'll force me to mention another disagreeable episode—the episode of Uncle Alfred's Will."

This was a thrust, and Merry flinched under it. He disliked that episode extremely; it jagged at his conscience.

"Lord Engleton," he said, "were you not your father's son I should refuse to handle the family affairs any longer, if that is your attitude."

"You needn't bother. When I handle my own life in a few months' time I intend to change my legal adviser. You can't gammon me that Peploe has any sort of case against me, either legal or moral. You are working for my grandmother and for her monomania about the financial status of the de Birketts, and you are apparently willing to blackmail me into a marriage that is distasteful. There has been nothing between Lily and myself. Do you believe that?"

Forced into a corner, Merry found it difficult to reply. At heart he *did* believe Henry, but being as anxious as anyone that the Peploe alliance should come about, had to take refuge in prevarication.

"How can I do otherwise than believe you when you assure me that there has been a mistake? But I'm a man of the world, and in view of Miss Peploe's own statement . . ."

"Lily never made a statement, as you call it. My grandmother has just got it all wrong, deliberately wrong, if you ask me. I've noticed, too, that when a man says he's 'a man of the world' it's always to cover up some piece of slime or dirtiness."

Merry positively bridled.

"How dare you, Henry! I'm older than you are, and have nothing but your real interests at heart."

"I repeat that you needn't bother. You can represent Peploe and my grandmother, but not me. I don't want 'a man of the world.' I'd prefer a man of God."

"Sheer melodrama! You are all worked up. Go away quietly and think things over." Merry felt that by rights he ought to be in a temper. Somehow he had ceased feeling indignation for many years, even righteous indignation. It just wouldn't come when summoned from the vasty deep of his heart. "You have been extremely rude to me," he said. "Did I not realize your youth, had I not served your family for years, I should . . ."

"Damn the Family!" Henry said tersely and without heat. "Damn the de Birketts! Damn the title! I wish I'd been born in a slum and called Smith. This Family obsession is getting us all down; it's driven my grandmother half-dotty and it's ruining my whole existence. Damn the Family!"

He seemed to get a peculiar satisfaction from damning the Family and mouthed the phrase affectionately. Just as Merry was opening his mouth to repudiate such blasphemy, the telephone on the desk buzzed. It is an extraordinary fact that men will break off any conversation, however important, in order to answer a telephone. A startled look came into his lack-lustre eyes.

"Dear me," he stammered. "This is most unfortunate. Mr. Peploe is in the outer office. What on earth are we going to do?" He glanced apprehensively at the window as if he half-expected Henry to escape over the roof or take a flying leap into the street below.

"Have him in. Let's have a show-down and see what happens."

"Mr. Peploe is not refined when in a temper."

"Good! Nature in the raw! When exactly *is* he refined, by the way?"

Further discussion was saved by the entrance of Peploe in person. He didn't know quite how to tackle his future son-in-law —whether to bully or placate.

"Ho!" he said when he saw the recumbent Henry, irritated that he didn't rise. "Stealin' a march, are you?"

"Good morning, Mr. Peploe," Merry remarked.

Peploe paid no attention.

"I was comin' 'ere," he went on rapidly, "to make a 'andsome settlement, but from what I 'ear it don't look as if it's welcome. Yes or no?"

"No," said Henry.

The simple monosyllable roused the Peploe temper more effectively than anything else could have done.

"No?" he said irritably. "'Ow d'yer mean—No?"

"Just that," Henry said with an insolence that surprised himself. He made an airy gesture, theatrical and irritating.

"You got a nerve! Are you telling me what I can do with it?"

"Yes."

Peploe's comb of hair rose like a parakeet.

"No! Yes! Yes! No! Can't you say anything else? Are you going to marry my girl?"

"No!"

"But your grandmother wrote and told me . . ."

"My grandmother can suck eggs!"

"Good morning, Mr. Peploe," Merry said again, feeling out of it. When all was said and done it was his office, not a battleground for clients.

"Do be quiet with your 'good mornin's,' Merry. This is serious. This 'ere young rip goes on the tiles with my girl and then comes and talks like this. Can we have the law on him, Merry?"

"I doubt it."

"But you can't go sedoocin' girls for nothin'."

"Indeed, no." Merry coughed. It was he who had arranged the hundred pounds for "that Gwendoline."

"Well, then. There you are!"

Henry jumped up suddenly and crossed over to Peploe, who quickly dodged behind a chair. He noticed the boy's clenched fist.

"Do you say," Henry asked angrily, "that I seduced your daughter?"

"Yes, I do."

"You are a dirty liar, then!"

"If I was a bit younger I'd give you a hiding, young man, lord or no lord."

"And if you say it again I'll sue you for slander and give you a sock on the jaw first."

Merry flapped his hands rapidly to restore order.

"No violence, please!"

"If 'e so much as touches me I'll 'ave 'im up for assault. Yes, and I'll tell the magistrate all about it."

"And I'll tell him about the whole dirty conspiracy."

"That's right. Drag your pore old grannie into it."

Henry picked up his hat.

"I'm not going to marry Lily. That's final!"

Merry sighed deeply, as one outraged by moral depravity.

"Think again, Lord Engleton. Think again! Say nothing in a hurry."

Henry turned on him savagely.

"As for you, Merry, you can thank your stars it's not Rat Week."

"Rat Week?"

"Think it over!"

He stamped through the outer office, scattering papers that were piled on desks. Mistaking the door, he went into a lavatory by accident, thinking he was going into the street, to the delight of the two typists. He emerged and made a blushing departure, covered with confusion. It was just his luck.

"Nice young hopeful, isn't he?" Peploe said, looking at the empty door. "If he was my boy I'd give him a good tanning."

"I'm horrified, my dear Mr. Peploe!" Merry said, scandalized. "But we'll draw up the settlement. Leave him to Lady Engleton. I've never known her fail."

"I'm not sure I want him for a son-in-law. But right's right, and I've got my pore girl to think of."

"Rat Week? I wonder what he meant by *that* remark."

"Ain't you got any sense, Merry?" Peploe lacked finesse. "'Ee meant 'e'd break your back."

"Strange," Merry said meditatively. "I've never known him behave like this before. He has always been so docile hitherto. I can't make it out."

"Scared! That's what he is. Blue funk."

"It seems the only explanation. . . ."

16

COUNTERPOINT

Vera had spent the day in Norwich and had returned to Mellingham in a bad temper. She had interviewed no fewer than three solicitors with the hope of getting them to consent to contest her brother's will. Two of them had politely declined, one because he thought she had no grounds and said so, and the other because he hadn't liked her face. This last had had clients like that before, and they had just been a nuisance.

The third, however, had been more hopeful. He hadn't much to do and thought there might be a few pickings hanging on to it. But he had been cautious; he must see the documents, interview Griffin before he would commit himself to any definite opinion. Had Mr. Griffin yet applied for probate? Probably not.

The result was a fit of peculiarly bad temper for Vera. It hung about her like a pall. Sophie was sufficiently used to her sister not to broach the matter till after supper. She was now doing all the housework, Noreen having stood by her resolution never to return to Woodfulls—never no more. Her mantle had therefore fallen on Sophie's thin little shoulders. It saved expense, anyway, but the mantle was a heavy one and Vera did nothing to lighten the burden, except a trifle of dusting on occasion. Even Sophie, who rarely complained, thought it a bit unfair, but then her sister was so masterful that she hardly dared mention the matter, nor had her temper improved since Sophie's acquisition of the house as a legal right. Clearly the visit to Norwich had not been the complete success that had been anticipated.

"Have some more hash, Vera dear?" Sophie said brightly, and with unconscious humour, added: "You need cheering up."

Vera pushed her plate away.

"Hash!" She gave her telling, bitter laugh. "Hash! It would choke me!"

Probably a case of the last straw and the camel's back, seeing that she had consumed the bulk of the dishful.

"I'm so sorry, dear. I made it with nutmegs, specially to tempt you."

"You do your best, Sophie. Far be it from me to deny it, but you also fidget me."

"I'm sorry." Sophie subsided; best let her sister do the talking. The rice pudding (made with milk) subsequent to the hash was consumed in a silence that was funereal, punctuated by Vera's little laughs; laughs that seemed to say: "How vile is the world and all that crawls on its crust."

Hash and rice did their work, however, and over the fire afterwards Vera became more communicative.

"I have had a disappointment," she announced. "No fewer than three lawyers have I seen to-day."

"What did they say?"

"They were not sanguine. Two of them declined to assist poor lone women, the other requiring a sum of money in advance to meet what he calls necessary preliminary expenditure. If that outrageous Will is overthrown, there will be enough and to spare!"

There was a pause.

"Vera, dear," Sophie put in timidly, "do you think it wise to fight this? I mean—you're right, of course—but we have enough to live upon. We are no worse off than we were before."

Vera turned a glassy eye on her sister.

"How can you say that?" she asked. "I only live under this roof on sufferance, whereas I should live at The Grange and take my place in Society as a right."

"Worrying about it is making you quite ill, dear."

"Lysol!" Vera said. "Think of it! After all I did for that man. Lysol! He must have been mad, influenced by that wicked woman. How dared she do it? Especially after the cruel indignities we suffered over that terrible medical examination, after we had been bamboozled."

Both sisters preserved a short and impressive silence when they thought of the insurance doctor.

"I asked this lawyer—a Mr. Lambton—whether we could cancel our policies, and explained the circumstances. Why should that boy benefit when I am called to my reward? He has robbed me!"

"It doesn't matter much either way."

"That is precisely what Mr. Lambton said. He also said that he had never met a similar case. But I'll fight it, if it costs me all I have."

As she had next to nothing, the remark was rhetorical.

"Dear, dear," Sophie said. "It's all very sad, but you mustn't say you are here on sufferance. We share everything alike."

"It's the vile principle of it. The foul insults! That legacy to Noreen. What talk that has created, what scandal! Why should that disorderly little slut rob me of five pounds?"

Vera was working herself into a frenzy that was becoming a chronic ailment.

"You need cheering up," Sophie said again.

"How Lady Tontine must be laughing! The story is widespread; Noreen has seen to that. I can't bear it!"

"Ssh, dear! Gently!" Then Sophie had a bright but lethal brain-wave. "Let us sample my home-made whisky. It'll do us both good!"

Subsequent events hardly confirmed her optimism, but the intention was sound, and she bustled off to fetch the results of her bootlegging.

"It is not a very nice colour, but it has stopped working and can be drunk at once!"

She poured herself out a thimbleful and a much more gen-erous portion for her sister. Vera had a weakness for home-made wines. She experienced all the joys of alcohol and yet remained a moral teetotaller. Home-made wines were somehow not in the category of "drink." She swallowed a large mouthful of the inauspicious-looking stuff, rolling it round with the air of a con-noisseur.

"It tastes odd and rather unpleasant," she said, "but the effect is warming."

Sophie sipped hers more gingerly.

"Not very palatable," she said. "It tastes of the preserving pan."

Vera poured herself out a further and even more generous portion with all the abandon of a Socrates, but when she had finished, there was nothing left for a libation. The result was the same for all that, with the difference that Socrates knew what he was doing and Vera didn't.

A few minutes later the two sisters exchanged a perfunctory, sisterly kiss and went to their respective rooms; Sophie had care-fully laid the breakfast.

A few hours later Sophie awoke, or at least regained conscious-ness. She had been tortured by hideous and hellish dreams. Some Satanic creature had been striking at her head with a hammer and she had screamed to her God for protection. Sweat was on her face and her limbs seemed froglike in their damp chill. The pulsating agony in her head went on with rhythmic insistence, and screams still echoed in her ears.

"Oh, merciful God, save me—save me!"

The realization dawned slowly in her aching head that she was ill, that she was in agony, that her heart was thumping painfully.

With trembling fingers she struck a match and lit the candle at her bedside. She was ill, desperately ill, dying perhaps. She must go to her sister, drag herself like some stricken animal. Vera's room was just across the landing—only a few feet, but it seemed miles to Sophie. The pain in her stomach was intense and she retched in agony. Oh, God, give her poor little legs strength! Confused thoughts chased each other over the screen of her mind. She thought of the eggs (new-laid) by the frying-pan. She didn't fancy eggs, probably would never eat an egg again. There was the cat, he who had watched Arabella as he ate illicit custard. Was he in?

"Puss, puss!" Sophie just framed the words with parched lips. "Puss, puss! Tibby!"

She felt the sweat course down her face and fall in great drops from her nose. Agony and bloody sweat! That was it! Why hadn't she thought of it before? She nearly laughed at the simplicity of it. Agony and bloody sweat. From Sudden Death, Good Lord deliver me. Perhaps she was dying. Sophie wished intensely that she hadn't given the bus conductor that foreign coin. A French coin it was, like a penny, with a man's head upon it. A bearded man, not a bit like our own King, The door—at last! She must get to Vera somehow, just over the landing, and wake her. Vera was not always very kind to her, but she would be thoughtful if her poor sister were really ill. She turned the handle and leaned against the lintel, candle in hand. Her head was in agony and she felt weak.

She fixed her eyes on the opposite door—Vera's door. Vera was awake, thank God, for a fitful light flickered at the key-hole; despite the pain in her head she could hear a hand groping for the handle. What was the matter, in God's name? Vera's door slowly opened and she saw her sister. She, too, held a candle in her hand. She, too, groaned and leaned against the lintel for rest. Sophie almost forgot her own distress at the sight. Vera's face was a mottled green, her eyes goggled from grey sockets. She heard a voice croaking:

"A doctor! I'm dying!"

Then the hand that grasped the candlestick drooped and sagged; the candlestick clattered to the floor and lay on its side still burning. Slowly Vera's great body slid to the floor and lay there unconscious. Sophie crawled over to her and setting the candle upright once more, peered into the other's ashy, blue-lipped face.

"Help!" she called, and could hear no sound.

Oh, God, give poor little Sophie strength! Grasping the banisters she heaved herself up and fell across the handrail. The sudden blow on her stomach made her violently sick. Her head swam and there was a filthy taste of metal in her mouth.

Somehow she must get down these stairs and get to Dodson next door. Dodson was a common labourer, and she felt ashamed that he must see her in her nightdress, but he was a good, kind creature and would understand when he knew how bad she was. At the top stair, Sophie let herself fall, grabbing the banisters as she went. That was quicker than trying to walk. Across the little parlour and into the front garden. How chilly it was, and there was rain falling! It was pleasant, though, and the thought entered her head that it would be good to lie there and let the rain just come down on her, soak her through. Then she remembered the face upstairs. No, that wouldn't be fair on Vera; she must drag herself on. The sharp stones on the path were cutting her hands and knees.

"Dear me, I hope Dodson won't think me immodest!"

Only a few feet more!

Her hands grasped the large, cold iron ring of Dodson's knocker. Panic seized her and she beat it till she fell fainting.

A few minutes later Dodson came out and saw the huddled little white heap, and wrapping it quickly in his overcoat, ran with it in his arms to the Vicarage.

The sickly light peered into Vera's bedroom. She was dead, and the doctor and the police sergeant had together straightened out the twisted limbs and covered the tortured eyes. The sergeant mopped his glistening forehead. Jobs like this weren't common at Mellingham Parva.

"First the Major," he muttered, "and now his sister. Pretty horrible sights, both of 'em!"

The doctor murmured his agreement.

"What did she die of, eh, doctor?"

"Poisoning of some sort. There'll have to be a post-mortem."

He stroked his chin reflectively. "It's lucky the other sister was sick, or they'd be side by side."

"Will she live?"

"Wouldn't bet on it."

They went downstairs slowly.

"Look here, sergeant," the doctor said with sudden resolution, "you go into Norwich as fast as car can take you. We both want help badly. Ask Dr. MacPherson to come back with you—and better leave this at the city analyst for immediate test. See?" He handed the sergeant a carefully-wrapped tooth mug.

"Good idea, doctor. It's all beyond me."

He was giving a constable directions to stay on guard when the doctor went over to the sideboard and eyed the "whisky" and the dirty glasses with suspicion.

"What's this muck?" he asked.

"Lord knows, sir. Home-made wine, I expect."

The doctor took the cork out and smelt the contents; the puzzled frown on his face deepened.

"I think," he said, "I think it would be worth while taking these as well. . . ."

The Vicar and his wife fought the Angel of Death for possession of Sophie. They were good souls and had not forgotten the first of the Corporal Works of Mercy. They fought for hours. The poor little creature seemed icily cold; her lips were blue and her limbs seemed paralysed; the pulse almost gone. An injection of strychnine almost literally tore her back as she was entering death's portal. Later she seemed in less pain; there was a faint tinge of pink in her pallid cheeks. It seemed that Sophie might live after all. Dr. MacPherson, who came over from Norwich, thought so, at any rate.

"She has all the symptoms of acute lead poisoning," he said. "However, we shall soon know; they are going to phone the result of that analysis, but I don't think there's much doubt about it."

"Are they analysing that 'whisky' stuff as well?"

"Yes. We shall get both reports at once."

Later that afternoon the reports came through and the opinion was justified. It was by no manner of means complete, but the first tests had revealed the presence of a large quantity of lead acetate and a trace of antimony; enough to kill an ox.

2

That same morning the Vicar had put through a trunk call and briefly informed Henry of his aunt's death and of her sister's dangerous condition. Henry had gone cold with apprehension and his spine had tingled. It was horrible, gruesome! He nerved himself to ask for details.

"It seems that they have been poisoned in some way."

"Can I be of any assistance?"

"None whatever. I thought you should be informed, that is all."

"Thank you . . ."

Arabella took the news calmly. She had not yet got up and Caraway was making preparations for the morning levee.

"I'm afraid, Grannie, I've got bad news for you."

"Indeed?"

"Aunt Vera is dead and Aunt Sophie desperately ill."

Caraway turned sharply and caught her breath. Arabella looked up from a letter she was reading.

"So that was why the telephone rang?"

"Yes. It was the Vicar of Mellingham; he thought we should be informed."

"Very obliging of him, I'm sure. And what did Vera die of?"

"Some sort of poisoning, it seems."

There was a crash on the washstand; Caraway had dropped a tooth mug and, white and shaking, was surveying the pieces. Arabella snarled at her.

"What on earth are you doing? Have you no consideration for my nerves?"

"I—I'm sorry, m'lady."

"So you ought to be. Aren't you well?"

"This bad news, m'lady—it gave me a turn."

"It is just as well we are to see Mr. Hamish this morning!" She turned away impatiently and resumed the even tones she adopted in normal conversation. "Your Aunt Vera," she said, addressing

Henry once more, "was not a pleasant woman, or an agreeable or even interesting character. My grief, therefore, is qualified."

Henry was revolted by her callousness.

"It surprises me that you take these things so calmly," he said. "It's just ghastly. First Uncle Hugh shot through the eye and now . . ."

"Please don't refer to Major Beamish. Dear me," she went on, "how annoying. They have sent the *Sketch* instead of the *Mirror*."

Henry noticed that Caraway was biting her underlip and could hardly hold the toilet articles she was setting out; her hands shook and her mouth was twitching. Arabella resumed the reading of her letter, turned over the last page of it and then removed her spectacles.

"Go away, Caraway," she said. "I wish to speak privately to his lordship."

Caraway turned on her heel and hurried from the room without a word.

"I think," Arabella said when the door was shut, "that it is highly probable that I shall dismiss Caraway before long. Her behaviour becomes less and less satisfactory. However, I have something more important than that to discuss with you, something more important even than Aunt Vera's death, though we must not forget the insurance. The mortgages on the Priory should quickly disappear—in fact, *will* disappear, if Sophie follows as well."

Henry waited through this rigmarole. He had a pretty good idea that the letter which lay before Arabella emanated from Merry and, hardening his heart accordingly, waited for her to come to business, to what was really the matter in hand. He knew Arabella's preambles of old. She tuned up, as it were.

"I'm not at all pleased with you, Henry."

Six months ago Henry would have been sincerely perturbed by this opening, but now he experienced a queer sense of elation; he was quite definitely glad she was displeased.

"Not at all pleased," she repeated. "It appears that yesterday without my knowledge you visited Mr. Merry and had an interview with Peploe; that you were rude and even, so Merry says, violent, though I can hardly credit that. Peploe is very angry, as

indeed he has every right to be, as we had already come to a preliminary understanding about his daughter, whose good name
you have soiled."

"Peploe has no right to be annoyed. He was insulting to me
and I threatened to hit him."

"An aged man?" Arabella lifted her eyebrows.

"If you like. He asked for it. And I have not soiled his daughter's good name."

"That is a matter of opinion."

"It is not. It is a stark fact that I've done nothing of the sort."
Henry clenched his fist and with the other hand clutched the
mantelpiece and prepared for battle.

"I suppose you will threaten to strike me, helpless in bed, if
I suggest that you are behaving like a cad and wish you to go at
once to Peploe and apologize?"

"You can suggest what you like, Grannie, but I shan't go."

Arabella suddenly lost her temper and stung by his obstinacy,
leaned forward and hissed at him:

"It's lucky for you, you young puppy, that this girl has no
brother, or I should tell them to buy a horsewhip. I loathe the
thought that you are a de Birkett, and if I didn't love the family I
should loathe *you*."

She was positively venomous in her denunciation; she shook
with rage. Never before had such a thing occurred; normally she
had only to issue an edict to have it promptly obeyed and without
question. Was she, who in attaining her ends had not been
thwarted even by death, to be obstructed by this callow youth?
Henry preserved a mulish silence.

"You make me feel," she went on, "that the de Birketts aren't
worth saving. You've no courage; you're lily-livered. Your ancestors may have been immoral, but they weren't skunks."

"I agree," Henry burst out, "the de Birketts aren't worth
saving. You may as well know now that I've no intention of
accepting Uncle Hugh's money or the insurance on those dead
bodies. Can't you see that I hate all this atmosphere of corpses
and intriguing? I'm sick of it! I want to breathe. I'd *rather* be poor.
If that's cowardice, then I'm a coward all right."

There was a silence after this tirade. Arabella was holding

her horn-rimmed glasses by the shank between her finger and thumb. Henry watched her shaking hand. Suddenly the shank snapped in two. The old woman said nothing, but carefully placed the broken piece on the side.

"That must go to the optician," she said at last. She seemed to have recovered from the violence of her fury and merely said coldly: "I wish you were dead, Henry, that the family might come to an honourable end."

"Thank you very much," Henry said. "I told you before, Grannie, that I'm sure you mean well by me. I'm really sorry to have to disagree, but our views just don't coincide, that's all."

Arabella leaned back, her gust of fury apparently spent.

"Ah, well," she said placidly and with a half-smile. "Ah, well, the influence of Age must, I suppose, make way for the influence of Youth. The March of Progress I believe it is called. I presume you have been aided and abetted in your ideas by this—this Miss Winslow?"

"I don't know," Henry answered. "Perhaps. We agree on the matter, anyhow."

"You have been seeing her, I take it, contrary to my wishes?"

"I'm afraid so, Grannie. You see, I love her and am going to marry her. Given life, that is inevitable."

"Ah, well," Arabella said again. "One must bow to the seemingly inevitable. Bow to the storm, as it were."

Henry knew his grandparent sufficiently well to realize that she was being dishonest. It was not her habitude to bow to anything, let alone the inevitable. She just didn't believe in it. He was, therefore, uneasy; apprehensive of the old woman's next move. He had been caught like that before and had no intention of repeating the dose. For all that, he felt glad to have cleared the air. At last he and his grandmother knew exactly how they stood in relation to each other. At least, that was what Henry fondly imagined.

3

An hour or so later he and Dora were seated on tuppenny chairs in the park; they were uncomfortable chairs and dear at the price as far as personal comfort went. There was, however, no other place where they could meet and just sit hand in hand. Teashops were inconvenient and gave them each a headache, with resultant irritability. Henry had gone over the whole ground once more. Uncle Alfred, the Major, Vera's death and the conspiracy over Lily. Without giving Lily away, he had been perfectly frank about the whole business.

"You do believe me about Lily, don't you?" he asked.

"Need you ask, darling? Of course I believe you."

"But I like to hear you say so, just as I like to hear you tell me you love me. I know you love me, but I like to hear the words; just as I know I love you and yet love saying it."

Dora gave his hand a happy squeeze.

"You are a darling, Henry. While we've been separated I've just tried to wrap you round with my love, said words over to myself to keep you safe, magic words."

They were silent for a minute or so, watching the passers-by and the scampering children. Suddenly Henry gave a little cry, almost of pain.

"Dora," he said, "it's no good. I try to keep certain thoughts out of my head, but they will come back, and not even you and the dear touch of your hand can dissipate them."

"I think I know what you mean, dear."

Henry shivered.

"I hope you don't," he said. "I hardly know myself."

"I'll tell you what I mean. You may dislike me for it, dear, but it's just got to be said. You're frightened, darling."

"Terrified," Henry whispered. "Terrified!"

Dora cuddled his arm as if it were a baby.

"I understand. Uncle Alfred dies and leaves you money, money that twenty-four hours before he had left to other people. Uncle Hugh dies, shot through the head, and does the same. Miss Beamish dies after threatening to contest that will, and you inherit under an insurance policy. In the first two cases your grandmother is present . . . that is what is tormenting us both, darling. We're becoming evil-minded. . . ."

"Or perhaps farseeing. You were always afraid of my grandmother. She recognizes that she can do nothing against us when we love each other, so she tries to part us, and is making the best of a bad job."

"I'm afraid *now*," Dora said quietly. "More afraid than I've ever been. Oh, I don't mean physically afraid, but afraid that she may succeed in the end."

"I told her that we were going to be married, that nothing could ever stop us, except . . ."

He broke off, appalled, as the significance of what Dora had said struck him. She turned and faced him, and for a few seconds they read each other's inmost thoughts, eye to eye.

"Exactly," Dora said at last. "That's what I'm afraid of."

"But it's fantastic. It just couldn't happen. No, there's some beastly curse on us all."

"Henry," Dora said, "when people start talking about being pursued by some curse or rotten luck they're in a bad way. Only atheists and materialists believe stuff like that. I don't believe you're cursed at all, nor any living thing. Not in that way. But I *do* believe in human wickedness, and human wickedness is capable of anything."

"But, darling, how can an old lady of over eighty—murder anyone?"

"I don't know. I don't even know that she did—probably not. . . . But she was glad they died; she hoped they would."

Henry cupped his face in his hands. Dora gently placed her slim young hand on his shoulder.

"Darling," she said, "it's no use mooning. We've got to do something."

"Yes, but *what?* Can love like ours ever be destroyed by malice?"

"No, I don't think it can. It can be chafed and hurt and irritated, just as I irritated you by running around with Monty, but I don't think it can be destroyed. There's a much more important point."

"Yes?"

"You or I might easily be destroyed by your grandmother."

"Good Lord!"

"You told her once that you wouldn't care what happened if I were to die. It was dear of you and I think you meant it, because I know that feeling."

"Well?"

"Others have died who got in her way. I may be the next. Oh, don't think I'm being morbid. I'm just facing facts as I see them. I just don't intend to die, my dear, to please your grandmother and to enable you to be hooked on to Lily plus a few thousands. I intend to lie in your arms and on your dear simple heart and have your children—jolly little people who'll turn cartwheels in the Name of the Lord."

Henry shamelessly held her in his arms and kissed her till he had no more breath left.

"And," he cried, "you've given me an idea."

"Yes?"

"We'll go and see Reginald. He told us to if we were in a jam. Well, we *are* in a jam. Come on, let's go now."

Dora glanced at her wrist watch.

"Not yet," she said. "The appointment is for half-past three."

"Appointment? You mean to say you . . ."

"Yes. I rang him up this morning."

4

Reginald leaned back in his chair and, finger-tips together, surveyed the ceiling. It was one of his characteristic attitudes, and was suave and aristocratic, like some clerical, good-looking Sherlock Holmes.

Dora had told him the whole story, exaggerating nothing, withholding nothing, Henry supplying details when called on. She felt it was better that she should do the talking, as Henry got so excited and romantic about it.

"I hope you don't think we're mad?" she said simply at the finish of the story.

Reginald glanced at her and treated her to one of his winning smiles, a smile that had its origin in laughter wrinkles.

"It sounds pretty crazy, I'll admit," she added.

"If you had heard as many confessions as I have in the last ten years," Reginald said quietly, "you would think no story too crazy to be true. No, I don't think you're mad, Dora. On the contrary, I think you're one of the sanest people I have ever known."

"I'm madly in love," she said with a laugh, annexing Henry's hand and blatantly kissing it.

"That's quite probably the sanest thing of all," Reginald retorted. His smile died as quickly as it had been born and he added gravely: "But I *do* think Lady Engleton is mad. That insurance business was so mad that ultra-sane people like Hamish didn't notice the fact. In my quaint, medieval way, I might say that she was possessed of a devil. Nasty things, devils! Devils that go to and fro, seeking what they may destroy. The love of God for you, of which your love for each other is a pale reflection, is the only real talisman."

Dora chuckled happily.

"Yes," she said, "I've just been telling Henry that."

"That's all very fine," Henry put in impatiently. "But what are we to do? I'm always asking that question. I wish to goodness I and Dora could run off and get married. I should feel safe."

"I understand that," Reginald said. "It's the great defence of taking a vow. It's the bond that gives you security and happiness, saves you from running amok."

"I decline to have a hole-and-corner wedding," Dora said. "And Henry doesn't want it really. We're not ashamed of each other. It's just the fear of losing each other that hurts and frightens."

Reginald said nothing and they waited patiently. Slowly he handed Henry his cigarette-case.

"Look here," he said, "I want you to promise me one thing, Dora."

"Yes?"

"To let me know at once if my great aunt makes any move, and to tell me exactly what it is. Will you do that?"

"I promise."

"Thank you. I wish I could help you more, but I don't quite see what I can do."

"D'you think that there's—that there's danger?" Henry asked anxiously.

"I don't want to scare you both, but I do, quite definitely. I find these sudden deaths disturbing and we must be on our guard, take precautions. Oh, I don't mean the police! That's unthinkable and they'd laugh at us. After all, there's nothing to go on, and God forgive us if we are wrong."

"I wish we were married," Henry said. "I wish we were one flesh and even more do I wish we were one heart and soul."

Reginald turned suddenly to Dora.

"Dora," he said, "do you believe in God?"

"Yes," she answered simply. "I do."

"Get me right," Reginald went on with a sudden, tense enthusiasm. "I don't mean 'the Good' or 'the Creative Force,' but God the Absolute, to Whom all things are known, to Whom the whole of knowledge is an open book, because He *is* Knowledge; to Whom the whole heartache of Beauty is known because He is beautiful; Who created you and became relative through being made Man and died and suffered degradation, Who loves you because He is the Quintessence of Love? Do you believe *that?*"

Dora took a deep breath and plunged into the turgid water of unforeseen Faith.

"Yes," she said with conviction. "I must believe it, because I love Henry."

Henry was rather bewildered by it all. This was a new Reginald, someone he had never known or met before, and Henry was at heart intensely English and thought it was rather embarrassing to talk like that. For all that, there was a ring in his cousin's voice which seemed an echo of the unspoken, unsayable things he had striven to find, an echo of the secrets he wanted to tell Dora, the secret that great composers have tried to tell the world with the wail of strings and the stridency of trumpets; have striven and never succeeded, because the last veil that hides the face of God can never be torn away by living hands, nor yet even by the imagination.

"Do you believe that, Henry?"

"I—I—feel that it must be true, Reginald. I don't know how to put it like you do; I've never really thought about that side of it."

"If you could tell the Absolute Source of Everything that you loved Dora, would you do it without a single reservation?"

That was talking, that was vital and real, that was something he could understand, that was personal. He leaped to his feet with shining eyes.

"By God I would!"

"And then by God and before Him you shall!" Reginald answered. "Don't think I'm proselytizing or trying to 'rope you in,' or anything like that. I want you both to feel sure, to make an open declaration to your Creator and to me."

Dora took Henry's arm.

"Please, Father Trefusis," she said.

It was the first time she had ever used his official title.

So these two young creatures knelt together and swore eternal love, hand in hand, the White Figure on the black gallows above them, and Reginald Trefusis blessed them and asked for God's help and protection.

"Thanks, awfully, Reginald," Dora said.

"Frightfully nice of you!" Henry added.

The tension had gone and Reginald had become once more his suave, smiling self.

"Not at all," he smiled. "Glad to help any time. Don't forget to ring me up if . . . you know what I mean. Don't forget that."

"I shan't forget," Dora said quietly.

Reginald watched them go laughing and arm in arm down the street until they turned the corner.

"Go in peace," he murmured to himself. "Go in peace!"

17

SANDWICHES AND SHIVERS

Hamish de Birkett was frightened; it would hardly be an exaggeration to say that he was bordering on a state of panic. It is one of the penalties of hyper-selfishness that it leaves the practitioner in a state of complete dependence when an emergency arises. This accounts for the fact that Hamish de Birkett of Wimpole Street, with a vast string of important letters after his name, saw fit to send for his brother and his cousin and to sacrifice the fees of no less than four patients, at three guineas each, between the hours of three and four on the day following the events described in the last chapter. Even so, he kept Bertram and Reginald waiting while he finished a lunch to which he had not invited them. It was a good lunch which even a state of emergency was not permitted to spoil. Bertram had seen the last course go in as he was arriving.

He and Reginald had been conducted into the consulting-room, where they sat eyeing each other in semi-silence. It was not that they felt any antagonism to each other; it was just that there was no common dialectical ground.

"Cold—what?" Bertram said at last. He had got into the habit of adding the word "what" chiefly because he read Mr. Wodehouse's novels and really thought his mother tongue was spoken in that quaint manner.

"Very," Reginald said concisely.

"Not that it matters much to you, Reggie. Churches are always steam heated; not like the Horse Guards. Terrible draughty place —what?"

He screwed a monocle into his eye and made gallant and soldierly efforts to keep it in position. To do so successfully was a mathematical problem and beyond his powers. It fell out.

"I'm not in church all the time," Reginald said. "In fact I sometimes go out for walks like a human being or even a dog!"

Reginald seemed nervy and took little trouble to hide the fact from his cousin, who in any case was quite unmoved by the small details of everyday humanity. Bertram began to wander round the consulting-room in search of his brother's cigars, the gifts of grateful patients, or even a possible drop of port. His eyeglass fell out again and was saved from destruction by the silk ribbon that secured it to his neck.

"Jolly good thing I had this thing made with a string to it," he said. "I bust five of the plain ones in four weeks; comes expensive at seven and a kick a time, what?"

"Must do," Reginald said vaguely. "Thirty-seven and sixpence!" His thoughts were elsewhere. Why had Hamish summoned them so peremptorily? Bertram had been thinking the same. Hamish was not of an affectionate disposition; there were more solid reasons than family love.

"Bet you Hamish has got the wind up about something," he said. "Bet you a million dollars to a sausage! He was always like that when we were kids. Windy as Hampstead Heath or an empty stomach. Sorry," he added. "Keep forgettin' you're a sort of padre, Reggie."

"Don't bother. Contrary to popular belief, even clergy understand empty stomachs!"

Bertram resumed his seemingly hopeless treasure hunt for cigars.

"Hamish is a mean devil," he said gloomily, as unsuccessfully he returned to his seat. "Not a smell of a cigar or even a fag. He was never the sort that shared his penny. Clever feller all the same." He added this as a sop to success and brotherly affection.

"Wonder what he wants?" Reginald asked.

"Probably in trouble with a woman," Bertram said, wise as any owl, "and scared he'll be struck off the register. Wouldn't think doctors would be interested in that sort of thing, would you? Not after readin' those books with coloured pictures. But I'm right; you'll see!"

He nodded sagely as one who knew the world and had seen life.

"It can't be money," he added. "Neither of us *has* any; that's one comfort."

The door opened with consulting-room noiselessness and Hamish hurried in, glancing at his wrist watch.

"Sorry to have kept you waiting," he said busily, after exchanging curt greetings and treating them to a miniature frown. Reginald felt that he was himself somehow to blame for his cousin's lack of punctuality. That was a trick of Hamish's and had been of considerable advantage in the pursuance of his highly lucrative profession.

"Enjoy your lunch?" Bertram asked. "That was a decent savoury I saw going in." He screwed his monocle into its predestined temporary resting-place and held it there for at least thirty seconds, which was very nearly a record.

Hamish disdained to reply. Quickly drawing up a chair, he sat down only to get up again an instant later. Reginald noticed that his cousin's hand shook, that he was in a pitiable state of jumps. Bertram dropped his monocle in surprise.

"I wish you wouldn't fidget, Bertie," Hamish snapped irritably.

This was unreasonable and Bertram said as much. Hamish pulled himself together. "I'm sorry," he said more quietly, "but the truth is I've had a shock, a very bad shock, so bad that I summoned you both. I think you should know—certain unpleasant facts."

"What facts?" Reginald asked.

"The truth is," Hamish said impressively, "our great aunt is mad." This was not so much a remark as an infallible pronouncement.

"That's nothing new," Bertram said. "She's always mad about something or another. It's chronic."

Hamish flashed a look of contempt at his brother and then addressed himself exclusively to Reginald.

"I mean mad, insane! In the medical sense. *You* might call it possessed of a devil." He added this with the superiority that Science adopts when addressing her elder sister, Theology.

"I might," Reginald conceded, "and it's possible I might be right. I've thought so myself for a long time."

"Come now," Bertram put in, "that's a bit steep! The old girl's queer, of course, Victorian and all that, what? But not potty."

"You're no judge. I didn't say 'imbecile.' Anything but. She's mad, dangerously mad, and I'm frightened."

"What has forced you to this conclusion?" Reginald asked. It was clear that there must have been some exceedingly untoward incident to have shaken his cousin out of his customary self-complacency.

"What I have to say," Hamish said quickly, "must be treated absolutely confidentially. Even now I don't know whether I'm doing right in telling you. This time yesterday I should have held my tongue, but something has since happened which has made me change my mind and I'm going to speak as I consider it affects our personal safety." He paused dramatically to allow the emphasis of his last words to sink well in. "Understand me —*personal safety*."

"Get on with it," Bertram said at last. "Not much use talking like that unless we know what it is you're talking about, what? What I mean to say is . . ."

"Yesterday," Hamish continued, paying not the slightest attention to the interruption, "our great aunt paid me a visit, ostensibly because her companion, Miss—Miss—" He snapped his fingers, trying to recall the elusive name. "Some sort of seed!" he said irritably.

"Caraway," Reginald prompted.

"That's it—Caraway. Because this Caraway woman was supposed to be ill. She wasn't ill at all."

"Women are like that," Bertram said wisely, "always imagining things."

"Shut up!" Hamish glared ferociously at the interrupter, and then, swallowing his irritation, continued: "She was pretending to be ill in order to have a private consultation with me, to lay certain facts before me which she thought I should know. It was the only method she could contrive to escape from Arabella, who won't let the woman out of her sight. Pretty smart, if you ask me."

"Exceedingly," Reginald said quietly.

"Mark you," Hamish said, "I don't know whether the woman was telling the truth or not, but I rather think she was. You remember that fool insurance scheme?" The others made affirmative sounds. "Uncle Alfred is dead. Henry inherits. Beamish and his sister are dead. Henry benefits again. Has it ever occurred to you that they were murdered—all three of 'em?" Hamish asked the question with fierce but whispered intensity.

Reginald displayed little surprise, but Bertram's monocle dropped from his eye and dangled unheeded. His face went a dusty sort of white as the significance dawned on him.

"I say," he muttered awkwardly, "that's all rot, piffle, road sweepings!"

"You think so, do you? I hope you go on thinking it's all road sweepings! I hope you'll be alive to think at all. You may be the next to go. You're insured, don't forget, and God knows, you're worth more to the House of de Birkett dead than alive."

"I say, old man, you've not got a nice way of putting things. . . . D'you mind if I help myself to a drink?"

"Help yourself to what you like, but I should avoid having anything, either to eat or drink, at Great Aunt Arabella's house."

"Got the key of the sideboard?"

Hamish flung it on the table.

"How do you know all this?" Reginald asked, as Bertram went towards the sideboard and scratched about for a glass.

"This woman Caraway told me."

"She may be lying."

"I think not. She actually saw Arabella squeeze a sponge full of cold water over old Alfred when he was in a critical condition. She was circumstantial in her account of it. I remember at the time that Grantley was puzzled."

"Would that be enough to kill him?"

"In the old boy's condition more than enough. The shock alone might be fatal."

"Dear Lord, how fearful!"

"Pretty grim, isn't it? But there's worse to follow. This woman Caraway, half asleep actually, saw our murderous old aunt pour chilblain liniment into some homemade wine which was afterwards drunk by the Beamish women. That liniment I prescribed myself—a solution of lead and antimony, which was exactly what they found in Vera's stomach. It's fearfully poisonous. Poor devils!"

For the first and last time in his life Reginald saw his cousin display a certain human compassion for suffering. Bertram had by now got a stiff whisky and was listening in an ox-like manner.

"Don't believe a word of it," he said. "Not a blessed word. It's just a damned libel."

"That's exactly the reason why Miss Whatshername didn't speak before," Hamish said. "No one would believe her."

"I should hope not, what?"

Reginald, experienced as he was in the seamy side of life, felt sick at the thought. Cold-blooded, agonizing murder!

"What," he asked, "happened to Major Beamish? Did Miss Caraway see him shot? She seems to have seen most things."

"No, she missed the shooting. But apparently the old woman makes no secret of it, boasts about it privately, in fact. Pretty cool, eh?" Hamish fired this out with grim relish, rolling it on his tongue like old port. "That, in short, is the story she told me yesterday in my consulting-room. What are we going to do? That's the question."

"Nothing," Bertram said brightly. "This Caraway woman

is either mad or malicious, perhaps both, what? Great Aunt is no murderess. She'd never do such a thing! After all, she *is* a de Birkett."

Hamish made snarling noises at the back of his nose.

"I wish to God she'd had a go at you first, Bertie. You make me vomit! For sheer, triple-distilled bilge, I've never heard anything to touch your talk. You make England what it is!"

"No politics, I beg you both." Reginald held up a deprecating hand. "May I ask what *you* propose to do?" he asked. "It seems to me to be your pigeon at the moment."

Hamish made a gesture of complete helplessness. "What on earth do you expect me to do? I can't go to the police. The old hag's right; we've no proof, and in any case the police wouldn't credit such a yarn. They don't like an old lady getting away with three murders. Does 'em no good. Anyhow, it would ruin my practice and Bertram would have to hand in his papers, so that's that. What would they do to *you*? Anything?"

He asked Reginald more out of curiosity than with any anxiety for his cousin's welfare.

"I haven't the vaguest idea and I don't care much, anyway. I haven't got a practice to consider."

"All right, Reggie. There's no need to get snappy about it. You parsons are so damned touchy." Hamish leaned back and wiped his forehead. "I confess it's upset me," he said. "I could hardly eat my lunch. My God, if people only realized how easy it is to commit murder if only you use your wits and wait for the right moment. Uncle Alfred's illness was a happy accident—for Aunt, I mean. She grabbed the opportunity. Same with the others. I can see it all. This idea of the Family is just a fierce monomania—and Bertram and I will be the next to go—unless, of course, she kills you, Reginald, just to keep her hand in. She always disliked you." He said it almost hopefully.

"You were always a rabbit, Hamish," Bertram said. "And you haven't altered. It's all piffle!"

"I wish I could agree, Bertie," Reginald said wearily. "Unfortunately it's not such a surprise to me as it should be. When you came in, Hamish, you said that 'something had happened,' something that made it imperative for you to get into touch with

Bertie and myself. May I ask what that something is?"

Hamish leaned forward.

"I'm coming to that," he said grimly. "Ever heard of botulism?"

"No," said Bertram. "Is it a new religion—or Black Shirts or something?"

"Don't be a damned fool!"

Bertram was nettled.

"Why the hell should I know what botulism is? It's all very fine, you scientific blokes think that everyone should know your beastly jargon and think 'em fools if they don't! Especially if they are in the Army. I should like to drill you for an hour or two. I'm not such a fool as I look—or at least," he added hastily, "as you think I look!"

"Loud cheers," Hamish said sardonically. "Hurrah for the Red, White and Blue! You probably *will* know what botulism is—or at least what the symptoms feel like—and so shall I."

"Botulism is some form of food poisoning, isn't it?" Reginald asked, therefore nipping Bertram's retort in the bud.

"It's one of the most violent and deadly microorganisms known. The chances of survival after infection are pretty well nil. There is no known cure. It occurs in preserved meat, rarely enough, thank God! But it's deadly—deadly and agonizing."

Reginald caught his breath in apprehension, dreading what Hamish was going to say.

"Go on!" he said.

"I've been making a culture of botulism. That culture is missing. Yesterday it was in my laboratory. To-day it can't be found. A housemaid saw Arabella coming out of the laboratory yesterday while I was talking to the seed woman. Draw your own conclusions!"

Even Bertram was impressed.

"That's bad," he said. "That's very bad. But probably you took it out and dropped it somewhere. Perhaps it was pinched from your car. Get 'em to broadcast an S.O.S."

Hamish controlled himself by an effort.

"No," he said. "I did not take it out—*or* drop it—*or* leave it in the car. I did none of those things. Would you carry Mills bombs about with you?"

"Such things should be kept locked up," Bertram said primly.

"It wasn't! Aunt Arabella pinched it, and she'll put it in someone's tea."

"Tea!"

Reginald leapt to his feet. Dora! Dora stood in the way of Henry
and Lily's thousands. Dora was an obstacle, a bigger obstacle than
any of them, and Dora was going to tea with Arabella that very
afternoon . . . was probably there already. Faithful to her pledge,
she had rung him up and told him. Arabella had been pleasant to
the girl, written her a placatory note asking her to tea. Tea!

"What's bitten you, Reggie?"

"Dora! Henry's sweetheart! She's going to tea with Arabella
this afternoon. . . ."

"What about her?"

Reginald made for the door.

"Haven't time to explain."

A few minutes later passers-by were surprised to see a bare-
headed priest running full tilt down Wimpole Street.

2

Dora had been more than surprised to receive a "cordial little
note" from Arabella that morning, inviting her to take tea at four
o'clock that very afternoon. Mindful of her promise to Father
Trefusis, she had rung him up and informed him. Dora was no
fool; she knew perfectly well that Arabella was to be profoundly
mistrusted, especially when issuing invitations to tea. Nor was
Reginald anything but apprehensive. He was of the opinion that
Arabella would endeavour to poison Dora's mind, refer to the Ely
incident or apologize for Henry's apparent defection and fickle-
ness. He was prepared for mental poisoning, but botulism had
remained outside his calculations. On the whole, he had been of
the opinion that Dora should go, if for no other reason than to
see how the land lay.

If Dora had been surprised at the invitation, she was even
more surprised at her reception. Arabella had beamed upon her,
held up a withered and lizard-like cheek for a kiss. No unpleasant
references had been made about Henry, in fact he was due to

join them a little later. Everything in the garden seemed not only lovely but in bloom.

Arabella had been of the opinion that they should have a little heart-to-heart woman's talk, unencumbered by male presences. The old lady had referred rather sadly to the time ("not very far distant now, my dear") when she would be gone, laid to rest quietly with the remains of her dear and gallant son ("he would have loved you, dear girl") and her much loved husband. It is very questionable whether Arabella ever believed in the reality of her own death. She referred to it frequently; it was a useful argumentative weapon, but she never visualized herself as a corpse. She had lived so long and despite the slight inconveniences of senility, had such a clear brain and vigorous body that its dispersal into component parts seemed outside the natural order of things. Dora found the old lady fascinating and seriously began to wonder whether they had not all misjudged her. How could such an old darling have squeezed a sponge in Uncle Alfred's gasping mouth? It was altogether incredible! She chatted like a book of Victorian reminiscences, glossing over unimportant details of her life, wars, rumours of wars and catastrophes, discoursing at length on the things that mattered, how she had been presented at Court, what she had worn and how gracious our dear Queen had been. Dora never forgot it, never forgot either the quick little gestures of those spider-like hands, covered all over with rings. Then tea came in, the usual array, presided over by a whitefaced Caraway. Dora was actually taking a cup when Reginald Trefusis burst in breathless and unannounced.

Eagerly and gratefully he noted the fact that no one had eaten anything. At the sight of her loathed nephew Arabella dropped her mask of cordiality. One could almost hear it rattle on the floor as it fell. Her lips tightened angrily, her hands shook and the blue veins stood out on her forehead.

"What is the meaning of this vulgar intrusion?" she asked. "I have given instructions that you are not to be admitted . . ."

"I know that, my dear Aunt. I forced my way in . . ."

"Do you wish me to send for the police and have you evicted? Do you wish to bring your so-called cloth into even greater disrepute?"

Reginald had regained his usual calm, it seemed, for he answered lightly, almost boyishly:

"By all means send for the police. Offer them the potted-meat sandwiches!"

There they were, lying in a neat little comestible tower.

Then he strode across to the tea table and, picking them up, offered them to the old lady.

"Try one yourself!"

Arabella shrank from him.

"Caraway! Ring the bell!" she gasped. "Ring it at once. You must be insane, Reginald. Go away!"

"Not without Dora."

Without further word, Reginald, crossing to the fire, pitched the contents of the plate into the flames. One sandwich lay in the ashes. This he picked up and began to wrap in his handkerchief.

"What are you doing that for?"

"To give the policeman, when he arrives."

Despite herself, Arabella paled.

"Hamish missed something from his laboratory yesterday and warned me that sandwiches might therefore become indigestible. Forgive plain speaking, but I haven't time for verbal niceties. He'd formed certain views and I had to come round unceremoniously, I admit, just to make sure his views were ill-founded."

"I dislike you, Reginald; you are an abominable fellow. Hamish is no better. Give me back my sandwich and go! You have not yet rung the bell, Caraway. Kindly obey me, and cease opening and closing your ridiculous mouth like some travesty of a goldfish."

Caraway stood motionless, trembling. Dora had been too astonished to speak, but had every confidence that Reginald had good reason for his seeming eccentricity. Reginald balanced the half-wrapped sandwich on the palm of his hand. His eyes met Arabella's and they stared glassily at each other for a full ten seconds. Arabella chuckled suddenly.

"You have an inordinate gift of the gab, Reginald. You typify everything I dislike, but I'll concede you a certain amount of moral courage. For all that, you daren't raise, or attempt to raise, a filthy scandal. You daren't do it, and you know it. You daren't make a laughing stock of your Order and your Church."

With a sudden movement Reginald sent the remaining sandwich after its fellows, and the butter crackled and hissed in the flames.

"You're right," he said. "I daren't. I might be wrong. I daren't risk it."

"Nor would you dare risk it even if you were right."

"No, not even if I were right. . . ."

His eyes blazed suddenly, his thin frame became rigid, and his hair seemed to bristle.

"But I dare beg you to turn from evil courses, beg you to turn your footsteps from the path to Hell."

Arabella sneered.

"What we used to call a sky pilot," she said. "You don't impress me, Reginald. Won't you ring that bell, or can't you ring it?"

Caraway, with a muttered apology, rang the bell.

"Don't think, Reginald," Arabella went on, having regained her nerve fully at the sight of the burning sandwich, "that I shall let this matter rest. I shall write to your Superior and complain of your conduct. I can only hope that you have been overworking in your efforts to reform Mayfair. Alice," she added, as the parlour-maid appeared, "kindly show Mr. Trefusis out. In future he is not to be admitted under any circumstances. Before you go, Reginald, perhaps you would like to throw the plate of cakes into the fire or to make a burnt offering of the bread and butter."

"It won't do, my dear aunt. It's unworthy of you—all that about making holocausts of cakes, I mean. Kindly bear in mind that I know all about it—*all* about it."

"I shan't forget," Arabella grinned. "Now get out, for goodness' sake. Take that dough-faced girl with you and leave me in peace."

"Thank God," she said to Caraway when the door had shut behind them, "that I have always been a staunch daughter of the Establishment."

And she meant it, too. There was nothing hypocritical in the remark.

Outside, Reginald put a perplexed Dora into a taxi, refusing to go into details or to offer any explanation.

"You have been nearer death than you have ever been in your

life," was all he would say. "Please ask your father if he would see me some time. I want to talk to him about Henry . . ."

Henry came in twenty minutes later to find his grandmother dictating a letter to the Archbishop of Westminster demanding that immediate disciplinary action be taken against her nephew, Reginald Trefusis, or alternatively that there should be an inquiry into the state of his mind. It was a good letter, and eloquent without being prejudiced or vicious.

"Where's Dora?" he asked in surprise at her absence.

"Reginald Trefusis arrived, threw sandwiches about the room and took her away," Arabella said calmly.

Henry had hoped for so much from the re-meeting of Dora and his grandmother, and his disappointment was acute.

"More trouble?" he asked wearily.

"We are born for trouble in this world," Arabella replied, unctuous as a tin of cold cream. Nor would she give her grandson any explanation. The whole episode, she said, was both absurd and discreditable to everyone concerned but herself.

"Kindly fetch me Whittaker's Almanack. I wish to know the correct method of addressing a Cardinal Archbishop. All such titles are purely courtesy titles, but if Queen Victoria could recognize Cardinal Manning, I suppose I must recognize the present fellow."

But troubles for that day were by no means over. Hardly had Henry begun to wade about in the Order of Precedence and Correct Methods of addressing titled notabilities for his grandmother's edification when the door opened and Alice appeared once more.

"What is it now?" Arabella asked testily.

"A Mr. Peploe, m'lady, wants to know if your ladyship could see him for a few moments."

"No," said Arabella coldly. "Tell him I'm not at home to callers."

"I said I thought you were not at home, m'lady. Then he asked for his lordship. He seems very upset."

Since her defeat at tea time, Arabella had made up her mind to discount the Peploes. Had Dora been taken fatally ill, Henry might have been cajoled into Lily's eager arms, caught on the rebound of his grief. She was annoyed, not unnaturally. There was, however, just a remote chance that Peploe had something to say that might yet prove advantageous to the family coffers. It was worth making sure, anyway. Another reason for seeing him was Henry's patent pleasure at her refusal, and she was not pleased with her grandson.

"Very well," she conceded. "Show Mr. Peploe in, Alice."

Henry rose quickly.

"I decline to see him, flatly," he announced. "I'm sick to death of the Peploes."

However, he had no time to get away. Twice that afternoon an agitated guest pushed his way in unannounced. Caraway remained, as nobody paid any attention to her at all, or even acknowledged her presence.

"Afternoon, m'lady. Afternoon, 'Enry. 'Ere's a pretty 'ow d'yer do!"

Peploe flung himself into an armchair and his agitation was plain to behold. He mopped his face with a huge silk handkerchief.

"'Ere's a pretty 'ow d'yer do," he repeated.

"Won't you sit down, Mr. Peploe?" Arabella said solicitously.

"But I *am* sittin' down."

"What's it all about?" Henry asked. He knew that old Peploe might take ten minutes to get to the point. He needn't have bothered.

"Lily's done a bunk," Peploe announced. "Slung 'er 'ook with a shuvver."

Down came the last remnants of Arabella's house of cards, away went the last chances of a fifty thousand dowry. It was a day of heavy defeats.

"I presume you mean she has eloped?" She asked the question with outward indifference.

"That's the idea. With a shuvver—dirty young 'ound!"

"With a what?"

"Shoo-fer—Show-fer, if you like to pronounce it 'igh-brow . . . a sleek-'aired young whelp what I paid four pound a week to! And it's your fault, young man," he added, fiercely turning on Henry. "Your fault and no other."

"Everything seems to be my fault nowadays," Henry said coldly. Then his natural curiosity got the better of him. "How did it happen?" he asked.

"Me and 'er 'ad a few words this morning about *you*, young man. Nothing out of the ordinary. When I come back from the shop—from business, that is—I find she's 'opped it. Broken open my desk, pinched a 'undred pound of *my* money. Gone off in *my* car with *my* shuvver. Taken nothing with 'er—not even a night shirt."

Henry felt himself blushing. Nightgowns were a prominent feature of Lily's elopements.

"I can't see what your daughter's vagaries have to do with my grandson."

"I'll soon show you. She left a letter . . ."

Peploe fumbled in his pocket and drew out a sheet of note-paper covered all over with Lily's untidy scrawl. It was a thick, cloth-like piece of paper, tinted and even at that distance scented.

"It's a nasty letter," he said. "Don't even begin 'Dear Father' nor anything like that. . . ."

He put a pair of folders across his nose and began to read.

"'I've gone off with Jennings because I 'appen to be fond of Henry.' Can you beat it? 'Jennings has been making love to me for months and he's quite decent-looking. You and that lawyer have tried to bully Henry into marrying me, telling a pack of damned lies about us. I won't have it. He doesn't want me and never has. Now I'm going to make certain you can't blackmail him any more. Let him marry the girl he loves and good luck to him. I shan't tell you where we're spending the night, but to-morrow the dirty work will be over.'"

Peploe surveyed the company over the top of his folders.

"Then the noospapers talk about the modern girl bein' trumps. Did you ever 'ear the likes o' that?"

"Never!" said Arabella definitely. "Never!"

"Ah," Peploe went on more in sorrow than in anger, "you 'aven't 'eard the worst yet neither. You and me is married people, Lady Engleton, so it don't signify, and 'is lordship'll 'ave to lump it, seein' as 'ow it's 'is fault."

He resumed his reading.

"'You've gone on at me about my morals long enough. I haven't been a virgin for years and to-morrow shan't be one officially.' After all the money I've spent on 'er education! After all 'er mother's good advice, to talk like that. 'I'll tell you where to send my things and come up to arrange about my allowance.' What a nerve, eh? 'You can tell Lady Engleton she's an old devil and you and that lawyer are a pair of rotters.' Well it don't signify. 'Love to Mother. Lily.'"

Henry had a fearful desire to laugh and shout "Good for Lily," a desire that he managed to restrain. Arabella seemed to be perfectly indifferent to the epithet that had been bestowed upon her.

"My grandson appears to have had a providential escape," she said.

"But it's 'is fault all this 'as 'appened. Deny that you can't. And to call 'er own father a rotter ain't nice. No! It ain't at all nice. Let alone what she called your ladyship. Love to mother, too. Poor mother's dissawlved in tears. Cryin' ever so. Shaken with sobs. Been sick!"

"Surely these medical details are unnecessary, Mr. Peploe. I'm deeply sorry for her mother, but there my interest ends. Neither can I profess to care an atom what abuse a young and foolish little slut may use about myself."

"It's all very fine and large to be aristocratic and upstage and call my girl a slut, but what are we goin' to do about it, eh? It's 'is fault that this 'as come about. Deny that you can't."

"Oh, yes, I can deny it," Henry chipped in with spirit. "I jolly well do deny it. It's your own fault entirely. In any case, what do you expect me to do?"

Peploe looked cunning; Henry half expected to see him tap the side of his nose.

"That's more like it," he said. "That's a better tone. Now, look 'ere. She's just been silly. You go and get 'er back, give that dirty shuvver a damn good 'idin', and I won't say as I won't pop another ten thousand on to 'er bit o' money. Now then, what about it, eh?"

"Don't be a fool," Henry said, flushing angrily.

"Not enough, eh? Look 'ere, I'll make 'er settlement up to seventy-five thousand pounds. Think of it! But I'll go no 'igher, so you can't beat me up any more."

Henry made for the door in indignation.

"Your proposal and your whole attitude are equally indecent, Mr. Peploe."

"Hoity-toity! Girls will 'ave their fun nowadays, same as the boys. They all do it; you read it in the papers every day. It 'ud only be like marryin' a widder."

Arabella watched the whole scene with birdlike eyes. The situation was grotesque and annoying. Yet seventy-five thousand pounds! It was a colossal sum. She was wise enough, however, to say nothing to Henry in his present mood. If only the wretched Dora were out of the way! That was out of the picture, however——

Henry turned on his heel and quitted them without a word.

"I must apologize for my grandson so far forgetting himself as to bang a door," she said.

Peploe got up and scratched his head.

"Bangin' doors don't matter," he commented. "But I'm sorry 'e takes it like that. Fair's fair and it's his fault. Deny that you can't, whatever he may say."

"If scandal could be avoided I'm not sure I don't agree, Mr. Peploe, though I must say your daughter has behaved very badly and that without reference to her offensive allusion to myself. Time will show."

In her heart, nevertheless, she knew that Time had got nothing to do with it, and when Peploe had gone she lay back in her chair crushed and exhausted by the magnitude of the disaster. For the first time she began to doubt whether her efforts for the Family had been worth the candle, worth the risk. Henry she disliked as an individual now, but still he represented the Family.

"Caraway," she said, "it is left to you to find out the correct method of address to a Roman Archbishop."

But the spirit had gone out of it and a few moments later she went dinnerless and dispirited to bed. The letter to the Archbishop was never posted.

18

JUST POSSIBLE

Once in bed, and after a glass of mulled claret and a cracknel, Arabella felt better, and was already formulating plans to retrieve her recent defeats. Caraway had been pressed into reading to her. Not that she listened, but the drone of the woman's voice and the fact that the book in question was *The Awful Disclosures of Maria Monk*, a copy of which had been secured on her return from Norfolk, and consequently distasteful to Caraway, gave it a pleasant zest. In fact, so refreshed did she feel that she told Caraway to stop and to give her her rice pudding, which together with the throat lozenges and the weak lemonade were placed in their accustomed readiness. She leant back amongst the pillows and slowly ate the pudding.

"Not a satisfactory day," she said. "It was unfortunate that Hamish noticed the loss of his poison. Hamish was always a coward, a fact that I foolishly forgot when the opportunity of taking his stupid microbes presented itself. I might have known that he would lose his nerve and blab to that priest. Reginald has an unenviable nature. By the way, did *you* notice I had taken that stuff?"

"Yes, my lady. I saw the glass tube in the dressing-table drawer, but I did *not* know that you had put it in the potted-meat sandwiches."

"Botulism!" Arabella said meditatively. "I read about it in the newspaper and remembered that it occurred in potted meat. I therefore ordered some potted meat from Fortnum and Mason's, instructing cook to let me see it. She brought it here while you were out of the room this morning. That was my chance. I availed myself of it."

"Lady Engleton! It's wicked! Terrible!"

"I wonder if Henry is worth the trouble? I'm inclined to think he is not, but I tell myself that having once put my hand to the plough I shall not withdraw. I should feel cheated and disloyal to myself, to the task I have set myself to do! By the way, you might have eaten one of those sandwiches, Caraway."

Caraway bowed her head and gripped it between bony fingers.

"I wish I could die," she moaned. "Better even such an awful death as that to the hell I endure . . ."

"Dear me," said Arabella, "I thought we had settled all that. I don't wish you to die. I counted on your partiality for sweet cakes. Your death would have been regrettable. I should miss your ministration and miss having someone to talk to. Poisoned potted meat might have proved unfortunate for Fortnum and Mason, which would have been a pity, as I have a great regard for that excellent firm of provision merchants. Though we might have got pleasant compensation from them."

Caraway shuddered.

"What on earth's the matter with the woman?"

"Was the rice pudding to your liking, my lady?"

"Yes, though now you mention it, one or two grains were rather hard and there was too much nutmeg to be altogether palatable. Don't let me have to mention that again. . . ."

"I put too much nutmeg in the pudding on purpose. . . ."

"I shall pay you no wages next week."

Caraway disregarded this threat altogether.

"I put it in on purpose to disguise the taste!"

Suddenly she flung herself on her knees by the bedside and with clasped hands turned a drawn, agonized face Heavenwards.

"God forgive me if I've done wrong," she muttered. "God forgive me, but I *had* to do it! To save innocent lives I had to do it."

"To disguise the taste?" Arabella asked sharply, ignoring the outburst. "What do you mean?"

Caraway made no answer but remained on her knees, her head bowed as if in prayer. Arabella became shrill.

"Get up, you fool, and answer my question. Don't sprawl about the place like something in a melodrama. Get up at once!"

Slowly Caraway got to her feet and surveyed the old woman in silence.

"Answer my question at once."

"My lady, you once referred to yourself as the Finger of God.

It seemed to me that I, the humblest of His creatures, might aspire to be His instrument. I was forced to keep the knowledge of your wickedness to myself, to watch poor Mr. Alfred and Miss Vera and the Major done to death, but I had to save sweet Miss Dora. You have just eaten that rice pudding. I have given you the rest of Dr. Hamish's tube of poison. You are going to die. God knows I've prayed for guidance." Her breath came in stabbing little gasps, her hand wandered to the bosom of her shabby, rusty dress to still the painful beating of her heart.

Arabella clawed at the bedclothes and for a few seconds said nothing.

"You're a liar," she said finally. "You're trying to frighten me. You wouldn't dare, you musty old weasel!"

"Oh, my lady, make your peace with the Almighty before it is too late. I'm giving you this chance. I couldn't allow these dreadful deaths to go on. It was my God-sent chance and I took it. You must believe me. . . ."

Despite herself, Arabella felt cold little drops of sweat gathering on her forehead. Supposing this fool were telling the truth? Was sweating a symptom? She seemed to have read somewhere that it was! Then she felt a little stabbing pain in her stomach —just a needle-thrust, no more. Perhaps those pains would increase, get worse—and worse . . .

"Nonsense," she said aloud. "It's indigestion . . . those hard grains of rice . . ."

She took stock of Caraway's bleak, rather puffy face. Better take no risks. The woman might be mad.

"You'll kill no more innocent people," Caraway said in a muttered monotone. "You'll understand a little of what poor Miss Vera endured. Perhaps your pains will be taken into consideration when God makes up your account. His mercy is infinite. . . ."

Arabella made little croaking noises, her throat contracting as panic seized her.

"Send for Hamish, you murderess; send at once! Get an emetic. . . . Rouse the house. . . ."

"No, my lady. . . ."

Arabella tried to scream, but only made a sound like rasping wood.

"Do as I tell you! Send for Hamish! I'll get better. I'll live to see you hanged. . . . Quickly . . ."

She began to shake, the ribbons on her breast stirred by the wind of her fear. Caraway crossed to the wash-stand and filled a sponge with water. With trembling hands she approached the bed.

"The poor reverend gentleman——" she murmured.

Arabella struck out at her with sudden vigorous venom, her eyes dilating with fear. Caraway easily evaded her. Then suddenly the old woman seemed to shrivel, to recede, shrink into her skin. She fell back, her nightcap grotesquely awry, her hand still feebly striking at nothing. As if some wind had passed over her face, so did her features suddenly distort. Her mouth was hooked up on one side and an eyelid sagged. Then she lay still.

Caraway waited and then returned the sponge to its usual position on the washstand. She looked down at the still figure lying there.

"The Finger of God," she murmured, "has touched her at last. . . ."

The house was roused and Hamish summoned.

"I think," Henry said over the 'phone, "that grandmother has had a stroke."

"Good," said Hamish cheerfully and without sufficient thought. "Good!"

"What do you mean?"

"Oh, nothing. Put some ice on her head and a hot bottle on her feet. I'll be round. . . . You should have sent for Grantley, Henry. I'm not a G.P., you know."

2

Apoplexy is a strange complaint, strange in its vagaries and the disorders that result. Arabella was unconscious for seven hours and then rallied, contrary to all expectation. She was alive, but almost entirely paralysed on her left side. Her left eye remained shrouded by the drooping lid, but the right eye regarded them all with undimmed ferocity. For a time Caraway wondered with a certain trepidation whether the old woman would regain her speech, but she need not have worried. To all questions and remarks addressed to her, Arabella had but one answer: "Just possible." How was she feeling? Would she like some chicken broth? "Just possible!" No other word of any sort. Nor was this phrase particularly clear, as the absence of false teeth fluffed the sibilants. She managed to convey many emotions in those two words, however—mostly hostile emotions. She would, for example, screw up every possible ounce of energy that remained to her and spit the words at Caraway, for whom she had conceived a savage dislike. It was clear that she understood everything that was said.

The household took the matter philosophically. Even Henry's concern was formal. He sat at the side of her bed, holding the tiny, fishlike hand, murmuring platitudes to which Arabella gave her usual answer. A night nurse weighing well over twelve stone was installed who, though quietly efficient, made no secret of the fact that she would be relieved when "the end came." She was due for another case, a maternity case, which was much more entertaining and which she had no desire to miss. "Poor old lady, it'll be a blessing for all concerned; she's a burden to herself and all around her," she used to say, with that comfortable knowledge that people have on such occasions. Hamish could hardly hide his satisfaction at the turn events had taken, in fact made no secret of it when left alone with Caraway and the patient, who regarded them with a hostile, beady black eye.

"How did it happen?" he asked Caraway one day, when they were all three alone. They were standing each side of the bed.

"I was reading to her ladyship, Mr. Hamish, when I suddenly noticed that she had fallen sideways on the pillow and was unconscious. Her face went dark for a few seconds."

Hamish stroked his chin.

"Hm. Interesting," he said. "Anything else?"

"No, Mr. Hamish."

"Just possible," said the old lady suddenly.

"By the way," said Hamish, "I want to have a look through her private drawers, bureau, dressing-table and all that. I've every reason to think the old brute was contemplating another of her murders."

"Just possible. . . ."

"Quite probable," Hamish said almost waggishly. "I missed a tube containing a germ culture—fearfully poisonous—and it's got to be found."

"I have it, Mr. Hamish," Caraway said evenly. "I found it in the washstand."

Hamish heaved a sigh of relief as the woman handed the tube nearly full of a viscous, dirty fluid.

"Did she try any tricks?"

"I greatly fear so. She dislikes Miss Dora and put some in some potted meat. I have that as well."

Hamish held the tube to the light.

"Not much gone," he murmured. "You did well, Miss Caraway." Carefully he wrapped up the tube and the potted meat.

"Thank you, Mr. Hamish. No one need ever know——"

"Of course not!"

"I have a suspicion, Mr. Hamish, that her ladyship thought she had eaten some herself, which may have brought about this stroke."

Hamish glanced sharply at Caraway, but on second thoughts decided not to ask needless questions. Things were very well as they were. Arabella twisted her head round laboriously and faced her companion, knowing she had had her stroke without real cause.

"Just possible . . . just possible . . ."

There was a concentration of hatred in it that surprised even Hamish.

"I suppose you thought I'd be the next to go, eh? I know all about your recent career of crime."

"Just possible. . . ."

"Reginald thinks you are possessed of a devil, which is just a pious way of saying 'mad.' I don't. I think you're just wicked. . . ."

"Oh, Mr. Hamish! The poor old lady can't answer back. We'll hope she is repenting. . . . It's just possible. . . ."

Caraway gave a little gasp; she hadn't meant to jeer at the possible penitent.

"I'm so sorry. . . ."

I regret to say that Hamish gave a grin. Hamish was not a pleasant individual.

"I shouldn't waste sorrow on that piece of skin and bone."

"Is there any chance of her recovery?" Caraway asked as he went to the door.

"Just possible," he said, "but not likely, thank God!"

It dragged on for ten days. Bertram called and dropped his monocle on the old lady's face. Reginald wisely kept away. Sophie Beamish wrote a sympathetic little note. She was better, she stated, though very shaken both by her illness and her double bereavement, but everyone had been so kind and attentive. She hoped her ladyship would soon be well. There must be no animosity at such times and if she would like the set of garnets back they should be sent by registered post. And so on. It was a sweet, typical little letter which did the sender credit.

Everyone was very kind. A clergyman called to render spiritual first aid, but his task was a difficult one in view of the monotony of Lady Engleton's replies. No one had warned him that she had only one sentence left in her vocabulary. Caraway enlightened him halfway through the interview, so he offered up a few prayers (Caraway chipping in with the Amens) and took himself off. What else could he do, poor man?

It was the night nurse who saw her die. Deeply engrossed in a novel by Ethel M. Dell, she heard a miniature groan and sharp, jerky, stertorous breathing. Arabella Lady Engleton had been summoned. The nurse leaned over her; she was a kindly woman as well as dutiful. She supported the worn old head in the crook of her elbow.

"God is very good, Lady Engleton. He will be merciful. . . ."

"Just possible . . ." said Arabella.

3

It was a grand funeral; quantities of flowers and messages of condolence had arrived from all manner of people, including notabilities and personages. Among the wreaths was an enormous and expensive harp from the Peploes, who, though uninvited, followed the *cortège;* and Mrs. Peploe, as usual, wreathed in silk (black, of course) and Mr. Peploe in the shiniest top hat that has ever been seen. As Mr. Peploe explained, he was nearly a "sort of brother-in-law" to the old girl. Anyhow, Mrs. Peploe liked funerals.

There wasn't much doing in the papers, so some of the more reputable published short obituaries. "Passing of a Link with Victorian Times." "One of the Old School." And all that. They raked up little bits of the family history and invented certain remarks that Arabella should have, but didn't, make about "make-up for girls," "short skirts," "jazz and the cinema." They were the usual views attributed to Victorian ladies, given a slight bias in the direction of broadmindedness.

The main mourners were, of course, Henry, Hamish and Bertram, the latter in imposing uniform with black tabs. The vicar went first with Processional Cross and a black cope. What Arabella would have thought of this Romish practice is naturally unknown, but the vicar had gradually been climbing the ladder and getting higher and higher. Bertram, the only true de Birkett, eyed the whole proceeding with disfavour.

"I doubt if our poor great-aunt would have liked it," he remarked to Hamish. "What next, I wonder? Incense?"

"Bacchanalian and Priapic dances if you like," was the facetious reply.

Bertram disdained to make direct answer, but broke into a miniature funeral oration.

"A grand old lady," he said solemnly, "has passed on. An example to all of us."

Just behind the remnants of the Family walked Mr. Merry. In spite of his row with Henry he still was official legal adviser, and hoped to remain so. There were still the pickings of Arabella's régime to be collected, no inconsiderable sum, as she had never paid his costs for years. He had submitted a regular account, but that was as far as it went.

("I am the Resurrection and the Life," saith the Lord; "he that believeth in Me, though he were dead, yet shall he live.")

"Those costs are over three hundred pounds," thought Merry. "Well over."

He was walking, as befitted his rank, just in front of Caraway and Mr. Bean, the agent, whose "black" was rudimentary.

("I know that my Redeemer liveth.")

"Dear God, forgive me if I have sinned," prayed Caraway, though her face was blank and expressionless.

("We brought nothing into this world and it is certain we can carry nothing...")

"She was good to me when I was little," thought Henry, temporarily discounting the last year.

("The Lord gave and the Lord hath taken away...")

"If I don't get that chicken house repainted," Bean said mentally, "the whole caboosh'll come down with a rush."

("Blessed be the name of the Lord.")

4

The Will was short and sweet. Henry was to have everything after the payment of funeral expenses and just debts. Merry drew attention to the just debts and diffidently mentioned his costs. The interpolation was not received enthusiastically.

"Damn bad form on an occasion like this," Bertram murmured, outwardly placid though inwardly grieved at not having been bequeathed "a single sausage" to quote verbatim from his inmost thoughts.

The main estate was, of course, entailed, the old lady having enjoyed its use, by courtesy, during her lifetime, but her private hoard was more substantial than anyone had thought. That dowry had been piling up.

Henry, though not a rich man, could face the future with equanimity and Dora.

One evening Henry came in tired and hungry from the fields of Engleton Priory. It was calving time and he had spent anxious moments in the company of the good Mr. Bean. In his hand he held a letter.

"Took it from the postman, darling."

Dora examined the costly envelope and the straggly writing, and smelt it.

"Lily!" she said promptly.

Lily, it appeared, had not made a success of her chauffeur, and was eagerly awaiting the decree absolute in order to have another shot at matrimony. Her letter was sprightly as ever in its details.

"It's just as well, Henry," she wrote, "that they never spliced us. I was made for divorces and expect to have at least four. Jonathan (my new fiancé) is an American and we see eye to eye on it. I'm restless, I suppose, but then I'm made that way and could never settle down on a silly old farm. My love to Dora and the baby. Fancy you having a baby!"

"Cheek!" Dora said and Henry blushed at the recollections.

"Poor Lily," she added a moment later, and her hand stole into her husband's.

"I just can't think of—of divorce—of being without you," Henry said quietly, "any more than I can think of not being born. I suppose it sounds trite, but you *are* me, my darling, ever since that day we knelt down and Reginald married us as it were. Being married is gloriously real—more real than Love even. . . ."

Dora laid her head on his shoulder and snuggled closer.

"How nice and earthy you smell," she murmured. "Of the earth, earthy. . . ."

A few minutes later there was a discreet tap at the door, but Dora didn't move, not being ashamed of loving. It was Caraway, who beamed sentimentally at the consummation of her vicarious adoration of Henry.

"The little nobleman is still asleep," she said unctuously, "but stirring. I think he wants his dinner. . . ."

Dora rose obediently. No patent foods for *her* child.

"Sit down, Caraway," Henry said when his wife had gone. "Sit down and have a Gin and It."

Caraway had a weakness for Gins and Its; a Caraway with a smoothed if slightly more wrinkled brow, a Caraway who had laboured long but not in vain.

"They go to my head," she said expectantly.

"Exactly," Henry said as he mixed it at the sideboard.

"Do you remember my giving you that whisky after poor old Uncle Alfred died?"

Caraway shuddered.

"I shall never forget those days," she muttered. "They seem like some evil dream. I'm afraid you gave me too much. . . ."

"God knows I don't want to rake it all up again, but I thought you might be glad to know that to-day I finished making such reparation as I could. Old Uncle Alfred's money has gone to his charities and little Sophie has plenty to spend on pleasant and indiscriminate and probably wasted village charity at Mellingham. All charity should be indiscriminate in my opinion. . . . Not a penny have I touched of all that—that blood money."

"It hurt me," Caraway said softly, "to have to tell you all those horrible things—pained me. . . ."

"You were quite right."

"But there's one thing I *didn't* tell you; I hadn't the courage!"

"What? Had the old lady any other deaths to her discredit?" Time had made him able to talk lightly of the past, though he never could eradicate the horror from his thoughts.

"No. It's about myself. I once committed a Terrible Sin."

"Get away with you!"

But Caraway was not to be jollied out of her penitential mood. "I did! I *did!*"

She spoke with passionate conviction and Henry paused, his much-needed drink half-way to his mouth. It didn't seem possible that this faded little woman could ever have committed a good thumping "blow-the-boys-down" sin.

"Does it weigh heavily on your conscience?" he asked. At that moment they heard a faint wail from up above. "The little nobleman" was being vociferous about his food supply. It became still almost at once, the stillness of satiety.

"No," said Caraway. "I'm afraid I think it was worth it."

Henry laughed.

"Well, here's how!" he said.

And they clinked glasses.

THE END

CPSIA information can be obtained
at www.ICGtesting.com
Printed in the USA
LVOW12s1630220916
505792LV00003B/616/P